Praise for previous Quintin Jardine novels:

'Perfect plotting and convincing characterisation ... Jardine manages to combine the picturesque with the thrilling and the dream-like with the coldly rational' *The Times*

'Deplorably readable' *Guardian*

'Jardine's plot is very cleverly constructed, every incident and every character has a justified place in the labyrinth of motives, and the final series of revelations follows logically from a surreptitious but well-placed series of clues' Gerald Kaufman, *Scotsman*

'If Ian Rankin is the Robert Carlyle of Scottish crime writers, then Jardine is surely its Sean Connery' *Glasgow Herald*

'It moves at a cracking pace, and with a crisp dialogue that is vastly superior to that of many of his jargon-loving rivals ... It encompasses a wonderfully neat structural twist, a few taut, well-weighted action sequences and emotionally charged exchanges that steer well clear of melodrama' *Sunday Herald*

'Remarkably assured ... a *tour de force*' *New York Times*

'Engrossing, believable characters ... captures Edinburgh beautifully ... It all adds up to a very good read' *Edinburgh Evening News*

'Robustly entertaining' *Irish Times*

Poisoned Cherries

Quintin Jardine

headline

First published in 2002
by HEADLINE BOOK PUBLISHING

First published in paperback in 2003
by HEADLINE BOOK PUBLISHING

5

ISBN 0 7472 6472 4

Typeset in TimesNewRoman by Avon DataSet Ltd,
Bidford-on-Avon, Warwickshire

Printed and bound in Great Britain by
Clays Ltd, St Ives plc

HEADLINE BOOK PUBLISHING
A division of Hodder Headline
338 Euston Road
London NW1 3BH

www.headline.co.uk
www.hodderheadline.com

This one's for Stewart and Susie, Mr and Mrs Baxter.

Acknowledgements

The author's thanks go to the real Ewan and Maggie Capperauld, of Thistles, North Berwick, for allowing themselves to be immortalised, and for their generous support of Riding for the Disabled.

1

Sometimes I think that if I was ever depressed enough to jump out of a window, I'd fall upwards.

We made a show of making our marriage work, my second wife Primavera and I, once I rejoined her in the States after our troubles in Spain. The deal was that I tried to put her past behind me, and she tried to do the same with mine . . . the parts of my past that she knew about, that is. I sold my flat in Glasgow, the one that had been Jan's and mine, to a willing buyer at a quick-sale price. Prim never even asked who it was; that's how keen she was to cut herself adrift from Scotland. We thought about getting shot of the Spanish villa at the same time, but put that on hold for a while and rented it out instead, for six months, to a Scots actor I had met on my first movie. That was just about as long as our reconciliation lasted too; not much more than half a year.

I suppose it was okay at first; after all, we were living a dream. After cruising my way through my thirties, fate and a trusting in-law had thrown me into an acting career. My confidence . . . never in short supply at the worst of times . . . had been boosted by some half-decent reviews for my performance in my debut film, and by some one-on-one coaching from an old theatre pro who taught me plenty about phrasing, timing, relaxation, and script retention . . . the stuff you can either learn or you can't . . . so I moved positively into my second role in a Miles Grayson production.

This one was supposed to be set in Chicago, but most of it was shot in Toronto, for a very good reason. Miles, who was, is and always will be married to Prim's actress sister, Dawn Phillips, as well as being the world's top box office attraction, is also a very sharp man around a pound note, dollar bill, yen, euro, or whatever currency happens to be appropriate at the time. When it comes to dollars, he knows that the Canadian version buys a hell of a lot more than its long green neighbour, hence his choice of location.

The downside of this selection was that Miles is not alone in knowing that. In fact, Toronto's new nickname is 'the Hollywood of the North', and on any given week in the year, there are so many American film crews roaming its streets that bumping into each other could be a real problem. Fortunately, thanks to our director's clout with the mayor, who was on a one-man crusade to round up as much big-name support as possible for his Olympic bid, that didn't happen to us.

The other problem with Toronto is its mooses, or mice, or meece . . . I never did find out what the plural is; let's just call them a herd, because there are more than enough of the things to qualify. The moose is the civic mascot . . . I asked many people why this is, but nobody could tell me . . . and they have really gone overboard on it. Life-size replicas of the gormless animals are everywhere, on just about every street corner, and outside every public building; replicas, save for one thing. Very few of them have horns; those have become a collectable item in the city by the lake.

Miles's movie had a long production schedule, since he was running a documentary project simultaneously, for Australian television. It didn't overrun, but I was committed to Canada on and off for more than six months. Whenever I could, on weekends and off-weeks, I went back, as was expected of one half of a happy couple, to Prim in Los Angeles, and to the beach-front house we were renting. When I was in Toronto, camping out in the spacious and elegant Royal York Hotel, I played the faithful husband to perfection. Almost. I won't say I never looked at another woman, but I certainly didn't touch. In fact, I spent most of my spare time in the gym, or watching baseball in the Skydome.

More fool me.

In spite of our director star's split commitment, we wrapped the movie two weeks ahead of schedule. The champagne corks were popped on set, I said goodbye to the lady publisher who had offered me serious bucks for US distribution rights to my ghosted autobiography... yes, that's how bizarre my life had become ... and headed home to LA, to the warm and welcoming arms of my wife and full-time dedicated matrimony.

As the Beatles sang, I should have known better.

It was a classic scene; you know it from a thousand movies and telly soaps. I actually did shout 'Honey, I'm home!' as I closed the door behind me. There was no sign of Prim in the big living room, and so I walked out onto the deck, which looked south over the beach and the Pacific.

There had been a new compact Jaguar in the driveway, but I'd simply assumed that my wife had been shopping again. So I frowned when I saw who was waiting for me; I knew right then that something was wrong. Still, I had an image to protect.

'Shit,' I murmured. 'What a memory I've got. I'm in the wrong house.'

I cannot imagine anyone less fitted for the breaking of bad news than my sister-in-law Dawn. She's a lovely Scots girl in every sense, and one of the kindest people I've ever met. She's the ultimate collector of waifs and strays, a trait that led her into some odd relationships before she met Miles. She cannot watch a charity ad on television without writing a cheque, or phoning in with a credit card number. She sponsors, personally, five hundred African children, and her own kid is well on the way to being spoiled rotten.

But she is flakier than a summer's worth of 99 ice cream cones. Dawn will panic at the drop of a hat. The first time the baby burped up some feed she wanted to call a paediatrician.

My nephew, Bruce . . . well, he's half Aussie, half Scots so what did you expect them to call him? . . . was in her arms as she turned to face me. As a matter of fact, he was plugged into the mains, as my old Dad would say. Dawn is an enthusiastic breastfeeder . . . and so, I realised as I watched him tuck in, is the boy Bruce.

She opened her mouth to speak but, inevitably, her pretty face wrinkled up and her chin started to tremble. Incongruous is too gentle a word to describe the way she looked, with her child sucking on her right nipple and tears streaming down her cheeks. Bruce paused and looked up as the first big drop landed on his forehead. LA babies aren't used to rain; it always gets their attention.

'It's P . . . P . . . Prim, Oz,' she stammered. 'She's . . .' And then she cracked up again. She didn't have to say any more, though. I'm no mind reader, but she'd told me the whole story in that one brief blubber. Besides, I knew my wife well enough by that time, just as she knew me.

My first thought was one of regret . . . not about Prim, but about what I'd passed up in Toronto with that publishing lady.

'Who is it?' I asked her, taking Bruce from her as she tucked herself back in, and struggled to get herself back under control.

4

'She's not dead,' I went on, not giving her a chance to answer, 'or the cops would probably be here, and she's come to like this lifestyle. So if she's gone there's a reason. What's his name?'

It was Dawn's turn to frown. Until then she'd only known the laughing-boy side of Oz Blackstone, everyone's favourite clown. She'd never seen the guy who was looking at her then. I think she expected me to cry too; she certainly expected me to care. Either way, I must have been a big disappointment to her.

'Nicky Johnson,' she whispered.

I actually smiled, as I held Bruce up to my shoulder and rubbed gently between his shoulder blades . . . I'm a well experienced uncle. Dawn's frown, and no doubt her disappointment, deepened. 'Ah, him. Nicky, the flying actor.' Nicky Johnson, the guy who'd given Prim a lift from California to Barcelona in his private jet, a few months before. He'd probably had it on autopilot for a good chunk of the way.

'Where have they gone?'

'Mexico. Puerto Vallarta, I think. Oz, you're not going to do anything reckless are you?'

This time, I laughed out loud at her concern; I wasn't trying to take the piss, I just couldn't help it. 'What, you mean like go after them with a shotgun? Nah, I won't bother. I'll probably punch the guy's lights out, the next time I see him . . . maybe on Oscars night, that would be good for a story . . . but only because it's expected of me.

'No, if he wants her, he can have her. Christ, whether he wants her or not, he's having her; that's the best revenge I can think of. Next time you talk to her, tell her to get a divorce when she's down there. I'll give her a million-and-a-half sterling, without haggling, less if she wants to argue about it.'

Bruce burped contentedly, and barfed a small amount of his mother's finest down my back.

'How can you be so calm about it?' Dawn asked, looking at me as if I was a stranger . . . and, at that time, I probably was.

'Easy.' I stroked the baby's head. 'It's better now than later, when there might be one of these guys to get hurt by it. Your sister would fuck anything in trousers, love; you must have known that.'

'My sister? Who, Prim?'

'Who else?'

'That's not fair!' she protested, showing some Perthshire spirit at last.

'Maybe not, but it's true.'

She was right, though, it wasn't fair. When Prim and I met up, she'd been on the straight and narrow. It was only after the first time I did the dirty on her that she started casting her eye around. After the second time, it was second nature to her, so I wasn't surprised that she'd gone off with Johnson. What did nark me slightly was that I'd been trying to behave myself. I didn't like the man I'd become . . . no, let's be honest, the man I realised I'd always been . . . and I'd been trying to clean my act up. Well, bugger that for a game of soldiers.

Love is blind, they say. It's also very stupid at times.

'Does Miles know about this?' I asked her. If he had, I'd have been major-league angry with him, for we'd travelled back from Toronto together.

'No,' she said at once. I believed her, of course; she couldn't lie to save her baby's life. 'I left a message with the maid, telling him where I was and that I'd be bringing you back for dinner.'

'Maybe I don't want dinner,' I suggested.

'Oz, you must look after yourself; I couldn't possibly leave you here to brood on your own.'

The fact is, I hadn't been thinking about brooding. No, I'd begun to mull over the possibility of calling Carmen Summers, who'd played opposite me in the Toronto movie, and trying my luck there. When it came to it, though, I couldn't say no to Dawn. You can't; it's impossible.

So I agreed. 'Let me wipe the sick off my shirt and I'll be with you,' I said, handing her son back to her. 'I'll follow you in the Corvette . . . that's assuming it's still there. I'll need to drive back later.'

'No you won't,' she replied, still snuffling a bit. 'You're staying with us tonight; just pack a bag and come in my car.'

I almost told her that this was nothing new to me, that I'd lost a wife before, big-time. But that was something else I couldn't have said to Dawn. It would have been too brutal, even for me. So I simply nodded, and did as I'd been told.

Miles was almost literally pacing the floor when we arrived at their place in Beverley Hills. On the outside it's every movie megastar's house you've ever dreamed of, but inside it's part spacious family home and part corporate headquarters. Naturally, Miles being Miles, the floor that he was pacing . . . almost literally . . . was that of his office, as he caught up on his mail and messages, but he was worried nonetheless.

'What's up?' he asked as soon as we walked in, sounding like an Aussie beer commercial. 'Where's Prim?'

The way that his jaw dropped when Dawn told him banished any last suspicion I had that he'd been in the know.

'That son-of-a-bitch Johnson,' he barked, when he could speak. 'He was a fucking hot-dog vendor when I found him, and he'll be a fucking hot-dog vendor again, when I'm finished with him.'

'Leave the sad bastard alone,' I advised him. 'He'll have enough to worry about. Please.'

'If you say so, buddy, but he'll never work on one of my projects again.' He looked at me, with those kind eyes of his. 'But are you all right? Oz, man, I'm really sorry; I was hoping that you two had yourselves sorted out for life. While I was waiting for you here, I thought that something had gone bad with Elanore. This never crossed my mind.'

'It's Mum I feel sorry for,' said Dawn, mournfully. 'She's only just got over her cancer scare, and now this . . . She'll take it very badly.'

I had to shake my head at that one. 'Elanore'll take it in her stride. Prim's a force of nature like her, in that respect at least. She can't be controlled or confined, and your mother knows that. I was wrong for her from the start; we should never have got back together after Jan died.'

'Of course you should have! You were an ideal couple, two peas from the same pod.'

'. . . Which is exactly why it hasn't worked.'

Miles laid a brotherly hand on my shoulder. 'I admire the way you're taking it, but you don't have to put on a show for us. You can let it out if you want.'

If I was a better actor I might have summoned up a tear for him, but that was beyond my skills. 'You know me,' I said instead, with what I hoped was an appropriately half-hearted grin. 'Laughing boy Oz; smiling on the outside, crying on the inside. It's my way.'

I thought to myself that if he had known the whole truth, my acting career might have hit a roadblock right there and then. As it was, he gave a sympathetic nod, and led me through the small kitchen beside his private office, and out to the pool, stopping to pick up a rack of cold beer on the way.

I don't drink the stuff much any more; I've become a wine buff since I bought a fully stocked . . . in fact, slightly overstocked . . . wine cellar with my Spanish villa. But to

8

please Miles, I took one . . . they were Victoria Bitter, imported from Australia . . . ripped off the ring pull and swallowed most of it in a gulp. It might have been bitter to an Aussie, but it tasted like damn fine lager to me. I finished it and held out my hand for another; all of a sudden it seemed like a good idea.

After the fourth, I began to realise just how tense I'd really been; and I knew why. It was sheer relief.

I hadn't really wanted to go back to Prim in the first place; I had only done it because of the leverage it gave me with Miles. Now she and that idiot Johnson had given me the perfect out. As my sympathetic in-law handed me another VB, I decided I'd play the part he wanted.

I took out my handphone, found Prim's stored number, and keyed it in. As I expected, it rang; she's embraced cellular technology more keenly than anyone I know.

She must have looked at the readout and known who was calling, for she sounded hesitant as she answered.

'Bitch!' I snarled at her. That was enough to end the hesitancy.

'At least I didn't screw anyone else on our honeymoon,' she snapped back.

'What are you talking about? Of course you did.'

'Well, yes,' she conceded, unabashed, 'okay I did; but only after I found out about you.'

'Is that what this is about? Do I still owe you?'

'No,' she answered, 'this is different.'

I thought I could hear seagulls in the background, and the sound of other people. 'Where are you?' I asked her.

'Puerto Vallarta.'

'I know that, but whereabouts?'

'In a café.'

'Does your drink have ice in it?'

'Yes. Why do you ask that?'

'Because I hope it gives you the shits. Is he there?'

'Yes.'

'Put him on.'

'No.'

'Listen, sooner or later, it'll happen. Might as well be now.'

'Okay,' she murmured, after a while. 'Nick.'

Johnson tried to sound cool as he took the phone. 'Oz, buddy, I'm sorry; you have to believe that. But these things happen; we just couldn't help ourselves.'

'Sure,' I said, as harshly as I could, for Miles's benefit. 'You just couldn't help banging my wife. Well here's something else that's going to happen; you'd better get ready to play ugly parts. When I'm finished with you, you're going to look like Brando did at the end of *On the Waterfront*.'

'Oz, please,' I heard the weasel protest. 'This isn't your style. Don't act the tough guy.'

'I'm not acting, Johnson; I am a tough guy. I've trained with tough guys. I know ways to hurt you that you couldn't even imagine.' That much was true; my time working with my wrestler pals had taught me plenty. I was beginning to look forward to showing him, too.

'Put my wife back on.' He did as he was told; I guessed I'd convinced him, because when Prim took the phone she sounded worried.

'What did you say to him?'

'I made him a promise. Miles was going to blow him out of Hollywood, but I want that pleasure for myself. Now listen, honey; I'll ask you this just once. Come home. Leave that bumhole sitting in the bar and catch the first plane back to LA.

'But I really mean it. Now or never; I won't ask you again.'

10

There was a silence. The longer it lasted, the more I worried. Christ, maybe I'd done too good a job, and she would catch the bloody plane.

So as she answered, I concentrated hard on wincing, and on not cracking an involuntary smile.

'I'm sorry,' she told me. 'I just can't do that. I don't love you any more, Oz.'

'You never did love me,' I murmured, with an Oscar-winning edge of bitterness in my voice.

'Maybe not; and maybe that cut both ways. Listen, I have to go. You do what you have to do, see a lawyer; I want a fair split, that's all. Just don't hurt Nicky, please.'

'That'll be difficult, but for you, okay; I won't touch him.' I decided that I'd leave that piece of business until she'd signed the divorce settlement. 'Take care; just don't trust that guy.'

'As if I would, after you,' she replied. 'Goodbye.'

I looked across at Miles, just as Dawn appeared at the poolside, and shook my head, slowly, and . . . I hoped . . . sadly. 'You heard me,' I said.

'Yes, mate, I did. I don't know if I could have done that in your shoes.'

'You'll never be in his shoes,' exclaimed his wife, indignantly. She looked at me. 'You called her after all?'

'Yes, more fool me.'

Miles opened yet another beer and handed it to me. I took it, but made a mental note to slow down. I didn't want to get pissed, not there, not then.

'Bruce has gone down for the night,' Dawn said. 'I thought we might cook steaks and bake potatoes on the barbecue, if that's all right with you boys.'

'Couldn't be better,' I told her.

We threw a few chunks of Texas beef on the outdoor grill and sat down to eat them with the spuds and a salad, at the big oval table at the shallow end of the pool. I was starving, but I made a show of shoving my food around the plate, and sipping morosely at my Long Flat Red . . . Miles imports most of his booze from his home country.

He watched me for a while, until eventually he leaned across towards me and punched me lightly on the shoulder. 'I can see this has blown you right out of the water, mate,' he began. He was speaking slowly; the Tyrrell's is heavy stuff. 'Me too, I don't mind telling you. I always thought Primavera was a straight arrow . . . and for her to go off with an arsehole like Johnson, that just makes it worse.

'But you must not let it get you down.' He rapped the table with his knuckles, hard enough to make him wince. 'You have a future in our business, buddy. You were good in your first movie, and better in the one we've just finished. You're a natural actor, Oz Blackstone, and you could be a big star. My advice is, concentrate on your career and use it to get over what Prim's done to you.'

I felt myself frown. 'What career, man?' I asked him. 'Okay, I've made a couple of movies for you, and I'm very grateful for the chance . . . not to mention the money . . . but my agent in London hasn't exactly been bombarding me with projects.'

'Fuck him,' Miles drawled, earning a nod of disapproval from Dawn. 'We'll get you a real agent, out here in California. But even before that, I've got a proposition to put to you. I was going to talk to you about it in a couple of days, but now's as good a time as any.

'I'm making a sack of money from the last Scottish project.' I knew this for myself; I was on one per cent of the gross and up to that point I'd made one and a half million dollars. 'So much, in fact, that I'm going back there for my next movie. I'll direct, not act, but Dawn will have the female lead. I want you in the second-guy role.'

'Oh yeah?' I felt my ears prick up, and my eyebrows rise. 'What is it?'

'It's a cop story, based on one of a series of novels. If it works out right it might even be the first in a series of movies.'

'Where's it set?'

'This is the bit you'll like most of all. It's set in your old home town; in Edinburgh.'

2

I made a show of thinking over Miles's offer of the Edinburgh part; I was even pretentious enough to ask to look at the script. Because of my grief, he humoured me, and I spent a few days at Malibu reading it between teleconferences with Greg McPhillips, my lawyer in Scotland, and meetings with Roscoe Brown, my brand new Hollywood agent.

I briefed Greg to draw up a legal separation from Prim, and a property settlement that was fair to us both, yet left me well fixed financially. He was gob-smacked when I told him, of course; he'd known us both when we lived in Glasgow and had played a significant part in our interesting lives. His shock didn't stop him giving me some pretty sharp advice, though, and promising me his personal loyalty in the event that my ex decided to cut up rough. I knew quite a bit about Greg's practice, having worked for him in the past, and I reckoned that I was on my way to becoming his biggest private client.

Roscoe Brown was positive too. Miles sent him along to see me the day after Prim dropped her bombshell. He was a young black guy, and he was offered to me as the coming player in the game. I figured out why, straight away; the reek of sharpness coming from him was as strong as his Eau Sauvage. I wasn't sure who was interviewing who . . . sorry, whom . . . at our first meeting, but whatever the truth of it was, we both passed.

It took him three days to make me realise that I didn't have to go back to Scotland. He came back to see me on the following Tuesday with offers of parts in three different projects, two of them to be shot in the States and the third back in Canada, in Vancouver this time.

He also brought with him an offer of a voice-over in a golf ball ad. I admit that I went a bit Hollywood when he tabled that one; I thought it was a step back down the ladder, until he showed me the money on offer. It was enough to change my mind. 'If it's good enough for Jack Nicholson,' I told him, 'it's good enough for me.'

When it came to choosing a movie, Roscoe was all for me staying in the States. He told me what I knew already, that sooner or later I had to cut the string that tried me to Miles. I heard him out but I decided that it would be later. I would take the Vancouver movie, I said, but first, since the schedules allowed it, I was going back home to shoot Miles's cop flick.

What I didn't tell him, or anyone else . . . least of all Dawn and Miles . . . was that I had another reason for going back to Scotland.

I had a promise to keep.

3

I wasn't sure how I'd feel, walking back into my old flat in Glasgow. It was part of a conversion of a classic nineteenth-century building: Jan and I had bought it on a whim, lured by its spectacular views across the heart of the city; but it had brought us only a few months of happiness, before it all went to rat-shit.

I should have moved on straight after Jan's death, but I didn't. I was pretty numb at the time, so I stayed there, until it became home to Prim and me as we renewed our ruptured relationship, drifting eventually into our brief, rancorous and disastrous marriage.

When I did sell it, I had misgivings about the buyer; call me superstitious if you like, but if the fucking place was cursed, as I thought, I wasn't sure if I should take the risk of passing it on to her.

But she had insisted, and when Susie Gantry digs in her heels it would take a pretty strong guy to deny her what she's after. Besides, she offered me twenty-five per cent over valuation.

'You cut it bloody fine!' she exclaimed as she opened the door that fair Saturday morning, but she was smiling, big white teeth, tan and freckles, all framed by lustrous red hair.

She was right too. Although we'd spoken about business a couple of times . . . I'm a non-executive director of her company . . . and exchanged a few text messages I hadn't seen Susie since January, eight months before. She'd been in fine shape then; she still was, only that shape was different. For all she was wearing a big white housecoat, you could tell she'd filled out a bit.

'So it seems,' I agreed as I stepped inside. 'Have you been hanging on for me?'

'Not quite,' she answered, 'but if you hadn't turned up this weekend I was going to get in touch with you. Officially, I'm due a week on Wednesday, but when I saw my consultant last Tuesday, he was talking about inducing her a few days early.'

'Her?'

'That's right, Pops. The heir to the Gantry empire's going to be an heiress.'

I wasn't sure how I felt about Susie G. When I'd first met her she'd been going out with my copper pal Mike Dylan, and her old man had been in his pomp as Lord Provost of Glasgow. Neither of them were around any more; Mike had succumbed to a terminal case of greed, and a policeman's bullet, while Jack Gantry had succumbed to several men in white coats, who'd taken him away to a place in the country, with a very high fence topped off with razor wire.

After those misfortunes, Susie was left to rescue the family construction group from potential disaster, which she did with a skill that made a nonsense of Darwin and his theories. Not many people knew that Jack wasn't her real father, and many of those who didn't insisted that his business skills were in her blood. (The same sycophants passed over the fact that he was barking mad, and that by their logic Susie might have been too.)

The business was all she had, though; that apart, she had been a lonely wee lass when she'd turned up on my doorstep in Spain, on the very day that Prim had gone off to be with her sick mother. She didn't stay lonely for long, mind you.

I learned a lot in those few days, most of it about myself; I won't say that Susie made me a better person, but she sure as hell made me more honest with myself. Until then, I'd gone through life subconsciously pretending to be like my father, who is unquestionably the nicest man I've ever known. Macintosh Blackstone does not have an enemy in the world, and that's the truth . . . made all the more amazing by the fact that he's a dentist.

The thing was that, as his son, I just assumed that everyone thought that the sun shone out of my arse as well. Everyone at school was my pal . . . it didn't occur to me for years that in a small town no one in their right mind would have wanted to fall out with the local dentist's lad . . . and afterwards I was everyone else's. I was good old Oz, short for Osbert . . . a laugh in itself . . . the finest lad you'd meet in a day's march. Okay, so my police career was so brief that afterwards I didn't even talk about it . . . well, we're not all cut out for a disciplined service. Okay, so I was a bit of a one for the ladies . . . well, we all sow our wild oats, don't we. Okay, so I was laid back to the point of indolence . . . well, we don't want to work any harder than we have to, do we?

Then I met Primavera Phillips; my luck changed, my life changed, and somewhere along the line, Oz Blackstone emerged from the chrysalis as the man who had been evolving, someone who wasn't nice all the time, but who stopped making excuses for his ruthlessness and his nastiness and who even enjoyed it on occasion.

I still think my Dad is the greatest man in the world; but I know now that he's too hard an act for me to follow. (Actually I think the same thing may have dawned on my sister Ellie. Since she dumped her apathetic husband, she's turned into a mid-thirties raver and she loves every minute of it.)

In time, I would probably have worked all that stuff out without Susie Gantry's intervention, but I thank her for it nonetheless. She opened my eyes to me, and she opened them to Prim as well, to what she was really like, and what we were like as a couple.

As for what she taught me about herself . . . let's just say that if the Glimmer Twins had met her, they'd never have written 'You can't always get what you want'. On the other hand, when Steve Winwood wrote 'While you see a chance, take it . . .'

Susie saw me there, on my own in Spain, and she knew me. She was needing, she saw her chance, and she took it. Love had nothing to do with it. As she said often enough, 'Susie doesn't love.' Just as well, I told myself; neither does Oz.

I liked her, though. I liked her frankness, and I liked her honesty . . . plus, she was tremendous under the duvet.

She didn't turn up in Spain with a game plan . . . not one that involved banging me, anyway. If she had, the baby probably wouldn't have been part of it. But when she happened, it just seemed right, somehow. It didn't alarm either of us, and it didn't add to our expectations of each other; we had sorted out our relationship by that time.

'What are you going to call her?' I asked, as I followed her into the big living space that I knew all too well.

'What are *we* going to call her, you mean. She's your daughter as well. Or do you want to keep that a secret, for Prim's sake?'

'There's no need for that. We're finished.'

'You haven't left her, have you?' she gasped. I thought I caught an edge of concern in her voice, one that had little to do with Prim, and more with the prospect of me as a single man. 'You said you were going to try to make it work.'

'No I didn't; I said I was going to go along with it at least until I'd finished the new movie with Miles. And no, I haven't left her.' I told her about Nicky Johnson and the Mexican lovenest.

'Serves you right, I suppose,' she said when I was finished, but with a smile.

'No; it serves him right.'

'That's not fair; Prim's not a bad girl. You treated her like shit on your shoe; that's the truth of it.'

'So did you. Fucking someone's husband on his honeymoon is not the act of a friend.'

'Ah, but I never said I liked her.'

I laughed. 'So you'll not be calling the baby Primavera, then.'

'Hell, no. Actually, I was thinking about calling her Janet, maybe Jan for short. I really did like her. How would you feel about that?'

I wanted to pick her up and hug her, but I hung on to my cool. One of my new life rules is 'Never get emotional'. It's the same as being drunk; you tend to say things without a thought of the consequences. Right then I might just have asked Susie to marry me, and I couldn't have been certain she'd have turned me down.

'I'd feel fine,' I told her . . . a considerable understatement.

'I was hoping you'd say that.' She smiled at me in a way she never had before. I think I realised in that moment that what we had between us was the closest we were going to get to total happiness for the rest of our lives.

'So what do you want to do, now you're here?' she asked.

I scratched my chin. 'Well, looking at the size of you, I suppose a shag'll be out of the question.'

'It'd be a bit crowded,' she agreed.

'In that case, you pack an overnight bag, I'll have a shower, a shave and whatever else, then we'll drive sedately up to Anstruther and see my Dad and my step-mother.'

'Sedately? That's not like you.'

'Girlie, I've just flown in from Los fuckin' Angeles, so my body thinks it's the middle of the night. I can fool it for the rest of the day, but please, allow me just one piece of untypical behaviour.'

She stepped up to me, then stood on tiptoe and kissed me. 'Nothing you do is typical, my love.'

'What did you call me?'

'Oops,' she exclaimed. 'Sorry . . . slip of the tongue; won't happen again, I promise. Okay, we'll do it your way. But how much have you told your Dad?'

'I've told him the same as always; everything. He's up to date; he knows Prim's gone. He knows I was coming here, and he's half-expecting us.'

'He knows I'm . . .?'

'That too; the day I keep secrets from him, I'm done.'

Susie grinned. Sometimes, when she does that, she can light up a room. 'The day you keep secrets from me you might be done, too. Listen,' she went on, 'I'd offer to drive us, but I have this problem with my feet just now. I have to put the seat so far back to get behind the wheel that they don't reach the pedals.'

She wasn't kidding either; since I'd seen her last, she had acquired a BMW sports coupé. It was low slung, and there was no graceful way she could lower herself into the passenger seat.

'I'm not so sure about this,' she muttered as I drove carefully out of the parking area.

'What do you mean?'

'I mean that I'd be nervous enough meeting your father, but looking like this . . .'

'Susie, you haven't been nervous since you were about ten, and anyway, you've met my dad before.'

'Maybe, but going up to him and saying, "Hey Mac, I've got your granddaughter in here!" . . . that's different. That's a pretty fundamental statement, sunshine.'

'My Dad has two grandsons,' I reminded her. 'He's bad enough with them, but a girl . . . He'll think you're offering him the crown jewels.'

I leaned on the accelerator as we turned on to the slip road to the M8 and had my first hint of the power under the bonnet. 'I'll have *your* crown jewels if you scrape this thing,' Susie hissed.

I took her at her word and stuck to 'sedate' as we cruised out of the city. I played with the CD controls and found that *Ophelia* by Natalie Merchant was lined up in the auto-changer. I was touched; I'd bought that album for her in January, but it's late night music and wasn't best at that moment for my advancing jet-lag. I moved on to the next and found Bob Dylan. 'Lenny Bruce' is one of his greatest and angriest songs, but there's a line in it that's pretty gross and not suitable for a lady in Susie's condition, so I hit the button again, quick, and settled for *Blue Views* by Paul Carrack . . . another of my January buys.

'No!' said Susie, and moved back to where I'd begun. 'I like that!' Until that moment, I didn't know she could sing; the mother of my child is full of surprises. She leaned back in her seat and let it all out, word-perfect on each track, her full, rich contralto complementing rather than fighting with Natalie's sharp soprano.

I didn't say a word; I just drove and listened as we cruised . . . sedately . . . out of Glasgow and along the motorway that cuts Lanarkshire in half. (Smaller pieces would be even better, a native of that county once said to me.) I didn't want her to stop, but eventually she did, during the long instrumental break on track four.

She smiled at me. 'Sorry,' she said, almost shyly.

'Don't be. Would you like to make a record? I could fix it.'

'I know you could. And if I wanted to be Sharleen Spitieri, that's who I'd be . . . but I don't.' She leaned back again and picked up on track five, with its simple piano backing, leaving Natalie in her wake as she embellished the song with some added twists that its writer never imagined.

She was into the last track, singing about golden bells, when she stopped, abruptly. I glanced sideways at her, worried that maybe I'd looked as if I was nodding off.

She switched off the music. 'Do you think you're up to driving a wee bit less sedately?'

'Probably, but why?'

She gasped, and winced. 'I could be wrong . . . I've never done this before . . . but I don't think I'm going to make it to your Dad's.'

4

For a while after that, everything became a bit blurred. I've been in a couple of dangerous situations in my time, and I've managed to stay reasonably cool, to keep thinking logically.

Looking back on that day, all I can remember saying is, 'Let's get you to the Simpson; it's nearest.' After that my brain went into meltdown; I drove that M3 like David Coulthard with Schumie on his tail, while Susie did all the sensible stuff like getting the number of the maternity unit and calling ahead to warn them.

Words broke in. Susie saying, calmly, 'Yes, my waters have broken,' although that was not news to me by that time. Then there was something about, 'Less than a minute.'

We got lucky on the outskirts of Edinburgh; I had to stop for a red light and I pulled up next to a police car. I honked the horn, the driver took one look and got the message; we had a blues and twos escort all the way to the new Royal Infirmary.

Even at that it was touch and go. I drove right up to the door of the unit; where a nurse . . . 'Hello dear. I'm Sister Mickel. A bit early, are we?' . . . and a porter were waiting for us with a wheelchair. If it had had a motor it would have been revved up. As the midwife helped her into the chair, Susie grunted, 'Christ, Oz, she's coming faster than you!' Somewhere behind me, I heard a policeman laugh.

It got blurred again; we were rushed along to a room with a funny-shaped bed. Nurses stripped Susie; just took all her clothes right off and stuck a gown over her head. There was shouting all round; 'Go on, that's a lass. Push hard now.' I realised that I was yelling as well, and that someone was grasping my hand hard enough to crush it. Then all at once, the pressure eased and there was a great collective gasp of satisfaction, into which intruded a thin wavering cry.

Sister Mickel held her up; a long, sticky, wet, pink, wriggly thing, crying full volume now that she was fully released into the world. I couldn't see her properly though, I blinked and realised that my eyes were full of tears. I held on to Susie, my head between her breasts, and let them all out. The last time I'd cried had been when one Janet had died; now I wept for the birth of another. Cry for sad if you must, but never be afraid to cry for happy; it's better.

'Well, look at you,' I heard her say, after a while; Susie as I'd never heard her before. 'Look at her, Oz. She's just like you.' I did; she was.

5

'Don't you ever think about tomorrow, son?'

'I gave that up a long time ago, Dad.'

'Maybe you should start again. What are you going to say to Miles and Dawn when they turn up in Scotland for this new movie? When they find out about the baby they're going to run out of sympathy for you bloody quick.'

That was a good question; jet-lag and the stress of the day were catching up with me fast, so I gave my brain a few seconds more than normal to come up with a good answer. I looked across the garden and out to sea; it was early evening, and May Island, bathed in sunshine, seemed to be smiling at the Fife Coast. I've seen a few pretty spectacular things in my life, but still I love that view more than any other. It's a doorway to so many memories, and, once the medical staff had pronounced Susie and wee Janet to be in the best of health, and had bedded them down for their only night in the Royal, there had been nothing for me to do but carry on up the road to Anstruther, to add another to the list.

'Who says they're going to find out?' I asked Mac the Dentist, still looking out to sea. Through the kitchen window, I heard the sound of rattling crockery, as my stepmother resurrected the meal she had readied for earlier in the day. There was a tension between Mary and me; I had expected it, but it didn't make it any easier to take. I'd been her blue-eyed boy for a long time, and she hadn't disguised the fact that she felt let down.

My Dad gave a half-snort, half-laugh. 'Will the pram not give them a clue?'

'There won't be any pram around. Susie and the baby will be back in Glasgow by the time they get here. I'll be in Edinburgh. We're not planning to put a birth notice in the *Herald* or the *Scotsman*, Dad.'

'You might as well. Susie's a prominent businesswoman, and now she's become a single mother. The tabloids are going to want to know who the father is.'

'And Susie's not going to tell them. Neither am I.'

'Are you not going to acknowledge your child, man?'

'Of course I am; I do already. I'm just not making any public announcements, that's all . . . not yet, at any rate.'

'Not until the new movie's well under way, is that what you're saying?'

'If you like, yes. I'm contracted already, so it would be bloody difficult for Miles to fire me. It would be a wee bit reckless of him too; I've become box office to an extent. Still, better safe than sorry. Once I've done this picture, I can cut myself loose, and look for other opportunities. I have a couple of them in the bag already.'

He frowned; I surmised that he wasn't that pleased with me either. 'So you have been planning ahead.'

'Of course I have.' I flashed him a grin. 'I might never think about tomorrow, but I'm fucking good when it comes to next week.'

'You've changed, Osbert, right enough.'

'For the worse?'

'No, I wouldn't say that. For the better, in some ways. For all your luck, for all your success, you've had too much grief in your life, too young. Your eyes have been opened to the evils of the world, okay. You've grown hard, and you're devious, but you don't seem to be bitter and you're not living in the past. You'll survive, and one day you might be happy again.'

'Today's not bad,' I told him.

'True,' he grinned. 'I canna wait to see my new grand-daughter. I still wonder about you and her mother, though. Is that it for the two of you? Your ships have bumped together in the night and now you're going your separate ways?'

'No, that's not it. I'll be a good father to wee Jan. I'm on the board of the Gantry Group, and I'll be a support to Susie that way.'

'But what if another father comes along? What if Susie meets someone else? What if you do? What if you find you miss Prim after all?'

'I never did miss Prim, Dad, any more than she missed me, really. We settled for each other; that's where we got it wrong. I'm not going to do the same with Susie. If she meets someone else, I'll handle that. I'll protect my daughter's interests, but I'll handle it.'

'Aye, son, I guess you will, in your own way, like you handle everything else. You know the thing that gets me about you?' I looked at him, but he didn't give me the chance to hazard a guess. 'You've never even had bloody toothache, not once in your life. Toothache is nature's way of letting the mightiest among us know that we're fallible after all, yet as far as I recall you've never had as much as a twinge.'

'D'you think Jesus had it, then?'

'Maybe not, but he had plenty in its place . . .' He stopped short. 'And so, I mustn't forget, have you.'

My father laid one of his massive hands on my shoulder. 'Don't be afraid of settling for Susie, son, if you want to put it that way, and if that's what's right for you. You and Prim should never have got back together, and if I'd been up to my job I'd have told you that. But you and Jan should never have drifted apart, and I kept that truth to myself too.

'You and Susie have this wee lass now, and that's not a bad basis for a partnership.'

'That's not just up to me, Dad. Susie's made her feelings clear.'

'Maybe, but it's a whole new world now. It changed about one o'clock this afternoon, when your daughter put in an appearance.'

The great hand squeezed my shoulder, hard. 'There's just one thing I want to know. If Prim hadn't left you, would you still be standing here right now, telling me about your daughter?'

I hadn't asked myself that question, but I knew the answer at once. 'Yes, if I'd had to make the choice, I reckon I still would.'

6

Mac the Dentist was right about the tabloids; was he ever. We weren't past the soup course before my cellphone played 'The Yellow Rose of Texas'. It was Susie, sounding a lot less tired than I did.

'The hospital's had a call from one of the Sunday papers,' she said, and I could hear the fizz in her voice. 'They've been tipped off about me having been rushed here, and that it was you who did the rushing.

'Who'd have done that, Oz?' she asked, indignantly.

'Take your pick. Police, hospital staff, another patient, it could have been anyone. I'd bet on the porters myself, but we'll never know for sure. The newspaper will protect its source.'

'Who's protected us?'

'We're not entitled to protection . . . at least I'm not. What did the hospital tell them?'

'They've referred the reporter to the Trust press officer. She's with me now, and she's asking how we want to play it.'

'It's decision time, then. What do you want to tell them?'

'That's up to you. If you just want to say that you're a friend and you happened to be with me when the baby started to come, that's okay by me. It would be the sensible thing to do, Oz.'

It was; I knew that. Nobody at the hospital knew for sure that I was the father, other than the people who had heard us in the delivery room, and I reckoned they were bound by medical confidentiality. If I played it that way there would be no comeback from Susie, ever. No lawyer would allow the paper to say any different and Miles would only find out if I chose to tell him.

There was only one problem.

'I won't deny our daughter, Susie,' I found myself saying, 'not for one second. Tell the press officer to give me the reporter's phone number. I'll issue a statement through my lawyer.'

'Saying what?'

'Saying that you've had our baby, that she's a wee cracker, and that we're both chuffed as hell.'

She laughed. 'I can just hear Greg McPhillips reading that to the press!'

'Word for word, I promise you.'

'And what'll he say about the fact that you're still married?'

'The truth; that Prim and I haven't been together for some time, and that the last time I spoke to her she was in Mexico with her new partner.'

'You sure you want to be that frank?'

'Certain.'

'What about Miles?'

'If he can't handle it, fuck him.' Mary frowned at me across the supper table. I mouthed an apology.

'Indeed I will not,' Susie chuckled. 'You might be making a scarlet woman of me, but I'm not going to live up to it.'

'Hey, I don't want to do that; we've got things to talk about.'

'No, we don't. I can take care of myself.'

'I know that. I didn't mean that.'

'Shut up, Oz. You're tired and emotional.'

'Okay, I will, for now. How're you feeling?'

31

'Sore.'

'How's wee Janet?'

'Hungry. Lovely too.'

'Look after her. I'll pick you both up tomorrow, mid-day as arranged. The only thing is, we're not going to be alone.'

7

I was as right about that as my Dad had been the day before. There was a posse of reporters and photographers staking out the maternity unit when I drove up in Susie's car. I recognised one bloke from my Edinburgh days, so I walked straight up to him, being as showbiz as I could.

'Hi, Freddy,' I greeted him. 'You guys expecting something?'

'Not any more,' he answered, as they crowded around me, shoving mikes and tape recorders into my face. 'You're a fucking dark horse, big Oz.'

'That won't be going out on radio,' I said. The newspaper reporters grinned; the woman from the local FM station scowled.

'Can we have a picture?' one of the photographers shouted. 'You and Miss Gantry and the baby?'

'That's up to Susie. We're going back to Glasgow...' I was still amazed that maternity units let patients home so quickly these days; I thought they'd have kept her in for a week. '... Maybe we could do something there.'

'We'd rather do it now, Oz,' said Freddy Everest. 'It'll get the picture desks off our backs ... and yours, for that matter.'

We did what they wanted; I had done some shopping for Susie on the way in from Fife, picking her up some normal-sized gear, since all she had packed for the weekend was maternity kit. I have to say she looked terrific, as good as

33

any movie star I've ever met, when we finally let the mob into her room.

She didn't look as good as Janet Gantry Blackstone, though, dressed in a tiny gown I'd also found at the Gyle Centre, and wrapped in my christening shawl, which my Dad had produced earlier that morning, from the box in which it had been stored for thirty years.

The drive home to Glasgow really was sedate; Susie sat in the back seat holding the baby as if she was made of nitroglycerine. This time there was no music allowed, although I don't think that *Bohemian Rhapsody* would have woken wee Jan.

'Have you spoken to Miles and Dawn?' Susie asked me, out of the blue, just as we passed Harthill.

'I called Miles last night.'

'Have you still got a career?'

I laughed. I'd been saving that one up. 'I surely do. He knew about you and me; Prim lied about that too. She told me that she'd said nothing to them about our thing, because she didn't want to hurt my movie prospects. That was rubbish, of course; as soon as she got back to the States, she spilled the lot to Miles and demanded that he fire me. He told her that he never let personal things influence business decisions, and he warned her not to say or do anything to upset Dawn.

'He was a bit pissed off that I hadn't trusted him enough to tell him myself, but we've sorted that out.'

'Well,' she muttered, 'that was easier than you thought, wasn't it?'

'I suppose so; I was never really, truly worried about that side of things, but I'm glad it's all out in the open.'

'Me too.' Susie paused. 'Tell me something, Oz. If all this hadn't hit the press, what would you have done?'

'About the baby, you mean? Exactly what I have done. In our own time, maybe, but I'd have gone public.'

34

'Why?'

I looked at her, in the rear-view mirror. 'You're sitting there, holding our daughter, and you have to ask me that?'

'I just want to hear you say it.'

'Okay. Because I've never been as proud of anything in my life as I am of being her father.'

She threw me a dazzling smile. 'Good. Because there won't be any more, you know. This one's going to be a spoiled only-child.'

'Susie . . .' I began.

She could read my mind, almost as well as Jan was able. 'Don't go there, Oz. Don't give me the "I'll stand by you" speech. I've got everything planned out. I'll run the business mostly from home; my managers and staff will have to get used to meeting me there. I'll have a live-in nanny, and domestic help; someone to clean and someone to cater when I have working lunches and the like. I don't need stood by, lover, especially not by someone like you. You're just starry-eyed over being a dad, so don't go noble on me.'

That shut me up; in fact neither of us spoke, until the Charing Cross turn-off. 'What are you going to do while you're shooting this new movie?' Susie asked me.

'You mean where am I going to live?'

'Yes.'

'I haven't made my mind up. I could take a suite in a hotel, but I had enough of them in Toronto, so I'm going to look for a place to rent for the duration. I'm not due there until the middle of next week, though; that being the case I thought I might bunk with you till then, and use the time to get myself sorted out.' I looked at her in the mirror again. 'Or is that not a runner?'

She grinned at me. 'I think I can allow that. The thought of sleeping with a movie star still has its attractions.'

8

It was clear to me from the off that Susie loved that apartment. Even if she had been ready and willing, I saw that as a big obstacle to us getting together permanently, since I couldn't conceive of myself wanting to lay down any roots there, not again.

Still, our time together was fun, while it lasted, even if I found it difficult to concentrate on the script of the new movie. A new baby is a bit like a quiet fart, in that its presence pervades all the surrounding space. A few months before, wee Janet hadn't been as much as a twitching in my loins, never mind a gleam in my eye. Prim and I had muttered things about children, but vaguely, quietly, as if we were each afraid the other might take us seriously.

My Jan had been pregnant when she died; Prim had been pregnant too at one stage, by someone else, so each of us had our own mixed feelings, even if they were unexplored and unspoken.

When Susie and I had flung our fling, I had made the classic male assumption that she was on the Pill. It had been years since a knotted condom had lain under my bed. Yet when she let me in on the truth, I felt my heart take flight in my chest; if Prim had given me the same tidings, it would have fallen like a stone.

I'd tried to explain my elation to myself, but I couldn't. And then wee Jan was born and I understood. Things don't have to be conventionally right; some just are. She was perfect, a doll, growing more beautiful by the day, as her face uncrumpled and her features began to define themselves. Both of her grandfathers came to visit, my Dad and Joe Donn, Susie's natural father. Joe didn't quite know what to make of me, but he made a fuss of the baby, that's for sure.

I watched her all the time. I watched Susie feed her, change her Pampers, dress her for the day, settle her down for the night. When she was asleep I couldn't stop myself from slipping into the nursery and standing there, staring at her. I'd always thought of myself as a clever bastard; I'd just never realised how clever I was, until her mother and I made her.

I was standing there, on the Wednesday after we'd brought her home, when I felt a small hand slip into mine. Susie stood beside me, looking down, just like me, her mouth hanging open in a smile as gauche as mine. Joe Donn had just headed back home to Motherwell, and we were alone again with our child.

'There won't be anyone else, you know,' she whispered. 'Remember all that stuff I spouted back at the turn of the year, about finding a titled twerp to give me a couple of kids and a place in the country that he could run with my money? That was all crap; I've got what I want.'

'So now I can piss off, is that what you're saying?'

'No. What I'm saying is that you can walk through that door any time you like, and come back any time you like.'

'Mmm. I don't know if that'll work both ways.'

'I don't care. As long as you provide accommodation suitable for Janet when she comes to stay with her dad, I don't care. She'll have a full-time nanny as of next week, and they'll arrive as a package.'

I hadn't given any thought to that one. In fact I hadn't given any thought to anything that might happen after the baby's birth.

'Christ,' I murmured, 'I don't even have accommodation suitable for me at the moment.'

'You still own the Spanish villa, don't you? She was made there, so where better for her to visit?'

'I'm selling that to Scott Steele. He's been renting it for a while, and he made me a good offer for it.'

'What have you got in America?'

'Nothing; the place where Prim and I lived was leased, and I've let it go. If I was asked what my permanent address is right now I'd have to say that I don't have one. I don't even have a car; I sold those to Scott as well.'

Susie stifled a chuckle. 'Oz Blackstone, millionaire vagrant; look, I mean it. You have to have something; I'm not having you take Janet to some crappy rented condo.'

'Okay, let's do some supposing. Suppose you fancied coming to visit Daddy with her, to play families for a couple of weeks? Where would you like it to be?'

'Anywhere safe, where they speak English.'

I gave her my arched eyebrows look. 'What the fuck are you doing in Glasgow, in that case? It's disqualified on both counts.'

She dug her nails into the palm of my hand. Janet started to stir, and so we crept out of the nursery, as quietly as we had come in.

'How about Fife?' I asked her, as she half-closed the door behind us. 'I've seen all these places, but I'm still a Fifer at heart. My Dad's house has been lying virtually empty since Ellie moved to St Andrews; I could take that over.'

She patted my chest. 'Whatever makes you happy . . . as long as it's good enough for our daughter.'

'Nothing will ever be good enough for our daughter.'

She squeezed my fairly impressive triceps. 'God help the lads when they come calling, in that case.'

'Indeed. It takes one to know one.'

Susie grinned up at me, slipped her arm through mine and led me along the hall.

'How're you feeling now, by the way?' I asked her. 'Still sore?'

She stopped at the bedroom door. 'Not so's you'd notice.'

9

I'd left the Edinburgh accommodation problem to Greg McPhillips. Life is ironic; he used to give me work, now he was getting so much from me that he'd almost become my personal assistant.

He called me on Thursday morning with a proposition. 'I know this chartered surveyor in Edinburgh,' he began. Everybody knows a chartered fucking surveyor in Edinburgh, there are so many of them, and especially in the city centre pubs, but Greg's a boy for long preambles so I let him stroll on.

The tale took a couple of twists before it settled down with a property developer who lived mostly off-shore but retained a duplex apartment on top of a building which he had refurbished in the Old Town, and which he was prepared to rent, fully furnished, of course, to the right clients, for the right amount of money.

Greg hadn't seen it himself, but his pal had assured him that the place was worth a look, so I drove back to the capital that afternoon, in Susie's M3 once again, but giving it its head all the way this time . . . subject to normal speed limits of course, officer.

The surveyor, a serious-looking, bespectacled guy named Luke Edgar, met me on the pavement at the Mound, about halfway between the Bank of Scotland head office and the temporary home of the Scottish Parliament. At first, I had no idea where we were going, but when he walked ten yards to an anonymous wooden front door I knew right away.

The building is probably the oldest surviving tenement in Edinburgh, and certainly the tallest. It wasn't the CN Tower, as I looked up at it, but it went pretty high by Old Town standards. I knew the story; it had been bought and tastefully refurbished by the developer, a well known Edinburgh guy with a celebrated Midas touch, and a reputation as the best spotter of opportunities in the business.

He had made a good job of the Mound, that's for sure. The apartment towered over Princes Street, and looked panoramically across the city, west, north and east. I knew I was going to take it as soon as I walked through the door, although I made a show of haggling with earnest Edgar.

There was a big reception room downstairs; I hit on that right away. We could use it for cast meetings, read-throughs and even rehearsals. I took a look at the kitchen; everything was state of the art. There were two bedrooms off the living area and two more upstairs; a couple more than I needed, but there would be plenty of room for a makeshift nursery if I could persuade Susie to bring the baby through to see her dad at weekends. To cap it all off, there was a superb Bang and Olufsen sound system, with speakers wired into every room in the place.

It didn't take long to do the deal. Greg's pal won the haggling hands down; he didn't budge on his price and I caved in quick . . . what the hell, Miles was picking up the tab anyway. We shook hands on a three-month lease, with an option to extend on a month-by-month basis if shooting overran, and arranged that I would sign next day and move in whenever I liked.

I was pretty chuffed as I drove back through to Glasgow. I knew that Susie would like the apartment, and I was pretty confident that we'd wind up playing house at weekends, for a while at least.

Life, I thought, was indeed a bowl of bloody cherries, and great big red ones, at that.

10

I persuaded Susie to help me move in on the Saturday, and to stay over, with the baby, for the weekend. She's always been very much a Glaswegian, and therefore pretty dismissive of Edinburgh, but when she saw the place, even she was impressed.

'You've got this thing about eyries, haven't you,' she said, as she looked out across the Mound. 'Your old flat in Edinburgh was a loft, then you bought the Glasgow place, which looks over everything, and the villa in Spain. I'll bet you had a view in California as well. Right?'

I thought of the crashing Pacific waves. 'True,' I admitted. 'It's the way I was brought up.'

'Rubbish,' she laughed. 'It's you, Blackstone. You've either got a voyeuristic streak, or it's sheer paranoia . . . you're afraid of the idea of anyone looking in on you.'

I hadn't thought about it before, but she'd a point. I've always liked high places. I broke my arm once falling out of a tree; not even that discouraged me.

'I don't think I'm a voyeur. As for being paranoid,' I said, as I thought about recent events, 'if I am, it's been justifiable a few times in my past. You know that well enough.'

A cloud crossed her face, briefly; I guessed who might have been behind it. 'Do you think about him much?' I asked her.

She chewed her lip. 'Mike? I think about him as

infrequently as I can possibly manage . . . which is still quite a lot. I envy you, in one way; when you think about Jan, you think warm. I can't do that. Funny, I don't feel bitter about Jack Gantry, but I do about Michael Dylan.'

'Then try not to; Mike was weak, but most of us are. He loved you.'

'No he didn't,' she snapped. 'If he had he'd have stayed with me, and not got involved in all the stuff that got him killed. And when that happened, he was leaving me, remember.'

I couldn't argue with that one; I'd been there, and I knew she was right. 'Did you love him?' I asked her.

'I thought so at the time, but not now. I really don't think I've ever loved anyone, not till last Saturday morning.'

'Don't let him put you off, Susie.'

'Ah, but he has. I wouldn't know where to begin loving a man. All I want is to feel safe.'

'Do you feel safe with me?'

'Most of the time. When we're together I do. I like being with you, Oz, but I'll never trust another man after Mike, and I sure as hell wouldn't trust you. I know you too well. How many women have you slept with since last January?'

'One.'

She threw me a quick, guilty grin. 'I've misjudged you, then; sorry.'

'No, you haven't. I never touched Prim after what happened in Spain; neither of us wanted to. She never forgot you and I never forgot Barcelona. There was someone else, though, someone in L'Escala, but it was complicated. It shouldn't have happened, but it did. I'm sorry.'

'You don't have to apologise to me, remember? You're a free man. Anyway, what's complicated about nooky?'

'In this case, the lady was married . . . to the guy Prim ran off with after she was tipped off about us.'

'I see. You were all getting even, then.'

'Vero might have been, but I wasn't. You had shown me the real Oz Blackstone by that time; you'd taught me about myself. Completely devoid of conscience, remember.'

Susie looked at me, indignantly. 'Sounds as if I taught you too bloody well!' The look became a frown; she doesn't do that too often. 'But you've told me about her. Why?'

'You asked.'

She snorted. 'And you told me, just like that! Do you think so little of me?'

'Far from it; I should have told you before. It was a secret between us.'

'Why didn't you let it stay that way? Are you just trying to put me in my place?'

I looked at her. I had come clean without thinking, but I knew why I had done it. 'I told you because I didn't want it there any more. It's a part of my past that I'm not proud of, and I didn't want it lying between us like a landmine.' I stepped up to her and put my hands on her waist. 'You said you felt safe with me, Susie. I want you always to feel that way, and I promise you that you always will be.'

Her eyes softened; so did her voice. 'What does that mean?' she whispered.

'I don't know. Just that you and the baby are now the two most important people in my life, and it will stay that way. I love wee Janet with all my heart; she turns my insides to mush. And how could I love her without loving her mother as well?'

She pressed her forehead against my chest and I held her to me. 'Shut up, Blackstone,' she murmured. 'Don't complicate things.'

'How am I doing that?'

She looked up. 'I'm afraid of you, man, don't you understand that? I'm afraid that you'll be another Dylan; he was a scheming, ambitious bastard, and so are you . . . well, ambitious, at least. Mike didn't have the wit or the balls to achieve his ambitions, but you do. I'm afraid that if I commit myself to you, those ambitions . . . not to mention your heretofore extremely promiscuous dick . . . will lead you away from me, and I'll get hurt again, only worse.'

'You're wrong about me there,' I protested. 'I've never had a properly thought-out ambition in my life. Everything that's happened to me has been by accident, until I've got where I am. I like doing what I'm doing now; I don't plan to do anything else, until I go out of fashion. By then, I'll have enough dough to enjoy a nice long retirement. Shit, I have now.

'And as far as my . . . sorry . . . our pal down there's concerned, he's had a right few opportunities over the last few months, in Canada and in California, and he hasn't risen to a single one.'

She was smiling again; I was happy about that. 'Are you telling me that from the time you went to the States at the end of January, until last Wednesday night, you were celibate?'

'I'm afraid so.'

'That beggars belief. Why?'

'I wasn't sure, until right now. Remember what you said the other night, about me being able to walk back through your door any time I like? Remember I said that might not cut both ways? Well it does. I don't want anyone but you.'

One of those long silences sprang up between us, like a barrier, until Susie knocked it down.

'Is that so? Well, do you remember when I said I didn't care if you did or not? That wasn't exactly true either. I care all right. You're not going to make me say I love you, but I care.'

46

She pushed me away and held me at arms' length. 'That doesn't mean I trust you, mind. When the baby and I go back to Glasgow, you'll be a boy-about-town again. It'll be just like it was when you were here before. You're on probation, Oz. I want to make damn sure you don't revert to type, before I start believing any promises.' Her eyes narrowed. 'You will be honest with me, yes?'

Mine widened. 'Totally.' I meant it.

'I'll believe that much, then. We tell each other everything. When you're working here we spend as many weekends as we can together. Agreed?'

'Agreed.'

'What happens when this picture's finished?'

'I'm going to Vancouver. You and Janet coming?'

'We'll see about that . . . if we get that far.'

11

I wasn't one hundred per cent sure what we'd agreed when Susie took the baby back to Glasgow the following night, to be ready for the arrival of the nanny next day.

I knew that whatever it was I liked the idea, and I felt more at peace than I had done since Jan had died. I knew also that I'd better get my head around Miles's new movie, since there wasn't that much time left.

Obviously, I'd skimmed through the script before I'd taken the part. The story was fast-moving and exciting, with a slam-bang climax, set in some familiar locations in and around Edinburgh, and I decided to read the book to get myself under the skin of my character. The hero was a senior police detective called Bob Skinner, a real hard bastard; I was playing his sidekick, a guy around my own age by the name of Andy Martin.

The first thing I read about Martin pulled me up short; the author described him as muscular . . . I could manage that okay, given the gym work I was in the habit of doing . . . and as having curly blond hair, and green contact lenses.

The dye job I could live with, but I saw a problem with the contacts. I can't stand having even a tiny piece of grit in my eye. I was sufficiently worried to call Miles . . . the apartment came complete with a phone and cable television.

He laughed when I told him about my problem. 'You say you're okay about the dye job? Did you ever see the remake of *The Jackal*? Christ, you might not be flavour of the month with Dawn right now, but I still wouldn't do that to you. You can forget the contacts too. Dark hair and blue eyes will do for the part.

'How's tricks, anyway?'

His amiability reassured me; Miles had given me an easy time of it as director of my first two projects. I didn't know if I could handle it if he started to have a go at me on set.

'Fine. Everything's fine.'

'How are the girls?'

'The baby's great and so's her mum. Susie's going back to work herself in a couple of days, once the new nanny's settled in.'

'Nothing changes, eh. She's a powerhouse, that girl. You two gonna live together?'

'Part-time, probably. I've rented a place in Edinburgh; that's where I am now. You'll like it, I think.' I described the apartment.

'Sounds great,' Miles said, when I had finished. 'You're right; I plan to shoot as much of this movie as possible on location, so we'll need a place for rehearsals, team meetings and so on.

'In fact, there's one I'll set up right away. I've hired a technical adviser, an ex-policeman. He's got the script, and he knows the book. I want him to brief the cast before we start shooting, but first I want to meet him myself. Your place will be perfect for that. Dawn and I get into Edinburgh on Wednesday. I'll arrange it for Thursday morning, ten sharp, then we'll have a cast meeting that afternoon. Gimme the address and phone number, and I'll circulate them to him and everyone else.'

I did as he asked then went back to the book. The more I read about the now dark-haired Andy Martin, the more I realised how tough he was supposed to be. I hadn't lifted anything heavier than Susie for ten days, so I called the Edinburgh Club, the best fitness centre in town, and checked out their opening hours.

I booked myself in for Monday morning, then went back to Detective Chief Inspector Martin. I'd have read it from cover to cover had I not begun to feel hungry, at around seven o'clock.

I checked the fridge and found it almost bare, apart from some milk, a few tomatoes and an egg. I was almost out of bread too . . . Susie and I had only picked up a few groceries and had sent out for pizza the night before.

I was also out of transport. A car can be an inconvenience in central Edinburgh, but these days not having one is a bigger inconvenience still. I had almost decided to take a taxi to Sainsbury's, when the obvious occurred to me. I was a lad alone in the city; where else would I go?

I hadn't seen Ali in a couple of years, but I knew he'd be there; the boy really was open all hours. His shop was a bit more than halfway down the Royal Mile, round the corner from my old loft and still no more than ten minutes' walk from my new digs.

He was behind the counter when I walked in, his back to the door as I closed it silently. As usual he was wearing a turban; if it was meant to be white it wasn't, so I gave him the benefit of the doubt and decided that it was cream. I don't know what religion Ali is, and I've never asked. I do know that with him the turban is a fashion statement, nothing more.

'Shop!' I called out; he spun round, eyes widening as he saw me.

'Hey,' he yelled, startling an old lady who was peering into the frozen food container. 'It's the fuckin' Oz man; the fuckin' movie star. Hullawrerr, Big Man, slummin' it the night, eh! Of all the bastards, eh!' As well as being one of the most accessible grocers in Scotland, my old friend is also one of the most foul-mouthed.

The old lady looked at me briefly, sniffed, and went back to perusing the frozen peas. I recognised her, vaguely, from the old days in the lounge bar in the pub down the road.

'Ah saw you wir back in town,' Ali proclaimed. He sells newspapers, so that came as no surprise. 'Fuckin' big dark horse you, eh. You don't jist dip yer wick, no' you. You dip it in the richest bird in Glesca'. Some man, right enough. How's the wean, onyway?'

'My daughter is very well thank you, Ali. Eight days old and growing more lovely with every passing moment . . . more than I can say for yourself.'

'Hey there, hey there,' he bellowed, in an almost cautionary tone. 'Where did you get the patter? You might be a big shite now, Blackstone, but I kent you when you were just a bampot round the corner.'

I smiled at him, happily. 'Aye, and you still are.'

He reached across and cuffed me lightly round the ear. 'Ach, away wi' ye.' He looked me up and down, as he rang up a packet of Bird's Eye fish fingers and a box of McCain's microchips for the old lady. 'You put on a bit o' weight?' he asked.

'I've muscled up a bit. I work out.'

'You onna steroids?'

'Nah.' I felt myself lapsing into Ali-speak. 'All protein and weights. Speaking of protein, gimme a pound of Lorne sausage, half a dozen eggs and four rolls. I'll take some beer as well, and a pint of milk . . .'

Between us, we filled a box with enough food to keep me going for three or four days. 'This still your only shop?' I asked, as he gave me my change.

'Aye, but it's no' my only business. I'm in partnership wi' ma cousin Sinjit; we do outside catering.'

'What kind?'

51

'Sannies for office meetings, and curries, bahjis, pakora, that sort of stuff; we're like everyone else around here, making a fuckin' bomb out of this new parliament. We're thinkin' about goin' after a catering concession in the new building, once it's finished. Be as fuckin' rich as you one day, son.'

'In your dreams, pal. I'll maybe give you some work though; we'll be having fairly regular meetings in my place up at the Mound. Give me some menus and I'll take a look at them.'

'Thanks. Ah'll get Sinjit to call you, if you gie' me the number.' As I wrote it down, his eyebrows rose. 'Hey, how's that fuckin' alligator of yours doin'?'

'Iguana, Ali. He's an iguana; he's with my nephews now, up in St Andrews.'

'Naw, naw. No' him, Ah ken what he is. Naw, Ah meant that bird of yours, that Prim. Right fuckin' man-eater she was.'

I frowned at him; anyone else, I might have done more than that, but Ali had always been an extreme liberty-taker. 'You are speaking, sir, of my soon to be ex-wife. I would take exception, only you're right . . . not that I knew it back then.'

'Ah did, but; she had you by the ba's, that's for sure.'

'On and off, Ali; on and off. It's all over now, though.'

'Jist as well. Oh by the way, another bird was asking after you. Member that lassie you went out wi' a few years back? Alison.'

I nodded. 'Of course I do.'

'She was in here the other day, askin' after you. She said she wantit tae get in touch; asked me if Ah hid yir number.'

'Pass it on tae her then. Ah don't mind. Shit, Ah'll have to get out of here, or Ah'll be talkin' like you all fucking week. See you.'

I picked up the box, making sure that my tins of lager were packed tight, and made a sharp exit.

12

I've looked all over Canada and California for anything that even approximates to the square, sliced Lorne sausage that my pal in the Royal Mile has stocked for years. I've never struck it lucky though; North Americans seem to go for quantity, not quality.

I had been looking forward to a good fry-up since I'd known that I was coming home to Edinburgh. There had been no chance at Susie's, since she was watching what she ate, both for the baby's sake and her own.

I called her, once I'd demolished my supper, and a can of Harp; the flat seemed empty without her and the baby. I pondered on the fact that here was I, back in what I regarded as my home city, shacked up in the sort of pad I'd dreamed about back in the old days, and I was bloody lonely. Not the sort of all-embracing loneliness that had engulfed me after Jan died, nor the vague sort from my twenties, when I was between steady women, but a sharp, biting feeling that I found unsettling, even when I was indulging myself with my spicy supper.

'How's the baby?' I asked, as soon as she picked up the phone.

'Perfect, as always,' she answered, with a chuckle. 'Don't worry, Oz. I really can look after her, you know.'

'I know; but I miss her.'

'I'm sure she misses you too, but I'm not going to waken her to ask her.'

'I miss you a bit as well, of course.'

'Glad to hear it. Let me know when you miss me a lot. Now go on out for a Chinky or something.'

'I don't need to.' I told her about my visit to Ali, and laid it on thick about the sausage.

'Stop it!' she said. 'You've got me salivating. I love square sausage too. If it's that good, then next time you come through, you can bring me some. Now bugger off and amuse yourself for a while. I'm in the middle of getting things ready for the nanny.'

I said goodnight, and went back to the Skinner book. The story hooked me, good and proper. Apart from cracking another can of lager, I didn't put it down until I'd reached the explosive conclusion. By that time I'd got to know Andy Martin pretty well, and I was beginning to look forward to bringing him to life.

For the first time since I'd left the States, I began to think hard about where I was going with the movie, and how it would be different from the first two parts I'd played. Actually, there was something I'd never told Miles; it wouldn't be the first time I had played a detective. In our middle and senior years at Waid Academy, in Anstruther, Jan and I had joined the school drama club; we'd worked our way up to the leading parts, and had got ourselves some decent reviews . . . albeit only in the *East Fife Mail*. We were pretty used to the greasepaint by the time we left for Edinburgh, but although we threatened to join the university theatre society, other things, like study and sex, got in the way.

I had enjoyed those schoolday plays, though. I never had any inhibitions as a kid . . . 'shy' is a word that has never been used to describe me . . . and I didn't have any trouble getting up there on stage and performing. I never had any trouble learning lines either; I was able to read the script a couple of times and my own part stuck; I could even prompt my fellow amateur thesps on the frequent occasions when they dried up.

Our acting highlight, Jan's and mine, came when our group took part in a county drama competition, and lifted the trophy. One of the judges was a Scottish Television producer, who thought enough of us to offer us parts, there and then, as gormless country teenagers in a forthcoming *Taggart* episode. Filming clashed with the run-up to our Highers exams, though, so we were forced to turn him, and his money, down.

When Miles gave me my first screen test, somehow it had all come back. He's still quite chuffed that he's taken a complete beginner and turned him into a feature player, and I've never got round to explaining that it wasn't quite that way.

I laid down the book and picked up the script and looked at the cast list; it was impressive, and I felt privileged that my name was on it. Right at its head, was Ewan Capperauld, undoubtedly Scotland's best known movie actor; apart, that is, from old 007. I had seen him many a time, in the television series that had launched his career, and in most of his films.

Miles had worked with him before, having cast him, for a ton of money, in a key cameo part in his remake of *Kidnapped* a couple of years earlier; that film had been Dawn's big breakthrough, in more ways than one.

The other feature parts would be played by my old chum Scott Steele, who more or less cast himself as Chief Constable James Proud, by Bill Massey, a smooth English actor who would be perfect as the bad guy, by Rhona Waitrose, an up-and-coming young Scot with big eyes and bouncy hair, just like Skinner's daughter in the book, and by Masahi Katayama, a celebrated Japanese actor, who had one of the key roles and who would give the project added international appeal.

I knew Scott well, and Dawn of course, in a professional as well as a family sense, and was comfortable with them, but the idea of working with the others started the hamster running around in my stomach. I didn't worry about it too much, though; I'd been in the business long enough to know that every performer has some nerves. Those who do best are those who overcome them best, and so far I'd managed.

There was one other guy on the cast list who would give the movie added value, and might widen its audience. One of the minor roles was a half-Irish, half-Italian detective called Mario McGuire. I'd persuaded Miles to give a test to my friend Liam Matthews, one of the stars of the Global Wrestling Alliance, where I'd cut my television teeth as ring announcer. All wrestlers these days are part-actor as well, and so he had sailed through. His major contribution to the story would be to get shot at the end, but no one can fake being hit like Liam.

I was smiling at the thought when the phone rang; so far only Susie, my Dad and Miles had the number, but I'd put my cellphone on divert when I'd come back in. I picked it up; Liam must have known I'd been thinking about him.

'How're you doing?' I asked him. 'Word perfect yet?'

'Christ, man, it's hardly going to take me long. I've only got about ten lines, then I go down in this big gunfight. I'm not exactly playing Hamlet.'

'No, but you get your leg over, and that's more than he does.'

'True; it has its compensations. Actually, I'm a bit worried about that.'

'What do you mean?'

'Well, when she gets her kit off, what if I sort of . . . You know what I mean, man.'

'Become aroused, you mean?'

'That's the polite term, yes.'

'Try to think of something else, like Jerry Gradi throwing your arse across the ring.'

'Mmm. It might take more than that, depending on the lady's appearance.'

'Look, man,' I told him, 'it's not a problem. They put something in your tea; that's what happened in Toronto.'

He bought it. 'Christ, man, are you fucking serious! How long does it take to wear off?'

'Not long. After a couple of weeks, you should see the first signs of life.'

I heard him gasp. 'A couple of weeks . . .' He stopped. 'Fuck it, I think I'll just wear baggy pyjamas.'

When I stopped laughing, I asked him why he had called. 'To wish you all the best,' he began, 'to ask after your new child, who is all over the funny papers . . . you never do anything conventional, pal, do you . . . and to pass on a message.'

'What's that?'

'The office took a call today, while we were all on the way back from a show in Cardiff. It was a girl, and she was looking for you. She said her name was Alison Goodchild; and that she was an old friend of yours. She said she needs to get in touch with you, and that it's urgent.' Liam paused. 'You haven't got another one up the duff, have you?'

'We took great pains not to do that,' I told him. 'But that was a few years back now. Did they take a number?'

'Yes.' He read it out, after I had grabbed a pen; it was a mobile, not a landline. 'She asked if you could send her a text message; she said she doesn't like speaking on the thing.'

Funny, I thought, then I remembered that Alison had always been a touch weird.

'If it makes her happy. I'll do that. Have you been told about the cast meeting yet?'

'No. When's that?'

I gave him the date and time, and told him how to find the apartment. 'See you Thursday.'

'Sure. Hey, were you serious about the stuff in your tea?'

'Nah. Did you mean it, about the baggy pyjamas?'

'What do you think?'

'A pair of boxers is probably all you'll need.'

I hung up, and thought of Alison; our thing had been doomed from the start. I could never take her as seriously as she had taken herself. I used to call her 'Tomorrow'; she thought it was after the song 'Tomorrow Belongs to Me', but actually, it was because she never came. Eventually I found someone who did, and that was that. Okay, I was a rat in those days; I admit it.

I looked at the number Liam had given me; then I switched on my mobile and keyed in a text message giving her my landline number and inviting her to call me.

I switched on the telly and was getting into David Attenborough telling me how important fieldmice are to the eco-system, when my cellphone bleeped twice to tell me that I had an incoming text message.

I accessed it and read. 'Can't phone. Can we meet?'

Strange, I thought, but I sent back, 'OK. Where? When?'

Two minutes later, I bleeped again. '9:30 tonight? Café Royal?' I read. I frowned; I was getting into those fieldmice, and there was a rerun of the afternoon's premiership match on Sky afterwards. Also, I didn't fancy the Café Royal; it's always busy and I'm at the stage of being recognised and accosted by punters I don't know. I don't mind, but they can be hard to shake loose. So I thought about it, then sent another message. 'Time okay, but not CR. George Hotel bar.' I waited, only partly focused on the mice. It took her less than a minute this time. 'OK. C U'.

There is no doubt about it; text messaging is changing the face of the English language, as it is rote.

13

The great thing about my new temporary home was that it was less than ten minutes' walk from anywhere in central Edinburgh. As I had hoped, the George Hotel bar was quiet; there were a couple of Japanese tourists and a table of loud American golfers, but otherwise only the barman and me.

He had just finished pouring what looked like a perfect pint of lager when Alison Goodchild appeared in the doorway . . . at least I guessed it was Alison. When we had been together, she had been a thin, pale, understated wee thing, with poorly cut mid-brown hair, little or no make-up, and a bad habit of catalogue shopping for clothes. In fact when I'd been watching Attenborough's mice, she had come to mind.

This woman had changed, and how. Her hair was shoulder-length, shiny, and honey-coloured, high-heeled blue patent shoes made her look a few inches taller, and her clothes were closer to Gianni Versace than Great Universal. Other things were different too; she wore eye make-up, and either she had switched to Wonderbra, or she'd been enlarged.

Still, it had been a while. I'd changed too, I guessed. I waved to her, then glanced at my reflection in the bar mirror. I was bigger in the shoulders than a couple of years before, and there were grey flecks in my side-burns and lines around my eyes that would be new to her. My clothes were much the same though, even if I was wearing Lacoste jeans rather than the Wranglers of old, and my jacket was antelope rather than cowhide.

'Vodka and tonic?' I asked her as she approached. My memory was spot on, because she smiled and nodded. The smile was new, as well. Where before it had been hesitant and a little pinched, to hide her slightly undersized teeth, now it was wide and open. I realised that she'd had them all expertly crowned. (You can tell these things when your old man's a dentist.)

'Thanks,' she said, 'but slimline, please, and just a spot of lime juice rather than lemon.'

The barman nodded and told us that if we'd like to go to a table he'd bring the drinks over. I dropped a tenner on the counter; I was pretty sure than a fiver wouldn't have been enough. I looked around for a spot as far away from the Japanese, and especially the Yanks, as we could get. As I did, a chunk of their discussion floated over.

'Hey,' one of them called out, intending that the whole bar should hear. 'Hey, did you guys hear that the Republican Party is changing its symbol from an elephant to a condom? It's perfect, see. A condom stands up to inflation, halts production, destroys the next generation, protects a bunch of pricks, and gives one a sense of security while screwing others.'

I threw the guy a 'sad bastard' look and steered Alison towards a table under the window.

She eyed me up and down as I settled into an armchair. 'You look just the same,' she said.

'Check your contacts, honey,' I told her. 'I don't.'

She shook her head. 'Oh you're older, sure, and there's a harder edge to you, more serious, but essentially you're just the same. I don't know, maybe I thought there would be sparks shooting off you now you're famous, but there aren't.'

'I still pee standing up,' I said.

'I hope you hit the bowl more often,' she murmured. Now that definitely was not the old Alison.

'So tell me about you,' she went on. 'I've read the odd article about you, but they weren't very informative. What have you been doing since you and I split up, apart from becoming a film star, that is?'

'I'm not a star,' I corrected her. 'I've taken to acting and I've been lucky to have made a couple of movies, but I'll never be top billing. Apart from that, I've just been living a life. I've been married, widowed, and married again. Now I'm in the process of getting divorced, and I've just had a child by a woman I don't live with. That's it.'

Her face fell a little; I wondered if she had pumped herself up somehow for our meeting. 'I knew the last part,' she said. 'That was in all the Sundays last weekend. But I didn't know you'd been widowed. I'm sorry, Oz.'

'It's not something I discuss with journalists.'

'What happened?'

'I don't like to discuss it with anyone. Now tell me about you, for you very definitely have changed.'

'For the better?' she asked.

'I don't know yet. I don't know anything. I don't even know why I'm here.'

'I'll come to that. Okay, about me. I've you to thank for it, in a way.'

'Why?'

'For chucking me. You were as nice as you could be when you did it, of course, but you still left me feeling that I'd bored you to tears. So I took a look at myself, and when I did, I realised that I bored even me. I looked like a bloody Sunday School teacher, I was hiding a pretty good body in drab, awful clothes, and I didn't even have the confidence to smile properly.' She paused as the barman arrived with our drinks and my change . . . even less than I'd expected.

'Plus,' she said quietly as she picked up her vodka, 'I wasn't any better when the lights were out . . . Not that you were any great shakes yourself, mind you. All cock, no technique, that was you.'

'Thank you very much, ma'am,' I muttered into my lager.

'Don't take it to heart; we didn't really interest each other so we didn't try very hard. That's the truth of it.'

I thought about it; she was probably right.

'Anyway,' she went on, 'I gave myself a makeover. I started with my teeth, then my hair, and then my wardrobe. I chucked my job, too. Remember I worked in the Scottish Office Information Department?'

'Yes.'

'Well I left, and got myself a job as an accounts manager with a public relations company. I did very well there and was promoted after a couple of years. I also got myself a fiancé. He worked for a rival firm, so we didn't announce our engagement, in case our respective bosses didn't like the idea, but we couldn't keep it secret forever. Neither of us was fired when it became public knowledge, but our client lists were scrutinised to make sure there was no conflict. I was taken off one account as a result, and I wasn't allowed on new business pitches in case I wound up competing with David.

'It wasn't an ideal situation for either of us, so we did the obvious thing. We both quit and set up on our own.'

As she told me her tale, I sensed something else that was new about her; she seemed to be brittle inside, in a way she never had been before. The old Alison might have been quiet, serious and ultimately boring, but she had never been nervous, or anything approaching highly strung; yet that was coming across the table in waves.

'So how did it go?' I asked, as she paused for refreshments.

'Very well,' she replied. 'We called ourselves Goodchild Capperauld . . .' She picked up on my frown at once. 'His cousin,' she said, forestalling my question.

'Does the name help in business?'

'It does until the prospects see the letterhead and realise it isn't him.'

'Still . . .'

'No, it doesn't work that way. He and Ewan don't get on; David's younger by about ten years, so they weren't close as children. Then something happened between them, when David was at university, and they haven't spoken since.'

'Let me guess, it involved a girl.'

'Naturally. She was a student too; David was going out with her and he took her to Ewan's younger sister's wedding. Big mistake!'

'It's worked out okay for you, though.' I glanced at her left hand, as she picked up her glass again. There were no rings; curious. 'Are you Mrs Capperauld now?'

'I was going to be,' she answered. 'We were going to get married last year, but we had so much business that we postponed it. We took on three new clients and set up a lobbying division, to help people put their cases to the Scottish Executive.'

'First things first, eh.'

'It's not like that,' she said, defensively. 'We love each other.'

'Lucky you. And you get your priorities right too.'

'We think so.'

'I'm not disagreeing with you. Now, before you eat the rest of that vodka, and the glass as well, do you want to tell me what this is about? You're in love, I've got a new baby, we could have said all this over the phone, but you wanted to meet me. Why?'

For a moment the old Alison seemed to creep out from behind the teeth, the hair and the make-up. 'I want to ask for a favour,' she murmured. I shrugged my shoulders. She gathered her confidence around her, sat up in her chair, and went on.

'I have a client who runs an office equipment business. His name is James Torrent.' I recognised it from vans I had seen around town, in Edinburgh and Glasgow. 'He supplies everything other than stationery; furniture, fittings, computers, photocopiers, the lot.

'It's a really big company; Mr Torrent plans to go public in a year, but first he's moving into new corporate head-quarters on the outskirts of Edinburgh, near the airport. He's a very important client for us, our biggest, in fact, but the thing is, he's very difficult to deal with. What he wants he gets, and if you can't give it to him, you're out; fired, no appeal, that's it.

'My problem is that when we got the business, part of my pitch said that we would arrange a big opening ceremony for the new headquarters, and that we would have a national celebrity to cut the tape. That's where I was hoping . . .'

I gasped; I couldn't help it. 'You want me to open this guy's office?'

She flushed, and let out a nervous sound that was somewhere between a laugh and a cough. 'Well, not exactly . . . I mean it would be great if you could come on the day as well, but . . .

'The thing is, Mr Torrent wants Ewan to perform the ceremony; in fact he's told me that if I can't get him to do it, he'll give his business to another company. He means it too. It would be a disaster for us, Oz, if we lost that account so quickly. He's our biggest client and word would get around the marketplace like wildfire. On top of that, he owes us quite a bit of money. He's a very slow payer, and I reckon that if he fires us we'll never see any of it. We've bought in things for him, printed material, high quality photography, and we've paid our suppliers already. We could go belly-up if he defaults on us.'

I had a sudden vision of Alison, belly-up. I also guessed what she was leading up to, but I played it out.

'I see your problem. So how do you want me to help? I can think of one way. Remember that guy Liam at GWA, who gave you my number? He could pay your man Torrent a visit, with a couple of the boys. You might not keep the business, but you'd get your money, even if it did have blood and snot all over it.'

'Let's hope it doesn't come to that,' she said gloomily. 'I'm not so sure they could frighten this man, though.'

'You've never met big Jerry.' I laughed to myself at the thought of my enormous friend. 'But if that's not a runner, do you want me to introduce you to a good lawyer? My guy Greg would sue him for you, I'm sure.'

'That would take too long. The bank's getting twitchy about our overdraft as it is. No, Oz, what I'm hoping is that you'll agree to approach Ewan on our behalf.'

My guess had been spot on. 'Christ, Alison, I don't even know the guy. Why can't you ask him? Okay, so he pinched your boyfriend's bird once. Big deal. If you talk to him he might fancy his chances of doing it again.'

'That's one reason why I can't,' she shot back. 'But it goes deeper than that. Ewan does not like his name being over the door of our company. He wrote to us and asked us to call ourselves something else, but David wouldn't hear of it. He can't do anything about it . . . I mean, he doesn't hold the copyright on it or anything . . . but his father told David's father that Ewan thinks we're cashing in on his fame, and he's furious about it. Even David's father and uncle aren't speaking now because of it.

'No, I can't talk to him; it would be difficult even if David would let me. Help me, Oz, you're our only hope.'

'Fuck me! You sound just like Carrie Fisher in *Star Wars*. Listen, I may have entered Jedi as my religion on the last census form, but it doesn't mean I am one. I'm a supporting actor; he is big time. I've got no grease with the man; he'll barely even say hello to me on set.'

'Oz, you could talk anybody into anything if you put your mind to it. My God, you talked your way into me, and no one had done that before.'

I raised an eyebrow. 'Oh yeah? You reckon I could do it again, then?'

She looked at me, over her glass; I saw that her hand was trembling, very slightly. 'If that's what it takes to get you to talk to Ewan,' she whispered.

I nodded towards the door. 'In advance?'

'Okay.'

I turned to the barman and made a 'two more' sign. 'You can relax,' I told her. 'You don't have to shag me into it; I'll talk to him for you. I'll do more than that; if Capperauld tells me to piss off, I'll ask Miles Grayson to do it. Mr Torrent will not turn him down, I guarantee you.'

Her face lit up; it reminded me of the time I gave her a week in Playa del Ingles for Christmas . . . hey, big spender.

'You will? You're wonderful, Oz. I knew I could rely on you. Hell, let's go to your place; I'll sleep with you anyway.'

I laughed. 'You must be really attached to that fiancé of yours.'

'Never mind him . . . this is a special occasion! We can call it for old times' sake.'

'My dear, bitter experience has taught me that going over old ground for the sake of it is always a bad idea. If it wasn't right then, it wouldn't be right now. And anyway . . . although I am astonished to hear myself say this . . . I can't.'

The way she smiled at me made me feel good. 'The girl in Glasgow? The one who had your baby?'

I nodded.

'What are you doing in Edinburgh, then?'

'Taking things one step at a time.'

'Is it really her, or is it the baby?'

'Until now I'd have said it was wee Jan, but the truth is, it's her too.'

'I'm happy for you.'

'Don't be, not yet. It might not work. Just let me be happy for you.'

A cloud crossed her face, as the barman put down two more drinks on the table. I gave him another tenner and told him to keep the change. 'What's up?' I asked as he left. 'You not so sure about him any more?'

'I was ready to go to bed with you, wasn't I?'

'Millions are. Has the business got more important than him, is that it? It could be that way with Susie and me, you know. Up to now, her company's been her life. There's a lot of adjusting to be done.'

'Maybe. Probably. Yes. But that's not what's wrong, or not all of it, at any rate. It's David. I don't know where he is.'

'What do you mean? Have you looked under the bed?'

'I'm serious. Anyway, we don't live together. No, I haven't seen him for nearly a week; he hasn't been into the office since Monday, and he hasn't been answering the phone at home. I went round to see him on Wednesday, and then again on Friday, but he wasn't in either time.'

'Has he done this before?'

Alison shook her head. 'No, never. He's Mr Reliable, usually. I don't know what to make of it.'

'One of two things, I'd guess; he's either lost his nerve over this problem client of yours and done a runner, or he'll turn up tomorrow morning smelling very faintly of a fragrance which is not on your dressing table.'

She pouted. 'He wouldn't do either of those things.'

'You were ready to do the second. Why shouldn't he be? What's his phone number?' She recited it; I took out my mobile, punched it in and handed it to her. She listened for a while then shook her head.

'Answering machine.'

'Doesn't mean he's not there; I do that all the time. Where does he live?'

'In Union Street, opposite the Playhouse Theatre. Why?'

'Let's go there now, the two of us, and thump on his door.'

'I couldn't do that.'

'You did already.'

'Yes, but not with you.'

'He'll answer the door if he's in there and I thump it. If he's got a bird in there he's hardly going to open it if he thinks it's you, is he?'

She killed half of her second drink. 'I suppose not. Okay, let's do it. But if he has got someone with him, will you at least pretend that you're sleeping with me?'

'How big is he?'

'About half your size.'

'Okay.'

14

David Capperauld lived in a main-door flat; that means that it opened directly on to the street. No lights were showing in the living-room window, or in the glass panel above the front door. It didn't look promising, but it had been my daft idea and Alison was pumped up to do it.

The Playhouse was emptying its audience into the night when our taxi dropped us at the end of Union Street. I didn't particularly want a large crowd to see me hammering on a door, so we slipped into Giuliano's for a coffee, to give them time to disperse, and to allow me to lose some of that beer.

Eventually we judged it to be quiet enough for us to go back. Capperauld's door was as solid and impressive as the rest of the building. He could be inside there and moving around and we wouldn't hear him through it.

I made Alison stand to one side, so she couldn't be seen though the spyglass, then I rang the bell. As we expected, there was no answer. There was a big black-painted knocker halfway up the door. I grabbed it and thumped it as hard as I could, then I did it again, and again, and again. If there had been anyone inside he wouldn't have stood for that.

'Nah,' I told her. 'Your boyfriend has definitely done a runner.'

Her face seemed to crumple; she was on the edge of tears. 'But it's not like him! David's a decent guy. He wouldn't run away and leave me to sort out the Torrent mess; he just wouldn't.' She looked at me with fear in her eyes; she was the mouse again. 'Oz, do you think we should go in?'

I looked at her, then at the door, then back at her, as if she was daft. 'I'm not kicking that fucking thing in. Do you see how thick it is?'

'You don't have to. I've got a key.'

'Jesus!' The night had turned sharp and cold; my breath came out as a cloud of steam. 'Now you bloody tell me; after we've wakened half the street. Is this what you wanted to do all along, only you wanted someone with you?'

She sniffed. 'I suppose so.'

'Well bloody do it, then! Get in there, see if there are any clues to where the boy might have gone, leave him an angry note and let's be done with it.'

Alison nodded, and fished a brass key from her bag. The lock was a complicated five-lever job, with dead-bolts built in for added security. When she turned the key it sounded like she was opening a cell. She pushed the door and stepped inside, with me at her heels, feeling more useless and awkward by the second.

'David!' she called out nervously. 'David, are you here?'

The place was pitch black and deadly still. 'No, he's fucking not!' I snapped at her; impatience is not one of my usual faults, but I had had enough for the night. 'Switch on a light and take a look around.'

She reached over to the wall and felt for the switch; eventually she found it, and in an instant the hall was light. 'Fucking hell,' I heard myself exclaim.

The floor was tiled, not carpeted; from that, and the solidity of the plasterwork and doorframes, I guessed that the house had either been restored to its original condition, or had never altered in the two hundred or so years since it was built.

The thing that lay at our feet was definitely not an original fitting. He was face down; his right arm stretched out as if it was pointing to something, and his left was by his side. His toes were tucked in, sort of pointing at each other. He hadn't been a very big bloke, but a bit more than half my size, as Alison had said.

She gave a sudden mewling sound that was half scream, half cry of fear, and seemed to stagger. Then she turned, as if to run. I caught her and held her. She looked down at him again, her eyes wide with fear. I was aware of a puddle forming on the floor.

'David, yes?' I asked her.

She couldn't speak, she could only barely nod. I held on to her until I was sure she could stand, then let her go and went back to close the door.

Taking care not to kneel on any wet bits, I crouched down beside David Capperauld and went through the formality of feeling for a pulse in his neck. But he was stone cold to the touch, so I wasn't going to find one.

Without moving him, I took a look at his face. It was almost purple, and he was staring wide-eyed to one side. I could see no signs of violence.

'What's happened?' Alison whimpered.

'I can't say for sure, but he might have had a heart attack, or a cerebral haemorrhage.'

'But he's only twenty-nine.'

'It happens.'

'How long has he been . . .'

'Love, I only know a bit of first aid. It'll take a pathologist to tell you that.' I did notice, though, that we hadn't smelled anything unusual when we'd stepped into the hall. Right at that moment, all I could smell was pee. So could Alison; she tottered off towards what I guessed was the bathroom.

71

I stood there looking down at Capperauld, looking for anything that might tell me what had happened to him, but seeing nothing. When Alison reappeared around ten minutes later, she was barefoot, and wearing a man's dressing gown, knotted tightly around her waist. She was red-eyed, and she had scrubbed off her make-up. Apart from the hair she looked just as she had in the old days.

'What do we do?' she asked me, her voice still shaky.

I wanted to tell her that she would call the police and I would get the fuck out of there. I didn't need any more publicity, and certainly not like this. I couldn't do it, though. I didn't answer her. Instead I took out my mobile and called directory enquiries. They gave me the number of the Gayfield Square police office.

There was no background noise when they answered; a quiet night, I guessed. It was time to liven it up. 'I want to report a sudden death,' I told the officer on the other end of the line. 'We'll need a doctor and an ambulance, in due course.' I gave him the address and the name of the occupant, and told him that the man's fiancée and I had just found him.

'Are you sure he's dead?' the young constable asked.

I threw him the line from *The Friends of Eddie Coyle*. 'If he isn't, he never will be.' The boy didn't laugh. Why should he have? It wasn't funny.

15

I woke up, dazed and confused; the phone was ringing beside my head and I had just emerged from a weird dream involving a stiff in a New Town flat, a girl pissing herself with fright . . .

Only, I realised, it hadn't been a dream.

I picked up the phone, and mumbled into it. 'You lazy so and so,' I heard Susie exclaim. 'Do you know what time it is?'

'No,' I answered, truthfully.

'Half past nine. Did you go on the batter last night?'

'Don't ask about last night.'

She laughed like a bell. 'That bad, was it?'

I pulled myself up in bed and told her the whole story.

'Oh, the poor girl,' Susie squealed, when I told her about finding David Capperauld. 'It must have scared the life out of her.'

'It scared something out of her, that's for sure.'

'Did you get the police?'

'Of course, and a doctor, and a wagon for the morgue.'

'Will you be in the papers again?'

'My name won't be mentioned; the guy who came round was a detective sergeant called Ron Morrow. I met him once; he's a good lad, said he'd leave me out of his report.'

'What did the doctor say?'

'Much the same as me; she said she couldn't be sure, but that it looked like a cerebral incident, rare but not unknown

73

in a guy of that age. They'll know for certain once they've done an autopsy.'

'When's that going to happen?'

'I don't know. Today, I guess.'

'Where's the girl now? Did you take her back to your place?'

'Did I hell as like! She phoned her mother and told her what had happened; the police took her there.'

'Mmm,' Susie murmured. 'I thought you'd have been there with a consoling shoulder.'

'She's better at her mother's. Besides . . .'

'Besides what?'

'Nothing. How's the baby?'

'She kept me awake half the night, but other than that she's perfect. Ethel's here now.'

'Ethel?'

'Ethel Reid, the new nanny; she arrived at nine sharp, and she's taken over already.'

'Ah, but can she breastfeed?'

'I shouldn't think so; she's about fifty. But we're going to get Janet on to the bottle quite soon.'

'Have you thought that through?'

'Absolutely. I'm going back to work, remember. I'm a builder, Oz; that's what I do, it's the world I live in, and I am not, repeat not, whipping out a tit halfway through a meeting with my site managers.'

'No,' I conceded. 'I can see that might distract them. You might have houses being built in inches rather than centimetres.'

'Was than an oblique reference to the size of my bosom?'

'Not so oblique; they're pretty spectacular just now, you have to admit.'

'Enjoy while you can.'

I paused. 'If that's an invitation, I thought I might come through tonight.'

'Why?'

'I have to see Greg McPhillips, about the divorce arrangements, so I thought I'd fit it in this afternoon.' I paused. 'Also . . . am I allowed to say I'm missing you?'

'You are . . . since I feel a bit that way myself.'

'See you later then.'

'Okay. You can take me out to dinner; I've got a sudden urge to get dolled up in normal-sized clothes. I haven't been able to do that for months.'

I hung up, swung myself out of bed and lurched into the shower. Half an hour later, after finishing off the Lorne sausage and the last couple of rolls, I began to feel human again.

I was looking out over the city, getting ready to go to the Edinburgh Club, when the phone rang once more. It was Alison; she sounded sad, but together. 'I want to thank you for last night,' she said. 'If I had gone in there on my own . . .'

'It's okay. You don't have to thank me.'

'You surprised me, you know,' she murmured. 'The way you handled it. There's more to you than I ever realised.'

I didn't tell her, but I've seen things that were a hell of a lot more grisly than her late fiancé. For some reason, I found myself thinking of a man called Ramon Fortunato.

'I suppose losing your wife must have had an effect on you. I understand that now, being in the same boat myself.'

I felt my forehead bunch into a savage frown. *Brain first, mouth second, Blackstone*, I tried to tell myself, but I was too late. 'What?' I said; actually it was more of a snarl. 'Was David pregnant too?

'You're not even on the same fucking ocean as me, never mind in the same boat. You were ready to screw me last night, remember. If I'd said the word we'd have been at my place, not his.'

75

'Don't, Oz,' she pleaded, and the wail in her voice got to me at once. 'I've been torturing myself about that all night.'

'Okay, okay, I'm sorry. That was brutal of me, but I still can't talk about that. I never will.'

'I understand. That's all; I understand.'

'Yeah. Truce.'

'Good.' She paused. 'About that thing we discussed last night?'

She was back to business already; she took my breath away. 'Torrent?'

'Yes. Will you still do what you said?'

'Of course I will. Ewan might feel a bit guilty now. He'll probably be a soft touch.'

'Maybe we should forget him and just go with Miles Grayson. You're right; Mr Torrent would love that.'

'No,' I told her. 'Miles is fall-back. You stick with Ewan Capperauld, if you can get him.'

'All right. When'll you do it?'

'This week, I hope. I expect to meet him on Thursday. I'll call you at your office when I've got something to tell you. I take it you'll be going to work regardless?'

'I have to; there's no choice.'

'Suppose not. I'll call.'

'Thanks. Goodbye.'

She hung up and left me shaking my head. I hadn't understood Alison before, and I sure as hell didn't now.

Her call had left me keener than ever to get into a gym, so I caught a taxi on the Mound and went straight to the Club. I signed up for a short-term membership and let the instructor show me round the equipment, although there was nothing there I hadn't used many times before.

I had a lot to get out of my system, so once I had warmed up with a few hundred sit-ups, I bench-pressed a shitload of weight, first legs, then arms, in increasingly large lumps. Once I was through with that, I worked my way around the rest of the machinery in my usual pattern, and finished off with a tough twenty minutes on the exercise bike.

'If Ali the Grocer could see me now,' I gasped as, finally, I swung off. I hadn't been a total stranger to physical exercise on my last sojourn in Edinburgh, but we hadn't been the best of pals either.

Once I had showered, for the second time that morning, I walked back up to Princes Street, picked up some lunch in Marks & Spencer's food hall, and made my way home, via the National Gallery, which stands at the foot of the Mound. It isn't the biggest in Britain, but it's one of the best, and it's always been one of my favourite places to chill out.

After I'd eaten, I decided to do some more work on my script; Thursday was looming up. I didn't know it, but so was something else.

I worked for nearly an hour, looking at my scenes, and going through them in my head at first, then aloud, my own very early rehearsal process. Eventually I decreed a coffee break and headed for the kitchen.

When the door buzzer sounded, it took me a second or two to figure out what it was, then another few to figure out where. I was puzzled as I reached out for it, too late to stop it from buzzing again. Apart from Susie and Miles, and neither of them were in town, nobody knew I was there. I guessed it had to be Luke Edgar.

I picked up the instrument. 'Hello,' I said, tentatively.

'Hello, Blackstone,' a deep voice boomed in my ear. 'Guess what; it's a blast from your past.'

It sure was, and one that I had hoped with all my heart, would stay there.

16

I could have left the bastard stood there in the street, but if he was determined I'd only have been postponing the moment, so I let him in and told him to take the lift all the way up to the top.

I left the front door open for him; he strolled into my living room, all swagger and menacing smile, came up to me and, without a word, threw a right-hander straight at my nose.

It stopped about an inch short; I'll never know whether he'd have pulled it, because I caught his wrist in mid-swing and held it steady. I squeezed the bones together until the grin left his face and he winced, then I threw him his arm back.

'Hello, Ricky,' I said, evenly. 'You're still underestimating me. I thought you'd have learned by now.'

'Only kidding, Blackstone, only kidding.' He rubbed his wrist. 'When did you get tough?'

'It happened along the way.'

I looked him up and down. Ex-Detective Superintendent Richard Ross looked older than before, and by more than the three years or so that had passed since our last meeting. He was a bit slimmer, too, but he was still a pretty formidable specimen for a guy in his mid-forties.

He and I had enjoyed . . . no, that's the wrong word; we hadn't . . . only a brief acquaintanceship, but it hadn't worked out too well for him. He had ended up in a very embarrassing position, after his piece on the side was charged with murdering her husband, and his shiny career had come to a tawdry end.

Serve the bastard right, though. He'd been keen to do me for said murder at one point, and had even broken into my flat in the process of trying to nail me for it.

Then the obvious hit me, and the pieces of the puzzle fell into place all at once. 'Let me guess,' I said to him. 'You're our technical adviser for the movie. Miles hired you; he gave you this address. I might have bloody known.'

He nodded. 'The boy detective lives on, eh. That's right; I just thought I'd pay you a call before we all get together, to get a few things out of the way.'

I sighed. 'If you really want to have a go, Ricky, try it. That window's toughened glass; you won't go through it, but I promise you this, you'll hit it bloody hard.'

Ross gave me that loaded grin again. 'No. If I was going to do you, son, it'd have happened by now, and I wouldn't have got my own hands dirty, either. I just wanted to say there's no hard feelings, about what happened back then. I've got a good chunk of pension, and I'm making more in private security work than I did on the force. In a way, I've got you to thank for that.

'I still think you or your bird, or her sister, did that murder, but I'm past caring.'

'Well you're wrong,' I told him. 'Yes, I know who did it, but he's dead. He was killed in an accident not long afterwards.'

He stared at me; I hadn't expected to take him by surprise. I thought he'd have worked it out by now. 'Yet you still let them charge Linda?'

'Too right. Did you know about a certain attempted hit-and-run incident, up in Auchterarder?'

'What are you talking about?'

'It happened. Linda Kane was the driver, in a hired car; she bloody near got all three of us too. It was you who told her where we were, Ricky. We both know that, don't we?'

He grimaced. 'I never thought she'd do that, though. First I've heard of it too. Did you make a complaint?'

'No. I told Mike Dylan about it, but that was all. Are you still porking her, by the way?'

'That'll be right. After they dropped the charges, she was going to bloody do for me. No, I steer well clear of Mrs Kane. You'd be well advised to do the same.'

He frowned. 'Mike Dylan, eh. A shame, what happened to him. I saw in the papers that you've moved in on his ex.'

Actually, he had it the wrong way round, but I wasn't going to tell him that. 'Susie and I have both had our bereavements,' I said. 'It suits us, the way we are.'

Ross actually looked sympathetic. 'Aye, I heard about yours. That was a damn shame too. That was some girl you wound up marrying. Mind that time I was following her thinking she was you? She led me a real dance.'

I never thought that he and I would share a laugh about that day, but we did.

'Before I forget, Ricky,' I said, 'and in case you do. My bird's sister, as you called her, is now Mrs Miles Grayson. I don't think Miles connects you with all that stuff, or he wouldn't have hired you. Best let it stay in the past.'

'Point taken.' He glanced back at me. 'I heard a story you were there when Dylan got it. Is that true?'

'All too true.'

'What happened?'

'We tracked the guy we were after to Amsterdam; Mike was with him. Apparently he'd been his accomplice all along. The guy made a move and the Dutch policeman shot them both.'

Ross heaved a sigh. 'Aye, that's what I heard, only the bloke wasn't a policeman. He was Dutch Special Forces, and he had his orders.' I had suspected that, although no one had ever admitted as much. 'Was it quick?'

'He said something to me, then died; that's how quick it was.'

'Ahhhhh, that Michael. He was always getting in over his head, was that boy. I knew when they let him into Special Branch that something bad would happen.'

'But not that bad. Mike and I became good friends, you know. I was gutted when it all went wrong.'

'Weren't we all, son. But it was his choice; remember that.'

'I'll never forget it; that made it even harder for Susie to deal with.' I paused and glanced at my watch. 'Speaking of whom, I've a train to Glasgow to catch.'

'Aye, I'll let you get on. See you on Thursday, then. By the way, if Grayson does remember it was me he was complaining about that time he phoned the chief . . .'

'I'll tell him it's sorted, don't worry. Just behave yourself around Dawn, and whatever you do, don't mention her sister.'

He threw me a wicked smile, with traces of his old nastiness. 'I heard about that too.' Then he laughed. 'This is going to be some job; taking a bunch of actors and chancers and trying to make them behave like real coppers.'

'Is that what you were, Ricky?'

'Most of the time, son.' He headed for the door. 'Most of the time.'

17

Ethel Reid opened the door when I arrived at Susie's with my travel bag slung over my shoulder. She eyed me up and down, with no pretence of subtlety.

'So you're Daddy, are you?'

'That's me,' I admitted, as she opened the door. 'What do you think of my daughter so far?'

She beamed at me like an auntie, and won me over there and then. 'She's an absolute wee treasure is baby Janet.'

'Takes after her mother, then.'

'Mmm,' Ethel murmured. 'I can see how you get on in the pictures and such.' I'd been called a smarmy bastard before, but never in such a pleasant way.

Susie was at her desk when I went into the living room, working on a pile of folders. The sight made my stomach twitch for a second or two. Jan and I had kept our desks in exactly the same place, looking down on the city.

'Pick it out, then,' I said to her, as I kissed her hello.

'What?'

'The restaurant; the place I'm taking you.'

'You'd have trouble seeing it from here. We're going to Rogano's; I've booked for seven thirty . . . in my name, not yours. Gantry still gets a better table in Glasgow than Blackstone.'

'Enjoy it while you can,' I told her. 'My fame grows by

82

the second. Plus . . .' I hesitated; she looked up at me, curious.

'What?'

'I just had a meeting with Greg; Prim's signed the divorce settlement and so have I. All we need to do is go through the petitioning process itself; we can do that in Scotland, right now. We don't have to wait for a year or anything like that. I'll be a free man in a few weeks.'

'And?'

'And all things will be possible.'

She held me at arm's length. 'What are you saying?'

'I never know what I'm saying,' I replied, defensively. It was true; I really wasn't sure. I hadn't planned any of this; the words were just falling out of my mouth like pebbles into a pond, and I had no idea how far the ripples would go. Until my meeting with Greg, I'd had no idea that the ties between Prim and me could be severed so quickly.

'Well, when you do know, tell me,' she said.

'You'd be interested in hearing, then?'

'Yes. Now if we've finished sparring; drop the subject until you actually are divorced.'

I felt myself grinning at her like an idiot; I couldn't help it. For the first time since Jan had died I could see real happiness stretching into the future. She laughed at me, then kissed me again. 'What do you think of Ethel, then?'

'Magic. Where did you find her?'

'My father . . . Joe, that is . . . knew someone whose daughter had her until her kid was ready for school. She gave me references going back twenty-five years, and was happy for me to speak to her last employer.'

'Wee Jan's in good hands; and so are you, for now.'

I went off to see the baby; she was awake and content so I did the Daddy thing for a while, carrying her around, showing her the view across the city from the windows.

'One day, kid,' I promised her, 'all this will be yours.'

Eventually, she became restless; maybe I was boring her, but I think she was hungry. I handed her back to Susie; she plugged her in for a while, then I burped her. I'd had plenty of recent practice with Bruce, but I still couldn't stop her barfing down my shirt.

Luckily, I had another. When the taxi turned up at seven-twenty, I looked not bad at all. Susie looked much better than that; she wore a blue sequinned dress which clung to her in a way that made the driver's eyes pop out like organ stops. I couldn't object; I'd just shoved mine back in.

The Rogano restaurant is one of the most famous in Glasgow; it's in the city centre and for several generations it's been the top watering hole for the top people. Its decor goes back to the thirties, when shipbuilding was king, and its dining room is after the style of a liner of that period.

The food has kept pace with the times, though; so have the prices. We went past the bar and straight to our table when we entered; on the way several drinkers and diners nodded to Susie; one even gave her a half bow.

'Who were they, then?' I whispered as we were seated.

'A mix of council and business; the woman near the door runs a staffing consultancy, and the guy next to her is a big wheel in the city Labour Party . . . New Labour, very much. The man who gave me the wee bow is a steel stockholder. I put a load of business his way.'

As if to prove it, a bottle of champagne arrived at the table, in a bucket. Susie looked across towards the bar; Mr Steel was smiling at her. He dropped another courtly bow as she mimed her thanks. I'd have shone up for the stuff myself, but I wasn't about to turn it down, so I gave him a wave also, as the wine waiter popped the cork.

For some reason, I thought back twenty-four hours, to Alison Goodchild and her tale. 'Have you ever come across

84

a man called James Torrent in business? He's very big in office equipment, they say.'

She nodded. 'Is he ever. Why do you ask?'

'He's my friend's awkward client; the one who's putting pressure on her to deliver Ewan Capperauld to open his headquarters.'

'I see,' her eyes narrowed slightly. 'I don't envy her, in that case.

'Yes, I've come across Mr Torrent, or at least the Gantry Group has. Back in the Lord Provost's time, when Joe was finance director, he leased some photocopiers from him. He never was the sharpest tool in the box, but still, Torrent's salesman took him for a real ride. The contract had copy charges built in, with a rolling inflation increase which was actually a blank cheque. We wound up paying a quarter of a million over five years for a machine that would have cost us six grand if we'd bought it . . . and Joe had leased six machines. One and a half mil., big bucks over five years, but capable of being overlooked when shown simply as annual group operating costs.

'It was Jan who spotted it, when I brought her in to look over my books. I'd have been angrier with Joe, but she told me that he wasn't the only guy to have been stitched up that way. She knew half-a-dozen law firms and at least two big-firm accountants who had signed similar deals with Torrent and with other companies.'

'Did you take it up with him?' I asked.

'No point; the leases had just about expired when we found out what had happened. I just didn't renew them, that was all, and I told Torrent's sales director that he would be getting no more business from me.'

'Was that the end of it?'

She grinned at me; Susie loves it when she puts one over on someone, especially a man. 'Not quite; Torrent phoned me himself, and asked me why I had put the black on him. He got quite heavy about it.'

After what Alison had told me about the man, I felt rising hackles. 'Did he threaten you?'

'Not in so many words.'

'What did you say?'

She lowered her voice, until it was little more than a whisper. 'I told him that I was about to ask our Group chairman, the Lord Provost, to call for a review of the City Council purchasing policy, and second, that I planned to show the original contracts to my boyfriend, a detective inspector, and ask him to have his experts check whether any of the figures had been altered after signature.'

'How did he react?'

'He got reasonable. He told me that I was clearly upset, and he asked how he could make it up to me. I thought about asking him for one and a half million, but if that had gone back into the books I'd have had to tell our auditors where it had come from. So instead I told him I wanted six free photocopiers for the next five years.

'He said yes, just like that. I told him that in that case he could tender for my business in the normal way. I've bought a few things from him since then; his service is very good, and his prices tend to be sharp too. I've let myself believe his story that he had a rogue salesman working for him when the dodgy contracts were signed.'

'But deep down, you still think he's a Great White Shark?'

'Yup.'

'What you've told me could be useful, in that case.'

'Don't tell your pal, for Christ's sake!'

'No, I wouldn't do that; but if I have to I might let Torrent know that I'm involved. If he's that smart he'll know of the connection between you and me and he might get the message to go easy on Alison.'

'There won't be a problem, though, if you can deliver Ewan Capperauld.'

'I'm not sure I want to, if the guy's like that.'

'Just do it if you can. Don't get yourself involved in an argument with Torrent.'

I grinned. 'As someone said to me today, I wouldn't get my own hands dirty. I know the very guy who could carry the message for me.'

'Who's that?'

'No one you've ever met, as far as I know; a blast from my past, that's all.'

18

Ethel knocked on the bedroom door just after seven-thirty, but she didn't really have to. Wee Janet had wakened the household by then.

Susie took the baby from her and plugged her into the mains once more. I tried to go back to sleep, but it was no use; there was too much gurgling and slurping going on.

'Do you two want breakfast?' Ethel called, once the process was complete and I was doing my burping bit. 'It's not part of the service, mind, but I'm making my own anyway. It'll be ready in half-an-hour if you want to get up for it.'

She makes bloody good scrambled eggs, does our Nanny; plus, she knows how coffee really should be made. I asked her if she'd spent any time in the States. 'No,' she said, 'but I did spend some time in Canada, when I was younger. I'm very fond of maple syrup as a result, but it's hard to find over here.' The woman was growing on me by the minute.

Susie wanted to get back into a working routine, so she was at her desk by nine-fifteen, sorting through the letters that the postman had delivered, and another bundle that had been couriered from the Gantry Group head office on the south side of the city. She was engrossed in it, and I felt a bit superfluous, so after I'd played with Janet some more, I said my goodbyes and headed back to Edinburgh.

I had nothing planned for that day, other than maybe another session in the gym, so I killed some time in the monster new shopping centre at the top of Buchanan Street. On a whim, I bought myself a new Rolex to celebrate my impending divorce and who knew what else, then headed for Queen Street Station.

I was almost there when my cellphone rang. I had put the apartment phone on divert to its number, so it could have been anyone, but part of me hoped it was Susie, saying, 'Hey, do you want to stay for lunch?'

It wasn't, though. It was Ricky Ross.

'Oz, where are you?' he asked tersely. No banter, no funny lines; he sounded like a copper again.

'Glasgow; I'm just about to get the train back through.'

'Okay; get off at Haymarket. I'll meet you there.' He hung up.

I must be getting too old, or too prosperous, for mysteries. I was more narked than curious; a couple of years before it would have been the other way around. I checked the incoming number on the phone and called it back, but there was no answer. Maybe Ross was heading for the station already.

I picked up a *Scotsman* at the station news-stand; it was just the right length of read for the journey. There wasn't much in it; a row in the Scottish Parliament, a Tory split over Europe, and President Dubya had pissed off his allies again. I didn't see any of that as news, but I'm not a journalist . . . even if I am cynical enough to be one.

There wasn't a lot on the back page either; Scottish football clubs were on their way out of Europe and Rangers had signed yet another striker. We were almost in Edinburgh when I saw the small story on page five about the discovery of David Capperauld's body. *Star's cousin in sudden death tragedy*, the headline read.

I glanced over the story.

The well-known parliamentary lobbyist and public relations guru David Capperauld (29) was found dead in his Edinburgh flat late on Sunday night.

The tragic discovery was made by Mr Capperauld's fiancée and business partner Alison Goodchild, when she called to see why he had failed to turn up for meetings. Police and medical services were called to the scene but Mr Capperauld was found to be dead.

A police spokesman said that it appeared that the victim had succumbed to a brain haemorrhage. Ms Goodchild (30) was said to be distraught. She was being comforted by relatives and was not available for comment.

'They should have phoned the office,' I muttered as I read on.

Goodchild Capperauld has grown into one of the most prestigious lobbying and PR groups in Scotland in the two years since its foundation. It blue-chip clients include banks, insurance companies and leading Scottish businesses, including Torrent, the office equipment giant which is said to be heading for a flotation.

James Torrent, group chief executive, said yesterday; 'I was shocked to hear of David's death. I will have to talk to Alison and see how it will affect our association.'

'Nice man indeed.' I growled, loud enough for the passenger across the aisle to glance my way.

Mr Capperauld was the cousin of film star Ewan Capperauld (41), who last night issued a short statement expressing his sorrow at the death. The actor is expected in Edinburgh this week to begin work on the film version of Skinner's Rules, *to be directed by Miles Grayson, and featuring his wife, Auchterarder's Dawn Phillips.*

Among Mr Capperauld's other co-stars is up-and-coming Fife actor Oz Blackstone (34), a former boyfriend of Ms Goodchild.

'Fucking hell!' I barked loudly enough to have attracted the attention of everyone in the carriage, but for the sound of brakes as the train slowed into Haymarket. I didn't mind them getting my age wrong, but I did take exception to a gratuitous mention in a story like that.

As I stepped down onto the platform, I ran through the list of people who had known about Alison and me, and who might have spoken to the *Scotsman* about us. I came up with a few possibilities from the Edinburgh days, and decided that the likeliest was one of my Tuesday football crowd who'd been going out with a radio reporter when I'd seen him last. I took a quick glance at the story, but there was no by-line.

Ricky Ross was waiting at the top of the stairs that led up to the exit; he saw the paper in my hand, and he saw the page I had been reading.

'All publicity's good publicity, Blackstone,' he began. 'Is that the way it goes?'

I glared at him. 'Not this. It's pure fucking cheek.' I took a deep breath. 'Mind you, it could have been worse.'

'Aye, I bloody know.' I looked at the ex-detective, in surprise.

'Come on,' he said, heading for a red Alfa Romeo parked in the station forecourt, 'get in my car.'

I hadn't time to wonder what it was all about; I simply followed him.

'Young Ron Morrow,' Ricky grunted. 'He was a DC in my division when I resigned. He's a detective sergeant at Gayfield now, and he keeps in touch. He asks me for advice every so often and he tells me things in return.' I knew what was coming. 'Like for example he told me that when the Goodchild girl found her boyfriend stiff and cold on Sunday night, you were with her.'

'That's right; and he said he'd keep my name out of it, too.' I waved the paper.

'He did. That in there had nothing to do with Ron. The quote in there came from the press office; he didn't speak to any journalists.'

'If you say so, fair enough.'

'Aye, but he wants to speak to you now. I said I'd take you to see him; otherwise he was going to pay you a visit up at the flat, and that might have been a bit public. I take my job seriously, son. I've been hired by Mr Grayson as security consultant as well as technical adviser; that covers a lot of ground.'

I felt a bit uneasy. I'd been on Cloud Nine for the best part of a day; now when I looked down it looked like a hell of a fall. 'Should I be worried about anything here?' I asked.

'You tell me,' Ross answered. 'Can you think of a reason why you should be worried?'

'No,' I said at once. 'No, I can't. So what the fuck's this about?'

'Young Ron asked me not to tell you, so I said I wouldn't. He wants to tell you himself, and see your face when he does. The boy's a good copper and he's going to be even better; I'm training him well.'

He swung the car out of the station and headed east,

through the lights, then left into Palmerston Place; the quickest way to Gayfield, I recognised.

We sat in silence for a while, till Ross broke it. 'Is it true, what it says in the *Scotsman*? You and the Goodchild girl; were you and she . . . ?'

'We went about for a while; it was four or five years ago though. It's ancient history; it's pure fucking mischief to bring it up now.'

'No it's not, son. It's news. Get used to it.' I thought about my pending divorce, and wondered if that would reach the press.

'So what were you and she doing together on Sunday?' Ricky asked.

I gave him a version of the story without going into the detail of Alison's business problem, but when I got to the part about opening Capperauld's door he stopped me.

'There was nothing wrong with it,' I protested. 'She was his fiancée and she had a key, even if she was bloody slow in bringing it out.'

'Fine. Just leave it at that for now.'

It took us over fifteen minutes, even taking the short route, to get to the Gayfield Square police office. The traffic's murder in Edinburgh, and getting worse; every daft management scheme the people on the council introduce just adds to the chaos.

There was a female constable on duty at the enquiry desk. She was only a probationer . . . as I was once, a long time ago . . . but she recognised Ross straight away. She even called him sir, when he told her to fetch DS Morrow.

The sergeant and I had met briefly a few years before when I'd given him a witness statement. He had remembered it straight away when he'd turned up in Union Street.

He was still friendly enough when he appeared from his office, but there was an air of formality about him that was new; it was as if he was keeping me at a distance. He called me 'Mr Blackstone', and asked me to come with him to an interview room. Ricky started to follow, but Morrow shook his head. 'Better not, sir,' he said.

Ross frowned, but stopped. 'You're right, Ron. Better do this by the book.' That got my attention. I won't say I was nervous, but I had a keen interest in whatever was about to happen.

Another officer, a woman, was waiting for us in the inevitably grubby room; she deferred to Morrow, so I knew she was a DC before he introduced her. 'This is Gemma Green; she works with me.'

'Nice to meet you.' I nodded to her then turned back to him as I sat in a hard steel-framed chair. 'Now, sergeant, what's this about?'

'David Capperauld,' Morrow replied. 'When you found him on Sunday, did you touch the body?'

'I told you at the time what I did; basic first aid stuff. I checked for a pulse, but he was as cold as the floor, stone ginger; I knew it right away.'

'Did you notice anything unusual about him? Anything at all?'

I began to see where this was headed, but I could do nothing but think back, and answer. 'His face was purple and he was dead; that's pretty unusual in my book.'

Morrow gave me a flicker of a smile. 'I'll be more specific. Did you notice any marks on him?'

'Nothing caught my attention.'

'Did you touch anything in the hall?'

'No.'

'Did you remove anything from the house?'

'Only myself, as soon as I could.'

'Fair enough. Now, when you found the body, how did Ms Goodchild react?'

'She was shocked. She screamed, sort of.'

'Did you scream?'

'Not that I recall. I think my exact words were "Fucking hell".'

'Her reaction; it was instinctive, yes?'

I glanced at the young DC, then back at Morrow. 'Remember when you got there, the floor was wet?' He nodded. 'She wet herself; that strikes me as pretty instinctive.'

'It would seem so; yes. She changed clothes, didn't she?'

'Yeah. You saw what she was wearing when you got there; his dressing gown. She took her clothes with her in a bag when she left with your people.'

The young sergeant leaned forward, a lock of dark hair fell over his forehead. 'That was my recollection too; I'm glad you confirmed it.'

'Why?' I asked.

He replied with another question of his own. 'Did you ever meet David Capperauld when he was alive?'

'I never even heard of him when he was alive.'

'Before last Sunday, when was the last time you saw Ms Goodchild?'

'Four years ago.'

'Did it strike you as odd when she contacted you?'

'Yes it did, until she explained that she wanted me to do her a business favour.' I told him about Torrent and his ultimatum, and about David's feud with his cousin.

'So how did you come to go with her to Union Street?'

I shrugged my shoulders. 'She told me her troubles. She and the boy hadn't been hitting the high notes, and she was worried about him not having turned up at the office for a few days. I told her that if she wanted to have another go at fronting him up, I'd come with her. It was a game, really, to see if he'd answer the door to me, rather than her.'

'I see.' Ron Morrow nodded and stood up; the silent DC Green, who had been taking notes all through the conversation, did the same. 'Okay, Oz, that's fine. Thank you very much for agreeing to talk to us. We may need you to make a formal statement. I'll call you if we do.'

I laughed. 'No, no, no, Ron. I'm not walking out of here till you tell me what this is all about.'

Morrow looked at me for a long time, as if he could tell by looking at me whether it was safe to trust me.

'Okay,' said the young detective, finally, 'but in strict confidence. Don't tell anyone about this . . .' He held my eye with a stare which I took to be meaningful. '. . . Especially anyone involved.'

I knew what, and who, he meant. 'Fair enough.'

'We got the PM report on David Capperauld this morning; he died of a cerebral incident all right. It was caused by someone ramming a needle-like implement into his brain through the base of his skull. He was killed instantaneously; that's why there was no blood. There wasn't a mark either, other than the puncture wound the pathologist found above his hairline.'

I'd guessed it had to be something like that, but I still whistled. 'When?' I asked.

'The time's been fixed as last Wednesday evening. Just for the record, can you tell me where you were then?'

I thought back. 'Sure, I was in Glasgow, with my baby daughter, my girlfriend and her father.'

'That's fine. You understand I may have to check that out.'

'Feel free.' I gave him Susie's phone number.

As I stood there, I found myself hoping that Alison had an alibi too.

19

I thought about phoning her to tip her off, but didn't, because I had given my word to Ron Morrow. Instead, when I got back to the apartment, I phoned Susie.

The sergeant had been diligent, right enough; he'd called her almost as soon as Ross and I had left Gayfield Square.

'What the hell was that about?' she asked, indignant as well as curious.

When I told her, she let out a soft whistle. 'Do you think your ex set you up to find him?' she asked.

I gaved her the same answer I had given Morrow. 'Mmm,' she murmured, with a dark chuckle. 'A girl would have to have pretty good bladder control to fake that. Still . . .' She paused. '. . . Some girls do.'

'No,' I insisted, 'she was just plain terrified.'

'If she had a key, why did it take her so long to go into the place?'

'Who knows? I just don't think there was anything suspicious about it, that's all.'

Ricky Ross, who was sitting on the couch drinking a beer and eating a sandwich, gave me a sceptical look.

'What's your problem?' I asked him when I'd hung up.

'Once a copper, always a copper, Blackstone,' he said. 'Nine times out of ten when a guy's found dead like that, it's a domestic.'

'Here, wait a minute; I was a copper too, once.'

He looked at me again; scornfully this time. 'No, you weren't. You were only a probationer, and you were no fucking good at it. That doesn't count. No, if I was Ron, I'd be having your girl Alison in for a good long chat.'

I could imagine him doing it too, and since, clearly, he was Morrow's mentor, from being mainly annoyed that she had got me into all this nonsense, I began to feel sorry for her.

I checked my watch and reached for the phone. 'Hey,' said Ricky, 'you promised Ron you wouldn't tip her off.'

'I'm not going to.'

Instead I dialled Miles; he had big bucks invested in the project and he was entitled to know about everything that affected it in the slightest, especially the fact that a member of the cast of his cop movie had been interviewed by the real police about a murder.

It was very early in California but he was up and about. 'If you'd left it much later you wouldn't have caught me. We leave for the airport in a couple of hours.'

'When do you get to Edinburgh?'

'I'll be there by ten a.m. Thursday to meet up with this guy Ross. We'll arrive in Scotland early tomorrow morning, but we're going straight up to Dawn's folks' place with Bruce and Maria, his nurse. Elanore and David are going to have their grandson for the duration. We'll rest up to get over the jet-lag the best way we can, then come down to meet up with you in the morning.

'Dawn'll check into the Caledonian; I'll come to your place.'

'You could stay here,' I offered, out of habit as much as anything else.

'Thanks, buddy,' he said, 'but you need your space, and so will we. You don't want to be living with the director. It's a bad idea.'

There were other reasons too, but he didn't need to spell them out. Instead, he asked me if that was the only reason I had called.

'Wish it was. No, the movie's had another bit of vicarious publicity, and it's my fault again.'

I explained what had happened, in detail. Miles didn't say a word until I was finished. 'Has our security guy been on our side?' he asked.

I saw no harm in putting in a word for Ricky; sooner or later Miles would remember their past connection. 'Very much so; he smoothed the way today at the police station. He still has strong connections in the force.'

'That's good. I'll thank him in person when I meet him.' He sighed. 'Capperauld's cousin, eh. Could you wind up being a witness?'

'Probably; I found him. But even if the police charge someone quickly it'll take months before the case comes to trial.'

'Okay, no worries, then.' I heard him grunt. 'Well, maybe there's one. I use a PR agency as publicists on all my UK projects. Part of their brief is to let me know whenever anything affecting me, even remotely, hits the press. They should have told me about this story by now, but they haven't.

'This friend of yours; do you think she could do the job?'

I took a deep breath. 'I honestly don't know, Miles. Maybe you should take a day or two to think about that. She's just lost her partner; could be she'd struggle with that sort of responsibility.'

'Yeah, I guess you're right. Hey, you've changed, buddy. In the past you'd have said hire her just because she's female. No harm in sounding her out though.'

'I suppose not,' I said, noncommittally. Then I thought of something else. 'Do you have a contact number for Ewan

Capperauld? I want to touch base with him on something.'

'Sure. He and his wife are staying with his parents; I've got his number noted somewhere. I'll send you an e-mail before we leave.'

'Fine.' I hung up the phone.

Ricky Ross had finished his sandwich. 'Thanks for putting in the good word with the boss,' he said.

'Remember it.'

'What do you want to talk to Ewan about?'

'I told Sergeant Morrow about it; a business thing, the reason Alison wanted to see me.' I sketched in the part of the story I had left out before, explaining the feud between the Capperauld cousins, and her predicament with James Torrent. When I was finished, Ross frowned. 'I didn't know about that,' he muttered, as if the omission was a personal affront.

'Thank Christ you don't know everything,' I snorted.

'I try to, though, Oz; I do try.'

'Why are you so interested in Ewan anyway?'

'I'm handling his personal security while he's in Edinburgh. It's part of the contract; his, Mr and Mrs Grayson's, Steele's, Massey's, the Japanese guy's, the Waitrose girl's and yours.'

'Mine?' I exclaimed.

'Aye. You're a VIP now, son. I've got a team looking after all the principal cast members. Ewan Capperauld's round the clock, and so will the Graysons be when they arrive, and the Japanese guy. The rest of you will have people responsible for you when you're filming on the streets, and you'll be given a number you can call if you're being pestered.

'Everyone will be told about the arrangements at the briefing on Thursday; apart from Mr Capperauld, that is. He knows already.'

Something clicked in my brain. 'Ricky, how did you get this gig?'

'Through a guy I know from the old days; a bloke called Mark Kravitz. You'll never have heard of him.'

He was wrong there; I know Mark all right. I've seen him in action too. He had worked for Miles on my first film project, when we'd had a bit of trouble. He's a man of mystery, and he has contacts all over the place, both sides of the fence, top to bottom.

If Ricky Ross was involved with him, maybe he deserved a new degree of respect.

'Do you want Mr Capperauld's contact details?' He took a diary from his pocket, flipped through it, then wrote an Edinburgh address and a phone number on the front page of my script, which was lying on the coffee table.

He drank the last of his beer and stood up. 'Better be going,' he said. 'I've got a lot of irons in the fire just now.' He scratched his chin. 'I wonder if young Ron's making anything out of the argument between the two Capperaulds? I don't know if it was wise to let that slip,' he mused.

'Don't be daft. He's not going to go after Ewan Capperauld.'

'I fucking would,' Ricky grunted.

He was just about to leave, when the phone rang again. 'Yes,' I said, as I picked it up. I never give my name these days when I answer a call.

'Mr Blackstone?' It was a woman's voice, high and twittery, and full of panic.

'Yes.'

'This is Mrs Goodchild, Alison's mother. She's in terrible trouble.' She started to cry, on the other end of the line.

'Okay, okay, okay,' I exclaimed. 'Now please try to calm down, and tell me what this is about.'

I had met Alison's mother a couple of times when we had been going out. She had been a widow for a couple of years then, and she hadn't been handling it well. Alison had said that she had been flaky at the best of times. Listening to her burble on the phone, it was clear that she hadn't improved.

'Mrs Goodchild,' I said. Ross's eyebrows rose. 'Please. Take a couple of deep breaths, and try to control yourself.'

Eventually she could speak again. 'Alison called me,' she said. 'She's with the police, and they've arrested her. She phoned me just a minute ago and asked me to call you and tell you. She said you'd help her.'

'Oh shit,' I murmured.

'Pardon?'

'Yes, Mrs Goodchild,' I replied, quickly. 'Of course I will. Now you just calm down; take a pill, or have a brandy or whatever, and try not to worry. I'll sort everything out.' I sounded like the Wizard of, rather than just Oz.

'I'll call you later.'

I hung up and looked at Ricky. 'Do me a favour and come with me.'

'Sure, but where are we going?'

'Back to Gayfield; I might need you to use your influence with your protégé.'

20

The woman in the public office looked a little more hesitant this time when ex-Detective Superintendent Ross marched in and asked to see Detective Sergeant Morrow.

'I'll see if he's available, sir,' she said, reaching for a telephone.

'He's available,' Ricky snapped. 'Now go and get him.'

Her face flushed up; but she stood and did as she'd been told.

'Did you really leave the force?' I asked him. 'They don't act as if you did.'

'Oh yes,' he replied. 'If you'd been a fly on the wall at the last discussion I had with the former chief constable, you wouldn't ask that. The only choice the old bastard gave me was whether I resigned as a superintendent or was kicked out as a sergeant.' He smiled, grimly. 'I had my supporters, though; coppers who've actually been out on the trail of villains, rather than building their careers pushing paper.

'When I left, they had a big dinner for me in the King James Hotel. It was organised by the Superintendents' Association. They invited the boss man, but he declined, so we drank a toast to him in his absence, only none of us stood up for it.

'There's a new chief now, a bright, young guy; he was a detective sergeant under me before he went south for a spell, so my face fits again, even in the executive corridor.'

The constable reappeared, stone-faced, with Morrow following her. He beckoned us through, and led us into the CID office. 'For fuck's sake, sir,' he began. 'I'm in the middle of an interview.'

'We know you are,' Ricky replied, 'and we know who you've got in there. You let her phone her mother, and she phoned Oz in hysterics. Now is the lassie getting home tonight, or what?'

Morrow took in a breath, then let it out. 'I don't know. It's actually the second time we've interviewed her today. I had her in this morning before I saw you. She's been formally arrested, and cautioned, but we haven't charged her yet.'

'What are your grounds?' I asked.

It was as if the sergeant was answering Ross. 'First she doesn't have an alibi for last Wednesday, and she's lying about it. She told me at her first interview that she was at home, but we've checked with the taxi firm that has a contract with her company, and they've got a record of her being picked up that evening and being taken back to her office. It's in York Place, and you could spit from there to David Capperauld's flat.

'On the back of that, we got a warrant from the sheriff to search her house.' He reached into a drawer in his desk, took out a clear plastic bag. 'We found that.'

We leaned over and looked down; it was a carpenter's awl, small and needle-pointed, with a red wooden handle.

'So,' I said. 'I used to have one of those. My Dad still has. Why shouldn't Alison, or are girlies not supposed to have DIY tools?'

'That one was found in her house, but it has David Capperauld's prints on it . . . and one of hers.'

'They were engaged. Maybe he helped her put up a curtain rail or something.'

104

'And maybe he cut himself when he did it,' Ron Morrow retorted. 'It also appears to have blood on it.'

'Maybe he did cut himself.'

'And hair.' Finally, the sergeant looked at me. 'I'm sorry, Oz, but there's a real chance that's the murder weapon. I'm just waiting for someone from the lab to come and collect it. They should be able to tell us for sure.'

'It might take a while, though,' Ricky pointed out. 'Can you not let the girl out on police bail meantime?'

'I'm scared she'd abscond.'

'Release her into her mother's custody then.'

Morrow's eyebrows shot up. 'Have you spoken to her mother? She's a Mr Kipling job.' Even I had to agree with that; there was a strong hint of exceedingly good fruitcake about Alison's mum. 'I might release her into someone else's custody, though. How about you, Oz?'

'Hey, wait a minute,' I protested. I thought about Susie, and, for all her independence, and her hands-off approach to me, about how she might feel about Alison spending a night or maybe more under my roof. Furthermore, what if she had bumped off Capperauld? All round, I felt uneasy. 'I'm not fucking idle here; I've got work to do,' I told him, grabbing the easiest cop-out I could.

'It's the only way,' said Morrow, firmly.

I looked at Ricky, then shook my head. 'Yeah, I know, Mrs Ross wouldn't have it either.'

He snorted. 'Mrs Ross hasn't been having it for a while: at least not off me. There is no Mrs Ross, not at the moment. Okay, I'll be responsible for the woman, for tonight at least.'

'If you're sure about that,' Morrow told him, 'I'll go and do the paperwork now.'

'Go on then,' snapped Ricky, 'before I change my mind.'

21

Alison was tearful when Morrow brought her to us; she wrapped herself around me straight away and set about soaking my shirt. Eventually I peeled her off, and once she had calmed herself down, introduced her to her new minder.

Ricky did his best to look like a friendly uncle, but he didn't come close. Like he said; once a copper always a copper.

We went to her place first, so that she could pick up some clothes. As usual, the police had been less than tidy in their search, and as usual they hadn't bothered to clear up once they'd finished. She wanted to start in on the mess right there and then, but we had more urgent things to do. She started to talk to us about her head-to-head with Morrow as she packed her overnight bag, but Ricky stopped her.

'Don't tell us anything,' he warned her, 'however innocuous it might be. We've got no privilege. Just get on with packing.'

The Ross residence turned out to be a grey stone semi-detached near King's Buildings, which are part of Edinburgh University. He showed his unexpected house guest her bedroom then sat her down in the conservatively furnished living room.

'Right,' he began, 'first off, who's your lawyer?'

'Alex Stein, of Stein and Rothman,' she told him. 'He does all my stuff.'

106

'He's no good; that firm doesn't do criminal work. Leave this to me.' He went out into the hall; within a minute we could hear him talking, earnestly, on the phone. The conversation didn't last long but when he came back into the living room, he had a satisfied smile on his face.

'Well?' I asked him.

He picked up a remote and switched on the television. 'Wait.' He flicked through the channels until he found an Australian rugby league match on Sky, dropped into a chair and settled down to watch.

There were still seven minutes to go when the doorbell rang. Ricky went to answer and returned with a short, balding, middle-aged guy in a dark suit. 'This is Charlie Badenoch,' he said. 'He's the best criminal solicitor in Scotland.'

The lawyer looked at me in surprise. Charlie and I know each other from way back; his firm gave me quite a lot of work in the days when I was a private enquiry agent.

'Alison's a friend,' I explained, before he had a chance to ask what the hell I was doing there.

He nodded, then shook hands with his new client as she stood to greet him.

'Give us a pound, Charlie.' It was my turn to be surprised, but Badenoch simply smiled at Ross, dug into his pocket and handed us each a pound coin.

'You are now both investigators in my employ in connection with this incident,' he announced.

'Fine.' Ross looked at Alison. 'Now we've got privilege. You can say anything you like in front of us and we can't be called as witnesses. Okay, did you kill him?'

'What?' she gasped. If she was acting, she was better at it than me.

'Did you drive an awl into the back of David Capperauld's head and kill him?'

107

'No! I didn't. And what's an awl?'

Ricky didn't say anything; he just turned on his heel and left the room. When he came back, a few minutes later, he was holding an implement identical to the one Morrow had shown us, only its handle was blue.

'That's an awl,' he told her, pinching its shaft between his thumb and forefinger so that she could see it. 'Also known as a gimlet. The police found one just like it at your flat. Your fingerprint's on it, and his, and they're going to prove that it has your fiancé's blood and hair on it as well.'

She went chalk white, even as I looked at her. 'I helped him fix something up a few weeks ago, in his kitchen,' she whispered. 'I handled it then.'

'Why did you lie to the police,' I asked her, 'about being at home on Wednesday night?'

'I didn't.'

'Alison,' Ricky said. 'They've spoken to the taxi firm; they know you were picked up from home and dropped at your office. They'll argue that you didn't go in; that instead you went round to David's place and killed him with that thing they've got.

'They'll then argue that you took it away with you, and four days later staged an elaborate charade with Oz, here, so that he could find the poor guy.'

'But I didn't!' she wailed, then burst into tears again.

Ross threw Badenoch a grim glance. 'Do you still want this, Charlie?'

'Like her boyfriend needed a hole in the fucking head,' the solicitor replied. 'But I'm in it now. I'll tell you one thing, though. I'm not pleading this one in the High Court myself, even though I could. I'm going to instruct a top silk.'

I did what I did best, and calmed Alison down again.

When she could, she looked up at Ricky. 'I was at home last Wednesday,' she said. 'But I got a phone call from someone telling me that there was a light left on in my office, so I called a taxi and went to switch it off.'

'Who called you?' Charlie asked.

'I don't know. He just asked if I was the Goodchild in Goodchild Capperauld. When I said I was, he said that he worked in an office across from mine and he told me what the problem was. He didn't give me his name.'

'When you got there, was there a light on?'

Alison shook her head. 'No,' she whispered.

'Why didn't you tell Ronnie Morrow this story?' Ross demanded. 'Is it because you've just made it up?'

'No, it's the truth. As far as I was concerned I was at home on Wednesday night. That was just an interlude; I never thought to mention it.'

I felt myself getting into the swing of this. 'Have you got call identification on your phone? Like a readout that gives you the number calling?'

'Yes, I have.'

I looked at the other two guys, then back at Alison. 'Have you had many incoming calls at home since then?'

'No, not really.'

'That's good,' said Badenoch, then glanced at Ricky and me. 'You two should get back to Ms Goodchild's place now and check that instrument, but be bloody careful not to erase anything.'

'I can't,' Ross told him. 'The girl's virtually in my custody, at this address; I can't leave her and I can't traipse her all over the city.'

'You and I'll do it then, Oz,' the solicitor declared.

I almost agreed, then I thought of the movie. 'I'm sorry, but I've got good professional reasons for not being involved any further.'

'Fuck me,' Charlie Badenoch moaned. 'Is that all I get for a pound? Okay, I'll do it myself; I'll take my secretary with me as a witness.'

'We could arrange for Morrow to go with you,' I suggested. The lawyer and the ex-superintendent both looked at me as if I was daft.

'Well?' I demanded.

Charlie took my elbow and led me towards the window, so that our backs were to Alison. 'What if there was no call?' he whispered. It must have been a flash of the old Blackstone; a poor, sad, gullible, trusting idiot where women were concerned.

'True,' I muttered.

We turned back to face the others. 'Let's not get too excited about this. If Alison was set up, whoever did it was probably clever enough to use a call-box. The police may argue that Alison could have gone out and made the call to herself and had it picked up by her answering service.'

'Yes, but if that was the case why didn't she volunteer that story to Morrow?'

'If I was going to kill David,' Alison interrupted, 'why did I take a taxi at all? And why did I book one that could be traced through the company contract?'

'The Crown could argue that you were either stupid or very, very clever, that you set up the whole call-out thing to explain your presence in the area, just in case you were seen.'

'What about the meeting with me?' I asked. 'If she set me up to find the body, then all that discussion would have been phoney; the James Torrent problem could all have been bullshit.'

'Oz!' Alison protested.

'Shut up,' I told her. 'The police haven't even started on you yet. It won't be Ronnie Morrow who interviews you

110

next time; it'll be someone nasty, like Ricky here. If we're going to keep your bum out of jail for any longer than a day or two we're going to have to have all these questions answered before you meet whoever that is.'

I ignored her and looked back at the other two. 'If the James Torrent story is true, it helps, yes?' They both nodded. 'In that case, I'll follow that up.'

'Are you sure about that?' asked Charlie. 'It's involvement, Oz.'

'Sure, but if the story is genuine . . .'

'It is!' Alison shouted.

'I told you before; shut up. If it is, I'm the guy who's supposed to be delivering Ewan Capperauld to open this bloody office, so it would be natural for me to come to see him. If anyone else turns up and starts asking him questions he might react by firing Alison and her firm on the spot.'

'You've got a point,' Ricky conceded.

'Besides,' I added, 'there's something else. I want to meet the guy who was brave or stupid enough to try to rip off my girlfriend.'

22

I knew one thing when I left Ricky's that afternoon; I had had enough of taxis for a while. Okay, Edinburgh may be a bit of a pisser of a city for a car-owner, but I can't help it. Ever since I've been eighteen I've had something at my front door into which I could jump and drive off at my whim.

The cab that picked me up from chez Ross was twenty minutes late; the driver pleaded traffic. 'Don't blame me, pal,' he moaned, when I shot a glance at my watch. 'Blame the fuckin' cooncillors.'

I wasn't interested in blaming anyone; I just decided that if I couldn't beat the problem I would add to it. So instead of taking me home I had the guy drop me at the Western Automobile showroom in Willowbrae Road, where an exceptionally friendly sales executive called Simon sold me a nice blue Mercedes demonstrator, with leather seats and all the toys, in about five minutes flat.

The smile only left his face when he asked me how I'd be financing it and I replied, 'Credit card.'

'You serious?' he said; surprised although still managing to be polite. I was quite chuffed to know that, clearly, there was still someone in Edinburgh who'd never heard of me.

'Absolutely.'

'It's a bit unusual.'

'I'll bet it is.'

'There's a surcharge.'

Once a Fifer, always a Fifer; I couldn't let that one pass, or my Dad would have turned in his grave, and he wasn't even dead yet. 'Why?'

'The companies charge us, we pass it on to you.'

'Do you hear me haggling over the price of the vehicle?' I asked.

'No,' he admitted.

'So?'

'I'll need to ask my sales manager.'

Simon disappeared into a glass-walled office at the far end of the showroom and spoke to a thin-faced man. He turned to look at me; I gave him a wave and a smile and saw the slight inclination of his eyebrows that told me that he did go to movies, or watched satellite television wrestling. He looked away, and I saw him nod.

The surcharge disappeared; my gold card was authorised and I signed the paperwork. I called Greg McPhillips' office, which also deals with my insurance business, and told them to have a cover note at the dealership next morning so that Simon could register the vehicle, and I could pick it up.

By the time all that was done, there was no point in phoning James Torrent's office to make an appointment. In any event, I still had to work out a line to get me in there; I didn't think I'd make it on my name alone. Back at the apartment, I sat down and gave it some thought, until eventually I settled on a pitch.

I called Alison at Ricky's. 'How's your business set up?' I asked her. 'Partnership or incorporated?'

'We're a limited company. David and I are . . . were . . . the directors.'

'Fine. You've just got yourself a new board member.'

'Eh? Who?'

'Me, you daft bat. I don't think it would be a good idea to

lie to this man Torrent, and I have to give a stronger reason for visiting him than the one we discussed earlier. That okay with you? It's a temporary measure, mind.'

'Of course it's okay. I've just had a one-woman board meeting and you're appointed. I'll minute it later. As for the length of your directorship, we'll have to see.'

Ross took the phone back from her when we were finished. 'Charlie called,' he told me. 'He and his secretary checked Alison's phone and it does show a call logged in at around the time she said. I checked out the number with a contact. It's a box, and it's in the entrance to Meadowbank Stadium.

'That helps, Oz. If it had been just round the corner from her place, the CID would just have laughed at her. The fact that it was further away even than her office gives it a wee bit more credibility.'

'It's pretty tenuous, though, isn't it?'

'Aye, it is that. A lot'll depend on what the lab turns up.'

'When will we know that?'

'I know it now. I'm dead certain they'll match the hair and blood to the boy. How else would they have found the thing at her place, if it wasn't hers like she says? And if it was . . .' He snorted. 'However it turns out, that'll be the murder weapon; either she's lying, or someone planted it there.'

'Which do you think?'

'I don't know, and that's the truth. If I was Morrow . . . or rather if I was Morrow's boss like I used to be . . . I'd probably sling it all to the fiscal and let the crown office decide whether or not to charge her.'

23

The bedside phone woke me at seven-forty-three next morning; as I reached for it, bleary-eyed, I thought that it might have been Susie, but it wasn't. It was Miles, calling from the VIP lounge in Heathrow.

'How's tricks up there?' he asked. 'Any more headlines we don't need?'

'No,' I told him, trusting that nothing had blown up overnight. 'Your security adviser's got it well under control.'

'That's good,' said my soon-to-be-ex-brother-in-law. 'Kravitz said he was a solid guy, and well-connected too. How you feeling, anyway?'

I suppressed a yawn. 'Rubber ducked,' I told him, lapsing in to Edinburgh rhyming slang.

Miles chuckled. 'If that means what I think it does, then it goes for me too. Any way you cut it, that is one long haul flight. I'll be wrecked by the time we get to Dawn's folks' place. Age is catching up with me, my man.'

'How's Brucie handling it?'

'Like it's an adventure; he slept most of the way across. Now it's just another new day to him. How's your little one doing?'

For some reason I thought of a tabloid feature that had appeared when we were in Toronto; Miles and Oz, men about town. If they could hear us now ... 'She's great,' I told him. 'She's mastered the typical ten-day-old's repertoire;

eats, sleeps and shits, and that's it. Speaking of which, I have a couple of those to take care of myself.'

'Sure. I'll have my assistant call you as soon as she gets to Edinburgh, to set up the arrangements for tomorrow. See you when I hit town myself.'

'Okay.' I hung up and rolled out of bed. I felt a bit stiff, a late reaction to my gym work, so I did some stretching exercises, then followed up with a quick hundred sit-ups, the same number of press-ups and fifty chins, using the top of the heavy bedroom door as a bar.

I was going to give shaving a miss, and was heading for the shower when I remembered that, with luck, I'd be meeting Mr James Torrent later. I still had half a face full of shave gel when Susie called. We talked about nothing much, other than the baby, for about ten minutes; the second half of my shave wasn't quite as smooth as the first.

By the time I had showered, dressed and eaten a healthy breakfast of wholemeal toast and black coffee, it was close enough to nine o'clock for me to take a chance on phoning Torrent to set up a meeting.

My call was picked up on the second ring, then I had to sit through one of those really annoying automated multiple choice responses. I didn't want to rent office equipment, nor did I want to buy it. I didn't want to buy specific items of office furniture, nor did I want to take advantage of their space-planning service. I didn't need any other office supplies, and since I didn't have any of their equipment, I didn't need their technical help-line either. However I did have a miscellaneous enquiry; I pressed button seven.

They must have had a few of those that morning, for I was told that I had been placed in a queue, without the option of listening to Lou Vega singing 'Mambo Number Five', or those two old geezers doing the Macarena. The Trio Los Bravos performing their only hit, 'Black is Black', were at the point of doing my head in completely when finally I heard a real, female voice on the other end, but by that time I had begun to work something out about Mr Torrent.

I asked for his office. 'In connection with what, sir?' the operator asked.

'His new suit,' I told her. 'This is his tailor speaking.'

I don't know if she believed me, but she put me through anyway. 'Mr Torrent's office,' said another woman; she pronounced the name with the emphasis on the second syllable. 'How can I help you?' Her voice was slow and cultured; for some reason she reminded me of an ad for Galaxy chocolate.

'By making an appointment for me to see your boss; this is Oz Blackstone speaking.'

There was a silence, of a sort I'd experienced before. '*The* Oz Blackstone?' she asked, in a tone which implied doubt.

'There's only one of me, as far as I know. I'll be carrying Oz Blackstone's driving licence when I come to see your boss. That'll mean either that I really am me, or that I've killed me and stolen it. Oh yes, and I'll also look remarkably like me.'

'What would you like to discuss with Mr Torrent?' she asked, without as much as a chuckle. This woman had no sense of humour.

'That's something I'd prefer to discuss with Mr Torrent,' I told her.

'I am his executive assistant,' the woman said, humouring the mystery caller.

'But you're not mine. Now do I get to see the man or not . . .' I paused for effect. '. . . Or do I have to pursue other means?'

She thought about that one for a moment or two, then, clearly having decided that she didn't want to know what I

117

meant, she told me to hold on. Finally, at least fifteen minutes after I'd dialled the number, she came back on the line and announced that Mr Torrent had a meeting in Glasgow that afternoon, but that he could fit me in at ten-thirty, for half an hour at the very most.

'That suits my schedule,' I told her, then hung up.

I was fairly chuffed with myself at getting in there without having to spill any beans, so much so that I almost forgot the reason why I was going there in the first place. Remembering, I called Ricky, to check that Alison hadn't done a runner in the night, and to let them both know that I was going to see the man.

She sounded more nervous than ever when I spoke to her, she was still waiting for the lab to report to Morrow, and Ross had warned her not to expect good news.

'You did tell me the truth about Torrent, Alison, didn't you?'

I half expected her to be offended by my question, but she wasn't. 'Yes, honest,' she said. Her tone took me back a few years. I guessed that the last of her carefully constructed image had been ground away by the pressure of the last couple of days. I wondered whether she'd be able to rebuild it; I should have known better.

I was about to call a taxi to take me to see Torrent when I remembered that I'd bought a bloody car . . . it's an everyday occurrence for us rich folk, see . . . so instead I had it take me down to Willowbrae.

The Merc was ready and waiting, shining in the morning sun. It seemed to have a personality of its own; I took to it at once, more than I had to Susie's M3. Say what you like, there is a difference between a Mercedes and a Beamer. I mean could you imagine Janis Joplin singing, 'Oh Lord won't you buy me a 3-series BMW'?

Once Simon had finished his delivery run-through, I

headed off, following the signs for the A1, then picking up the by-pass and heading for Edinburgh Park, following the directions that Alison had given me. The car handled like, like . . . like a pram; fatherhood was having its effect on me, right enough.

She had told me I wouldn't have any trouble spotting the new Torrent headquarters, and she was right. It had a bloody great red 'T' on a pole in front of the main entrance, high enough and garish enough to be seen a mile away.

The visitors' car park was full, but I spotted a space in the directors' area and slid carefully in there, right in the middle of the bay to cut down the chances of my shiny car being bumped by one of its neighbours opening a door in a hurry.

The brand new, ready-to-be-opened office was a four-storey building of fairly conventional design. It looked as if it had been built out of solid stone blocks, and it shouted 'Money!' at me as I approached. There was a man in uniform standing just inside the big marble-clad atrium; I could see him as I trotted up the steps, and as he swung the heavy glass door open for me. Some job; still, it was better than being a traffic warden. 'You know you can't park there, sir,' he said. He had the same instincts, though.

'Yes,' I answered . . . one of my finest lifetime moments was being sick over one of those guys . . . and headed for the desk which was positioned in the centre of the hall, under the high glass roof. 'Oz Blackstone for Mr Torrent,' I announced, loudly. The receptionist was Chinese; a plastic card clipped to her blouse identified her as Anna Chin. She had a very nice one too, with a dimple that deepened as she smiled at me. On her desk, there was a big wooden bowl, full of red cherries, and beside it a small ceramic dish for their pips.

'Good morning, sir,' she said, in an accent which might have been honed at Mary Erskine or St George's School, then slid a thick folder across the desk. 'If you'd just like to fill in your details there.' She pointed. 'And sign alongside . . . a Health and Safety requirement.'

'Sure,' I told her, flashing her a quick twinkle. 'I'm pretty healthy, and relatively safe.' I filled in the form, and signed it; she ripped it from the pad and tucked it inside a plastic holder, then produced a small book from beneath the desk. 'If you could sign here, too, I'll let Mr Torrent's chief personal assistant know you're here.'

I couldn't help it; I hesitated. I think I probably frowned as well. Doesn't matter how often it happens, I reckon I will always be just a wee bit embarrassed when someone asks for my autograph. She misunderstood me; Anna's Chin seemed to fall and her dimple almost vanished. 'I'm sorry,' she began.

'Don't be,' I reassured her. 'I'm flattered, honest. I'm just a dentist's son from Anstruther.'

Her smile returned, even brighter this time. 'Not any more,' she said, firmly. 'You're a film star now . . . and I'm still just a doctor's daughter from Barnton.'

I shot a quick glance at her left hand as I took the autograph book from her; no ring. 'Stop it, Blackstone!' I told myself, and signed the blank page she offered me. I flicked through some of the other pages; it's always good to know whose company you're in. In the few pages back from mine, I recognised the careful signature of Scotland's First Minister, the flamboyant scrawl of my friend Scott Steele, the names of two members of Texas, augmented by a tiny cartoon guitar, a well-known Edinburgh novelist with a noughts and crosses trademark, a football manager who had printed his name below his signature to make sure that everyone knew who he was, and a couple of others which were just plain indecipherable. Of these the least decipherable was one that looked just like the picture on the screen of a heart monitor. I wondered whether, over time, the signature would get flatter and flatter, until one day, it was a straight line.

'Where did you pick all these up?' I asked her, as I handed back her book, and helped myself to a couple of cherries.

'I got all of them here,' she told me. 'Mr Torrent has been running a series of cocktail parties for celebrities. You won't tell him though, will you? He might think I was abusing my position.'

'I couldn't imagine you abusing anything.' I almost added, '. . . except me'; old habits and all that, but I stopped myself.

Anna picked up her phone and pushed a button on her console. 'Mr Blackstone,' she said, her accent still impeccable, without a hint of an oriental 'r' . . . even though she was from Barnton. She nodded into the handset, replaced it then turned and pointed to two glass-walled lifts behind her desk. 'Please take the one on the left,' she told me. 'It goes directly to the top floor.'

I jerked my thumb in the direction of the guy in the uniform. 'Does he get to open the door for me?'

She gave a quick tinkling laugh. 'No, it's automatic,' she answered, quietly, as if we were sharing a secret. I liked that; I gave her a wave through the glass as the lift started to go up.

It went fast; I counted off the floors as I rose. I assumed that it would stop at the fourth, but to my surprise it kept going.

James Torrent's office suite was on the roof of the building; out of sight from the car park, surrounding the glass panel of the atrium. Like the capsule that had brought me up, it appeared to be built almost entirely of glass, although part of it was smoked to the point of blackness. The back wall of the reception area was not. Through it, I could see the tops of the two Forth Bridges, and the hills of West Fife beyond.

A woman approached me, hand outstretched. 'Mr Blackstone.' I felt as if she was telling me who I was, not welcoming me. The Galaxy chocolate voice, and more imperious in the flesh; somehow I knew that this woman was not going to ask for my autograph.

She looked me up and down as we shook hands, so I gave her the same treatment. She was tanned and tall, with legs that seemed to be reaching for her armpits; I touch six feet and I was barely looking down on her. Her dress matched her voice; it was a warm brown colour, in a clinging fabric that could have been cashmere. It fitted from her throat to just below the knee, and she looked as if she might have been poured into it. There were no visible lines; if she was wearing anything under it, then it was even sleeker than the dress. What she definitely was not wearing was a label, like Anna Chin's or like the one she had given me. I glanced beyond her to an empty desk; there was a triangular metal bar on it, bearing the name 'Natalie Morgan'.

'Natalie Morgan,' she said. 'I'm Mr Torrent's chief of staff.'

'That makes him sound like a general,' I murmured. She wasn't smiling, so I didn't either. A while back, a woman like her could have eaten me for breakfast; I think I must be less digestible now.

'He is,' she replied, soft and low. 'You're a few minutes early, but he'll see you. Follow me, please.' She turned on her heel and led me along a passageway. The roof of the atrium was on my right; on the other side was another panelled wall. It was double-skinned, with a Venetian blind between the panels, but the slats were open and I could see through into a long room that looked eastwards, towards Edinburgh and the castle. If I'd looked, I could have seen my apartment from there. I guessed that was where Torrent held his celebrity parties.

At the end of the passage there was a black glass wall, which stretched the full width of the suite. A door was cut into it, but you wouldn't have seen it, but for its round gun-metal handle. Natalie Morgan opened it and moved aside, for me to step into the sanctum. As I passed her, I caught a strong fragrance that I recognised from Hollywood. That place floats on Giorgio of Beverley Hills.

I stepped into the office, and looked around. For a while, I thought that it was empty. The door opened more or less into the middle of the room; on my right there was an oval meeting table, and beyond that a wall which looked as if it could have been made of ebony, but also of the blackest glass. Another door was set in it. To my left there was a big kidney-shaped desk with a plasmatronic computer screen and three telephones. Two leather armchairs faced it, and behind it there was a third, which turned slowly towards me as I looked at it.

James Torrent pushed himself to his feet and moved round the desk to greet me, a great podgy hand outstretched. He wore what might have been described as a smile on someone else, but which looked on him like something halfway between a leer and a grimace.

The man looked to be in his early fifties, and he was massive. He was no taller than me, but tremendously solid; not so much fat, but more like a small mountain on legs. He had sleek black hair, which swept back from a receding forehead. His facial features were as gross as the rest of him; thick rubbery lips, piggy eyes and ears and a great bulbous nose. His complexion was so swarthy that I knew at once that my earlier guess had been right.

'Oz,' he said, in a gravelly voice, devoid of accent. 'So glad to meet you.'

'Likewise,' I lied, with the same mock politeness. 'Spanish?' I asked.

'My father was; he left during the Civil War. I was born and educated here. How did you guess?'

'From the way your staff pronounced your name; I've encountered it before.'

'You've travelled in Spain?'

'I lived there for a while.'

'More than me, then; I won't go back there. Franco shot my grandfather.' He pointed me at one of the two visitor chairs. 'Sit down,' he said, returning to his swivel chair. 'You'll have coffee?'

'No, thanks. I've had my dose for today.'

'Yes, we tend to drink too much of it, I always think. So, to what do I owe the pleasure of this visit? I have heard of you, of course; quite the coming man in the film industry, so they say.'

'It's more than I'd say, in that case. I'm getting along though. But that's not the only string to my bow.'

Torrent raised his heavy black eyebrows. 'No?'

'No. I have a couple of business interests; non-executive directorships. I'm on the board of the Gantry Group; you'll have heard of us, I'm sure.' I looked him in the eyes as I said it. Not a single lash batted, never mind an eyelid; he didn't give as much as a twitch.

'Of course,' he rumbled. 'You and Susie have a personal connection, don't you?'

'Yes. She's my fiancée.' The word came out without my even thinking about it. *Christ, Blackstone*, I said to myself. *What's got into you?*

'You're in for an interesting life, then. She's quite a lady; a businesswoman after my own heart, as a matter of fact.'

'I'm glad to hear you approve. But that has nothing to do with my visit. No, it's my other directorship that brings me here. I know you've heard of the unfortunate death of David Capperauld.' This time, James Torrent did blink. 'Well, as it

124

happens, Alison Goodchild's an old friend of mine. She's asked me to join her board, to help her through, and I've agreed.'

'Mmm.' The murmur sounded like a drill cutting into rock. 'There's a turn-up for the books.' He paused. 'But you did say non-executive, earlier.'

'I did, but I take my responsibilities seriously. I have some time on my hands, so I thought I should visit all of our major clients, to assure them personally that David's loss isn't going to cause a vacuum in the management of the business, and that its quality of service will continue as before.'

Torrent gave me that half-leer again. 'I'm delighted to hear it, Oz. I value Alison's advice greatly.'

'I'm glad to hear that too. I confess to having had a doubt about that, given the emphasis you placed on the importance of securing Ewan Capperauld to perform your opening ceremony. She gave me the impression that it was a condition of continued employment, in fact.'

He shrugged his shoulders. 'I'm sorry if she took me so literally. It's my style, I'm afraid. I like to keep my people on their toes. This is a hard business I'm in, son, and I've been growing it for a long time. I didn't get here by being everyone's favourite uncle.

'I have the greatest respect for Alison, and admiration for her as a professional. Of course, it would be good to have someone as eminent as Ewan Capperauld visit this building, and even more to have him open it, but there are others. I'm sure the First Minister would be pleased to do the job.

'If Alison thought I was being threatening when I mentioned Capperauld's name, then please give her my apologies and tell her not to give it another thought.' He shot me a quick, perceptive glance. 'Of course, you're making a film with him, aren't you?'

I nodded. 'Yes, and I'll ask him, first chance I get. I've never met him, you understand, but most actors are ego-maniacs. The chance to have his name on a plaque on an important building might be too much for him to turn down.'

'Let's hope so. Tell him he can name his own fee . . . within reason, of course. Or if he'd prefer it, I'll make a substantial donation to a charity of his choice, in recognition of the event.'

'Okay, I'll put that to him.' Torrent's affability had thrown me; I had gone in there partly to check Alison's story, and partly to do battle. I had expected him either to deny everything, or to give me a hard time. The last thing I had anticipated was that he would be reasonable. I began to harbour my first doubt about Ms Goodchild; maybe she wasn't good at all.

Still, having Torrent in this sort of mood was an opportunity too good to miss. I decided to push my luck just a little further. 'One of the areas Alison's asked me to look at is the company's cashflow. This has all happened very quickly, so I haven't had a chance to look at the debtor lists. Can you recall if you're holding any outstanding invoices?'

That grin again; cheesy this time. 'I'm sure we are,' he chortled. 'We're bloody slow payers. I'm good at cash management too, Oz.' He picked up one of his telephones and pushed a button. 'Nat,' he said into the phone. 'Dig out all the pending Goodchild Capperauld invoices, total them up and make payment in full today, through the system, then send out the usual notification.'

He hung up and turned back to me. 'The money, whatever it is, should be in your bank by close of play this afternoon. We pay all our regular suppliers by electronic transfer these days. This is a cashless business. I hired a security consultant a few years back, and that was his first recommendation.

Good chap; he's an ex-policeman. He was pretty senior, before he decided to retire.'

'His name isn't Ross, is it?'

The great head nodded. 'Yes, it is. Do you know him?'

'He's looking after security for the movie.'

'You'll be fine, then. He's a very sound man, is Richard.'

Fucking tight-lipped as well, I thought. Ricky had known I was going to see Torrent, and he'd said nothing about his connection with him.

'That's reassuring,' I said. 'I knew him as a copper; he was a real collar and front then, I can tell you.'

He looked puzzled at my slang for a moment, then worked it out. I stood, and he followed suit. 'I mustn't keep you any longer,' I told him. 'I'm grateful to you for putting me right on Capperauld, and for your payment. Alison will be pleased on both scores.'

'That's good.' I glanced at him; he seemed genuine. 'Oh yes,' he continued, 'I should have mentioned this earlier. Please give the young lady my deepest condolences. David's death must be a terrible blow to her, both in personal and business terms. I had very little to do with him, but I found him a very pleasant young man when we did meet . . .' He gave a small sad laugh. '. . . Even if he didn't get on with his famous cousin.' He pushed a button on his phone.

'I'm a great believer in family values, Oz,' he rumbled as he walked me to the door. 'I've never married myself, but I treat my late sister's daughter as my own. I couldn't do without her, in fact.' At that moment, the door opened and Natalie Morgan appeared. 'Could I, my dear?'

'Could you what, Uncle James?'

'Do without you.'

She smiled, for the first time in my presence. It was supercharged, and it made her eyes shine like deep blue pools. 'Absolutely not,' she said.

24

I drove straight to Ricky's place, without calling to let him know I was coming.

'Thanks, pal,' I said, when he opened the door. 'You might have bloody told me you work for Torrent.'

'Why?' he retorted. 'I treat all my clients on a confidential basis. I'm in the security business, for fuck's sake. Anyway, what difference would it have made?'

'You might have saved me a trip.'

'How? I don't bug his fucking office. I don't know what he did or didn't tell Alison.'

He had a point; I cooled down. 'How is she, anyway?' I asked him.

Ross shrugged his shoulders and nodded towards the kitchen, at the back of the narrow hall. 'Nervous; we still haven't heard from Ronnie Morrow. She's in the kitchen knocking up some lunch; go and ask her yourself.' His tone was as he looked; offhand.

I did as he suggested. She had her back to the door as I stepped into the room. 'Do you want HP sauce on your corned beef?' she asked. There was something in her voice too, and I knew at once what it was. Even in that simple question, she sounded just as she had a few years back, when she and I had been together and she'd been making breakfast at my place. Alison always sounded guilty after sex, as if it was something she shouldn't have been doing.

For some reason, she also consumed large quantities of brown sauce the morning after.

'I'll take mustard on mine, thanks.'

She jumped at the sound of my voice and turned round. She caught me frowning at her, and turned red. 'Did you shag him?' I asked her. She turned even redder.

'That's . . .'

'None of my business, I know. Except for the fact that I'm out there trying to help my old friend, the grieving fiancée, and all the time she's doing the fucking horizontal mambo with her minder.

'You know what? I'm starting to have serious doubts about you, Alison.'

'Why?' she protested. 'I'm frightened, and I was lonely; I needed to be with someone. You made your feelings clear the other night, and Ricky was kind to me, so . . .'

I reached out, opened one of the kitchen drawers and took a look inside. 'What are you doing?' she asked.

'Checking for ice-picks, or other sharp objects,' I told her.

'Oz!' She squealed my name.

'No, listen. Did you have any sort of a relationship with David, other than business? Were you really engaged to him?'

The blush left her cheeks; she looked down at the floor, and gnawed her lip. 'Not any more,' she whispered. 'He broke it off a month ago.'

'Did he tell you why?'

'He was seeing someone else.'

'Who?'

'I don't know.'

'And all that carry-on on Sunday night; getting me to thump on his door. What was that about?'

'I was hoping she'd be there, whoever she was. I wanted to cause a scene, to embarrass him.'

'So you used me?'

'Yes. I'm sorry.' A spark of the new Alison flared up in her. 'But why should I be? You used me often enough in the past.' She had me there.

'I taught you bloody well, then,' I shot back at her. 'Okay,' I went on. 'So David dumped you a month ago. How did you manage to conduct a business relationship after that?'

'We didn't. He walked out of the business as well, and he demanded half the assets.'

'What assets? You told me the business had a cash problem.'

'It's still worth quite a bit, though, as a trading entity. David had the shares valued by our auditor. He was insisting that I buy him out or that the company bought his shares in. I couldn't afford that and neither could the business. Anyway . . .' her voice rose, and hardened; '. . . it wasn't fair. I would never agree to that. He never pulled his weight at work. I won most of the clients, and I serviced most of them myself.'

'I'll bet you did. That's probably why he chucked you.'

She ignored my wisecrack. 'He did ten per cent of the work yet he wanted half the value. I wasn't going to let him away with that. I offered him one fifth of what the auditor claimed his shares were worth. He laughed at me, and told me that if I didn't give him what he wanted he'd withdraw his personal guarantee of our overdraft, and the bank would pull the plug on everything.'

'Oh shit,' I heard myself bellow, just as the kitchen door opened again behind me, and Ricky Ross walked in.

'Indeed,' he said. 'I'm afraid you're cooked, dear.'

I stared at him. The offhand look had gone; now he looked very interested, and bloody pleased with himself too. 'You son of a . . .' I hissed. 'You might not have bugged Torrent's place, but you've done your own, haven't you?'

White teeth gleamed. 'Once a copper, Oz, always . . .'

That was as far as he got before I sank my right fist deep into his gut. The breath rushed out of him and he folded up. Alison just stood there, bewildered, staring at us, both hands pressed to her mouth.

'Ohhh,' Ricky groaned, then bizarrely, he smiled up at me from the floor. 'Sorry, Oz,' he gasped. 'I couldn't tell you, though; not with you having been close to the girl.'

'Did you and Morrow cook this up?'

He pulled himself to his feet. 'No, it was all my idea. If I'd got Ronnie involved, the tape probably wouldn't have been admissible as evidence. Maybe yes, maybe not, but it wasn't worth the risk.'

'What?' Alison screamed. We both turned to look at her. She was holding the big kitchen knife with which she had been slicing the corned beef, and pointing it straight at us. 'You . . .' She screamed again and rushed at Ricky. He dived for his life, but slowly, as he was still feeling the effects of my punch. He might not have made it, but I grabbed her arm as she went past, and twisted it up and round behind her, compressing her wrist until her hand went numb and she dropped the blade.

'Keep her here, Oz,' said Ricky, breathlessly, as he picked the knife from the floor. 'I'll get Ronnie.' Alison was still struggling against my grip, straining, wild-eyed, to get at him. Once, her head twisted round and down as if she was reaching for my hands, to bite them. I didn't fancy that at all, not with the fleck of foam in one corner of her mouth.

'You keep her here yourself,' I suggested. 'I'll make the call. That seems like a better deal to me.' He wasn't that daft though; he was through that door like a greyhound out of a trap, leaving me wondering how long I could hang on to this mad woman and wondering whether there were any more lethal kitchen implements lying around within easy reach.

She muttered something incoherent, then snarled a bit,

then gradually began to calm down. She still twisted and wrenched against me, trying to free herself, until finally she ran out of strength. I still held her tight, though, keeping her arms pinned from behind; I couldn't be sure she wasn't faking it and that she wouldn't go for my throat.

'That bastard,' she exclaimed, the words punctuated by a great gasping sob. 'He made love to me, and it was all a trick.'

'Come on now,' I said, 'be fair. He didn't make love to you; you shagged him. That was the way it came out earlier. And if the guy wants to plant listening devices in his own house, I suppose he's got the right to do that. Let's stop blaming other people here, Alison. If you hadn't killed your bloody ex, none of this would have happened.'

'But I didn't kill him!' she said. Her voice was weak now, with a wheedling, frightened tone to it.

'What?' I had to laugh at her. 'After you try to fillet the two of us with that boning knife, and after the story you told me about what David was trying to do to you, you expect me to believe that?'

'Yes,' she whispered, 'because it's the truth.' She tried to look back at me, over her shoulder. 'I wasn't trying to stab anyone, Oz. I was just furious; I'd forgotten I was holding the knife. Let me go, please.'

'I can't do that,' I told her. 'Ricky's calling the police; apart from anything else, you're on bail and we have to hand you over.'

'Well at least stop holding me so tight; I won't do anything silly, I promise.'

I thought about it for a bit, then finally relented. 'Go and sit on that stool,' I said, 'and keep your hands where I can see them. If you try to run for it, or have another go at me, then I promise you, girlie or no girlie, I will knock you into the middle of next week.'

She nodded; I let her arms go and she did as I had told

her. She looked up at me through blotchy eyes. 'I really didn't do it,' she whispered. I could see that she was desperate for me to believe her, but I couldn't.

'Sure,' I replied. I crossed to the kitchen door and shouted to Ricky. 'Is that tape switched off?'

'Yes,' he called back. 'Morrow's on his way. I phoned Charlie as well; he'll go straight to the nick. He's not exactly speaking to me. Oh aye,' he added. 'The lab report's in. That was the weapon all right.'

I closed the door and turned back to Alison. She was still on the stool, behaving herself; I guess she'd believed what I'd said about thumping her. Wise girl. 'Now listen to me,' I told her, 'before the coppers get here. You should say nothing at all to them until you've spoken with Badenoch again.

'Then you should come up with a story that he can use to persuade the fiscal to reduce the charge to culpable homicide, rather than murder. You went to his house to plead with him, he laughed in your face and you just lost it. The awl was there, on the hall table; you just picked it up and swung at him, blind with rage. You were in such a panic that you took it home with you, where it was found by the police.'

I paused to let her think about it. 'That is how it happened, isn't it?' I asked.

Tears started to run slowly down her cheeks. She shook her head. 'No, it isn't. I really didn't do it. You have to believe me, Oz.' Again, I thought that if she was acting she was worth a BAFTA.

'Okay. Let's say, for the purposes of this discussion, that I do. That doesn't matter a damn. This is what will happen. You'll be charged with murder, on the basis of what's on that tape, the fact that the weapon was found in your house, and the fact that you can be placed in the vicinity at the time of death.

'I'll almost certainly be called as a witness to what you

said earlier and I'll have to confirm that the tape hasn't been doctored and that it's a true record. If I try to add that you're a good wee lass really, and that you didn't do it, the judge will give me thirty days for contempt.

'Long before I'm out, the jury will have brought in a fifteen-nil verdict of guilty and you'll be in Cornton Vale, starting a life sentence. It's time for damage control, Alison. If the Crown offers you a plea to culpable homicide, take it. Charlie will instruct the best criminal QC in the business; he'll put in a plea in mitigation that will make David Capperauld sound like Bill Sykes and you like Nancy. With a lot of luck . . . a hell of a lot, but it's happened before . . . the judge might just take a fancy to you and put you on probation for a couple of years.'

'But I can't do that,' she wailed. 'I'm innocent.'

'Until you're proved guilty? That's not the way it works, love. The way the evidence is you're as good as in the prison van already. You've got one way to protect yourself; use it. Co-operate and Charlie might just get you out on bail, until the trial at least.'

She frowned at me. 'After Ricky tells them I went for him with that knife?'

'That never happened. He won't say a word about that, otherwise I'll tell the world about him giving you one last night. He's spent too long rebuilding his reputation to want that to happen.'

As I looked at her, I could almost see her brain start to work again. I could almost see her start to pick up the pieces of herself and put them back together. 'You really believe that's what I should do?'

'Yes. But don't do it on my word; ask Charlie what he thinks.'

'What if he doesn't agree with you?'

'Then get another lawyer.'

25

Badenoch did agree with me, though. Once Morrow had let him read the lab report and had played him what was on the tape, he knew what the score was, and he advised his client to face the facts.

I wasn't there when they had that conversation, but he told me later that when she protested her innocence, he had said straight out that if he found it hard to believe, any jury was going to find it impossible.

He didn't let her make a formal statement to the police, but they didn't expect that. Instead, Charlie went to the fiscal and told her what the defence would be if she proceeded with a murder charge. She weighed the cost of a full-scale trial, took an educated guess at the likely verdict and agreed to take a plea to culpable homicide.

She even told the police not to oppose bail, which they had been inclined to do. He's some operator, that Charlie Badenoch.

Once the deal had been cut, they let me in to see Alison again, to deliver her some clothes for next day. She had to make a formal court appearance next morning, and she had opted for a night in the cells rather than the alternative, which was still open, of going back to Ricky's place. I hoped that, to quote the King, one night of sin was all he'd been praying for, because I reckoned, sure as hell, that was all he was going to get after his trick with the tape.

I saw her in the usual interview room in the Gayfield Square office; a constable stood on guard outside the door, but they gave us privacy, after they had checked what was in the bag I'd brought. The police had still been at her house when I'd got there, and they had watched me pack it, then it had been searched again at the police station. I thought that in the circumstances, a cake with a file in it was an unlikely find, but they'd given the stuff a going-over nonetheless.

She was calm, even if she still seemed slightly stunned by what had happened. 'Do you really think I'll get probation?' she asked me, quietly.

'I don't know,' I told her, honestly. 'There are plenty of precedents, but it still comes down to what the judge thinks is the punishment that fits the crime. There are a couple of women on the bench now; maybe you'll get lucky and draw one of them.'

'But I could go to prison?'

I had to tell her the truth; I mean, I could only jolly her along so far, couldn't I. 'Yes, you could.'

'Even though I didn't do it?'

I sighed. 'Okay. If that's the way you want it, plead not guilty; go back on Charlie's deal with the fiscal. But if it goes to trial and you're convicted, even if it's only of culpable homicide, the judge'll throw the book at you. You fancy ten years?'

'No,' she whispered; her eyes glistening again. 'That's why I've agreed to do as Mr Badenoch said. But it still doesn't make me guilty, Oz. Please,' she begged, 'believe me.'

I have always been a sucker for a crying woman; plus, she had agreed to the plea. She was going to get off lightly, so why keep up the pretence now? 'Suppose I do,' I said, grudgingly. 'What difference does it make?'

'It'll make a big difference to me; it'll mean that there's someone in the world, other than my dizzy old mother, who's on my side.'

'I've never been against you. I've never thought you killed him in cold blood. I was prepared to accept that you did it in a flash of blind rage at his deceit and his threats to destroy your business, just as you're going to admit to in court. But if you promise me on your heart's blood that you didn't, then I'll believe you.'

'I swear,' she burst out, in a voice loaded with relief. 'Even if I have to go away for a while, it'll make it easier just knowing that. Even though I'll have nothing when I come out, and I'll have the bank on my neck, I'll get through it somehow.'

'When you get out tomorrow, and go back to the office, you might find that you're suddenly in good standing with your bank.'

'What do you mean?'

I told her about my meeting with James Torrent, and about his clearing her outstanding invoices. 'He did that?' she gasped. 'How did you manage it?'

'I take my responsibilities as a director seriously. He also told me that you'd taken him too literally when he asked you to get Ewan Capperauld for his ceremony. He said he didn't mean it to sound like that, and he apologised.'

'Well it did sound like that,' she insisted. 'How did you manage all this, Oz? How did you get him to pay, especially? Did you threaten him, or something?'

'I don't think it would be a great idea to threaten that man. He may have been impressed by my connection with Susie. Whatever it was, I just mentioned your bills, sort of in passing, and he whistled up payment on the spot. The money's probably there by now.'

Her face brightened; there's nothing like cash for cheering

you up. 'That's great. I was going to have to pay someone off at the end of the month; now I won't.'

Time for a reality reminder, I thought. 'Don't be so sure. You're going to be in court tomorrow, and the charge will go public, even if the press can't report any details. You're going to have a hell of a job holding your clients in those circumstances.'

Her sudden burst of optimism was hard to suppress, though. 'Most of them will stick by me; I'm sure of that. And if I can announce that you've become a director, that'll convince people too, won't it?'

'Jesus, Alison, it wouldn't even convince me. What are my skills? I'm a ham actor, that's all.'

'But they'll assume you're investing in the business.' She paused. 'You wouldn't, Oz, would you?'

That was a shot I hadn't been expecting. I did some quick thinking. 'What are Capperauld's shares worth?'

'The auditor valued them at a quarter of a million.'

'Fine, but now he's dead, and the business is in trouble. Offer his estate fifty grand, on my behalf, and I'll pick them up, with a formal agreement that you or the company itself will buy them from me at valuation in three years' time.'

Her eyes narrowed. 'You could make a tidy profit on that. When did you pick up the business brain?'

'Along the way.'

'Why three years?'

'If you do go away, I reckon you'll be out in a year, eighteen months at the most. You draw no pay, other than what it takes to cover your mortgage, and we appoint a manager to run things during that period. I'll supervise from a distance, and keep an eye on the cash. When you come out, you pick up the reins again, and at the agreed time, I get paid off.'

'What about the bank? My manager's a grim-looking man; he frightens me a bit.'

'No problem; I'll tell them to give you someone who doesn't.'

'How can you do that?'

'I'm not without influence. By that I mean money; it's the only language these guys understand. I still do most of my banking in Edinburgh; I'll fix it for my guy to take over your account.'

She looked at me as if she'd never known me. 'First Torrent, now this; is there anything you couldn't fix?'

'I can't fix your problem with your late ex-fiancé.'

'I'll bet you could if you put your mind to it.' There was a crafty gleam in her eye now.

'Listen, I am here to make a movie. I am being paid a hell of a lot of money for it, I'm still new to the game and it needs my one-hundred-per-cent attention. You want that problem solved, hire a detective.'

'I don't know any detectives.'

'You fucked one last night,' I pointed out.

Alison did not appreciate that reminder. 'Him!' she exploded. 'Ricky! After what he did, I wouldn't employ him if he was . . .'

'. . . the last private eye on earth? Okay, do your time, if you have to. Ross might be a slippery bastard, but he is very good. You don't get to be a Lothian and Borders detective superintendent without being shit hot at the job. Okay, he set you up today and maybe he shouldn't have. But he took it hard when he got kicked off the force. I reckon he was trying to prove a point. Still, if you want help and he'll take it on, he's the man.'

'It'll stick in my throat.'

'An unfortunate remark, in the circumstances.'

She giggled, then suppressed it, 'Well, if you'll talk to him for me, I'll consider it. But where would he begin?'

'With the murder weapon. If you didn't do it, someone

139

planted it in your flat. You didn't see any signs of a break-in, last Thursday or later, did you?'

'No; and I would have. All my windows secure from the inside, and I always double-lock my door when I go out.'

'So how was it done?'

'David had a key.'

'Didn't you ask for it back when he chucked you?'

'Yes, but he still had it. The killer must have found it and used it.'

'Could be.'

'Will that help?' she asked brightly.

'Who knows? But at least, it's a place to start.'

26

Ricky wasn't too keen to take the commission when I told him about it later that evening. In fact his exact words were, 'No fucking way!'

He hadn't been totally pleased to see me when I'd rung his bell; I think he was still smarting over the way I'd rung it earlier on, when I found out he'd recorded my conversation with Alison. I didn't really feel like apologising for that, but I did, for her sake. 'Sorry about that, mate,' I told him, 'but if I hadn't belted you, she'd never have believed that I wasn't in on the act as well.'

'You think that quick, do you?' he grunted, doubtfully, as he dug a couple of beers out of his fridge.

'Sometimes.'

'That'll be right. I'm still not taking the job, though.'

'Of course you are. Come on, Ricky, you can't turn down a challenge like that. I'll bet that somewhere inside that conniving head of yours there's a mad dream that your pal the new chief constable might reinstate you in the force. If you could pull off something like this . . .'

He looked at me scornfully. 'There's no chance of that. Anyway, I told you; I'm making too much bloody money to even think about going back in.'

'Fine. So clear Alison's name, then sell your story to a tabloid. You never know, Miles might even fancy it as a movie plot.'

I saw pound signs rolling in his eyes like two-thirds of a one-armed bandit. 'Maybe. But there's a problem, Oz; she fucking did it!'

'I don't think so.'

'Don't give me it. You thought so when you left here; you were as sure as me. So what's made you change your mind? Did she flash her eyes at you? Did she say, "Hold me, Oz, I'm scared"? Was that it?'

'She tried that last Sunday and it didn't work. No, she swore to me, on her life, that she didn't do it. She's taking the plea, but she still maintains that she's innocent.'

'Silly lass. She'd better shut up, or the crown office might hear her and call off the deal.' He sighed. 'Okay, if you're convinced, I'll give it a go. I owe her, I suppose. I feel a bit shitty about the way I set her up.'

'Did you bug the bedroom as well?' I asked him, jokingly.

'Of course I did.'

I'm not easily surprised any more, but that one made me gasp. 'You're serious, aren't you? You were banging her, and all the time you were hoping she'd confess to murder.' Ricky looked at the floor. 'Go on.' I said, 'get the tape out and play it. I've got to hear this.'

'I wiped it afterwards,' he muttered.

'Very sanitary of you; now get the tape.'

'Give it up, Blackstone. I feel guilty enough without you taking the piss. Especially now that I'm starting to like the girl.'

'What? After she went for you with that knife? Mind you that's appropriate, I suppose; you bone her, she tries to bone you.'

'I've told you, chuck it!' he shouted, but a smile crossed his face at the same time. 'She's got spirit in her, has Alison; she can hide it well at times, but it's there. Right, I'm going to help her, and what's more, I'll do it for free. So where do we begin?'

'You're the detective.'

'I know that. I was talking to myself, not you. We start with the murder weapon; she didn't kill him, so someone must have planted it at her place. We'll go there and look for signs of a break-in.'

I shook my head. 'No. You'll go there. I'm not involved in this. But you'll be wasting your time; there were no signs of a break-in, and there was no need for one either. David Capperauld still had a key to Alison's flat.'

Ricky scratched his chin. 'Had he now?' He was even starting to sound like a copper again. I know that chin trick; I worked for a lawyer once who did something similar. In his case, he used to light his pipe in the middle of a discussion. What he was actually doing was giving himself time to think.

'I'd better get into his place,' Ross said, eventually. 'If the key's missing, we need to know. That could be a bugger, though; I don't want Ronnie Morrow to hear I'm doing this, or it could put Alison's deal in jeopardy. But I can't break into the place.'

I recalled that once, not that many years in the past, the same guy had broken into my flat, but I let that pass. I also let him off the hook. 'Not a problem,' I told him. 'She had a key to his place as well, remember. That was how we got in last Sunday.

'It was on the bunch of keys she gave me today, so I could pick up her stuff . . . although as it happened, I didn't need them.' I took a brass Chubb key from my pocket, laid it on his kitchen work-surface, and slid it across to him. 'It isn't there any more.'

Ricky whistled, and smiled.

27

He was still smiling when he stepped out of the lift next morning. I wasn't, though; I had phoned Susie as I was having breakfast and told her how the Alison thing had developed; all of it. Not to put too fine a point on it she had done her nut.

'You're telling me that this woman, one of your many old flames, is about to plead guilty to killing her boyfriend, you've taken his place on the board of their company, and you're in the process of buying his shares in the business, at a knock-down price? How the hell do you think that's going to look to the police when they find out? Are you completely off your head?'

That aspect hadn't occurred to me for one second.

'Put it that way, and the answer's yes; I probably am. But I've made the offer, love. I can't back down now.'

'Don't "love" me. You're a director of the Gantry Group; what's trouble for you is trouble for me. Tell me straight; are you still lusting after this woman?'

'No, I'm not; I never did, either.'

'Just as well for you, or I'd cut your balls off. Now you must get out of this daft agreement, now.'

'How am I going to do that, without leaving her in the lurch?'

'I'll put up the fifty grand, or whatever figure the boy's estate settles for eventually. I'll advance the money to her solicitor, in confidence, and he'll buy the shares on my behalf. She can repay me on the same basis you agreed. I'll protect myself by putting my own accountants in place to oversee the business.'

'But . . .'

'No arguments, Oz; that's what's going to happen.'

'But why would you do that for her?'

'I wouldn't. I'm doing it for you.'

'Why?'

'Because you're the father of my daughter and I won't let you make such an arse of yourself.'

'And that's all?'

An intake of breath so deep that it sounded like a wave winding up to crash on to a beach. 'No. Because I love you, and I don't want you to get into any more trouble than you can help.'

After that, I had to agree. I was still thinking about it when Miles phoned from the Caledonian Hotel, to say that he and Dawn had checked in, and when Ricky Ross rang the entryphone buzzer at ten minutes to ten. What I was thinking about, was being my own man.

'What's tickling you?' I asked him.

'I went to David Capperauld's place,' he answered. 'He had her key all right. He'd still have it, if he was alive. It was in his kitchen cupboard, hanging on a row of hooks with lots of other keys. Every one of them was on a ring with a plastic tag, with a label in it. Hers said "Alison". I took it up to her flat and tried it, to make sure, then I put it back where it was.

'His door key was hanging there too, labelled "spare". Whoever killed him must have taken a look around, or known where to look, found Alison's key there, and used it to get in to plant the awl at her place.'

'And then put it back,' I said. 'That was bloody crafty. It doesn't really help her at all, does it?'

'Yes it does. Everything helps, Oz, everything that backs up an alternative solution to the one the police are going for. It doesn't prove anything, but it suggests something. If we can gather in more suggestions, enough of them, we can maybe . . . okay, it's a big maybe . . . we can undermine the prosecution case.'

He smirked again. 'There's another thing. I dusted the key with powder, and lifted a couple of prints from it. They might just be Capperauld's, but I don't think they are . . .'

'What makes you so sure?'

'Because I took prints from the razor I found in his bathroom, and from his shaving gel canister; they don't match, none of them.'

'Maybe they're Alison's.'

'They're not.'

'How do you know?'

'I printed the knife she tried to slice me with.'

I was impressed. 'Clever bastard, eh, Ricky?'

'I have my moments.'

'Okay, so where to now?'

'CID manual page two,' he replied. 'I'll check on known associates. There were no signs of a break-in at Capperauld's house either, so whoever did it, he let in there. Not just that; from the position of the wound, he didn't feel threatened, because he turned his back on him.'

'How do you start tracing them?'

'I'll talk to Alison once she gets . . .'

He was interrupted by the entryphone; I picked it up, said, 'Lift; top floor,' pressed the button to release the lock, then walked across to the front door and wedged it open. Less than two minutes later, slightly bleary-eyed, but still tanned and looking rock-hard as ever, Miles Grayson stepped into the apartment.

Miles and I greeted each other like long-lost brothers,

which was not a million miles away from what we still were, then I introduced him to his new security consultant. The change in Ricky was instantaneous. I'd never seen him awestruck before, or even nervous, but he was right then. Miles can have that effect on people. The first time I met him was in the bar of a hotel in Connell Ferry; he bought me a pint. He's always buying me beer; it's the Australian in him.

'So you're Mr Ross,' he said. 'It's good to meet you in the flesh after all these years.' Ricky blanched; so Miles had remembered their first, indirect, encounter, and his phone call to the chief constable.

'Don't worry,' he laughed, breaking the tension. 'I don't let personal things get in the way of business . . . unless they're really personal. I hired you on Mark Kravitz's recommendation; that's always good enough for me.

'Oz tells me you've been a big help already, in smoothing a couple of things over.'

Ricky grunted and gave me what might have been a nod of thanks; then again it might have been a bad attempt at a head-butt.

'I've already met the guy you've assigned to Dawn and me. He was waiting at the Caledonian as you said he would be; I've left him there with Dawn. Word will get around that we've moved in, so it's as well that he stays with her.'

Ross nodded. 'Yes. He's a good guy, is Mike Reilly; he's ex-army and he did a stint in the SAS. Mark sent him to me when he was mustered out. My people are a mix of ex-police and ex-military. None of them are gung-ho types, but they can do the business if they have to.'

'None of them are carrying, are they?' asked Miles.

'No, sir. That's illegal in this country.'

'I know; that's why I asked.'

'They don't. The people who are with you don't need them.'

'People?' I asked.

'Brucie has his own minder up at Auchterarder,' Miles explained, 'as back-up to his nurse.'

I felt my eyebrows go up. 'His nurse?'

Miles grinned. 'Maria's a fully qualified children's nurse; she was also an undercover officer with the LAPD. She was a detective sergeant working South Central Los Angeles when we hired her out of there.' Then the smile vanished. 'People like us, Oz, we can't be too careful. We're the super-rich, and to the wrong people, that can make our children valuable commodities.'

A cold shiver ran through me; I thought of wee Janet, and of Ethel Reid facing up to a determined kidnapper, in a block to which there was relatively easy access, for anyone seriously inclined to get in. I decided that Susie and I would have to discuss that as soon as possible; between us, we were worth more than a pound or two.

Miles looked around the apartment, then took in the view from the big window. 'Hey,' he exclaimed, 'you've struck it lucky with this place. Pretty damn good; better than a hotel.'

'You and Dawn can have it, if you like,' I offered, in a flash of toadying generosity that drew me a sidelong glance from Ricky. 'I can always stay at Susie's and commute.'

'That's good of you, buddy, but you stay here. It's ideal for the sort of cast get-together we're having this afternoon; if we're using it for that, I'd rather not live here as well.'

'Fine. I don't mind cleaning up the left-over sandwiches.'

He laughed. 'Don't worry, that's down to the caterers. By the way, my assistant followed up that contact you gave me, the Asian firm, but they're too small. We need a specialist operation, one that can keep the cast and crew, especially the crew, fed and happy all hours of the day and night. And there'll be quite a few night shots on this one.'

He paused. 'Okay, this afternoon's meeting. Mr Ross . . . Hey what do I call you? Is it still Superintendent?'

'Not for a while now; Ricky usually gets my attention.'

'Fine. Ricky, I want all your people here, so that everyone knows from the start who'll be looking after them and who's looking after everyone else. We'll start at two-thirty sharp. I'd have made it two, but our star is having lunch with his agent.'

He made a sound that I took to be disapproval and glanced at me. 'Have you met Capperauld yet?'

'No, only his dead cousin.'

'You may have seen the family at its best,' he said, emphatically.

'Uhh?'

Miles grinned. 'Maybe I'm being unkind. Ewan's an "Actor", of the old school . . . or he thinks he is at least. I'm a movie-maker; I haven't been on the boards in twenty years, and I've never done anything like the West End or Broadway. I've used him once before, and he was a royal pain in the ass; he made it clear that he didn't regard me as qualified to direct him. I made it clear that I was qualified to pay his fee, and that that allowed for everything else.'

'He's going to look down on me from a great height, then.'

'He'd better not try; I don't allow that on my movies, from anyone. But the word on the grapevine is that he's usually in humble mode just now, being nice to everyone, because he's next in line for a knighthood. A couple of the old acting "sirs" have fallen off the perch lately, so there's maybe a vacancy.'

'Who's his agent, that he has you reschedule for him?'

'For her; it's his wife, Margaret.'

'You're kidding. Couldn't they have had a working breakfast, then?'

'A good question; but Ewan said that she's going back to London to work on the negotiations for his next two projects and that they have a lot to discuss. She's a very capable woman, is Mrs Capperauld; she's as imposing as he is in her own way. They make quite a team.'

He chuckled. 'Fuck it, Oz, I'll humour him for now. Once I start spending real money, I'll have less time for any shit. But the thing is, he's the obvious man for the part. I wouldn't have done this project if I hadn't been able to get him. You've read Skinner?'

I nodded.

'He is Skinner.'

In that case, I thought, *he must be one impressive actor.*

28

He was. When he walked out of the lift and across the hall into the apartment, five minutes after two-thirty, I almost said 'Hello, Bob.'

I'd seen him on screen before, and on television, in costume parts, contemporary parts, comedy and tragedy. In all of them he'd looked handsome and slightly patrician, a tall dark-haired man in early middle age.

The Ewan Capperauld who walked into my apartment was tall, okay, around six-two, but that was as far as the comparison went. His hair was steel-grey, flopping loosely over his forehead. His shoulders were wide and he walked loose-limbed, almost like a gunfighter. It was a mild autumn day, yet he wore a long black leather overcoat.

He looked as if he had stepped straight off the front page of *Skinner's Rules*.

'Hello, Mr Director,' he said, spotting him across the room and extending a hand. His accent had the same rough edges as the rest of him. I took a closer look at his face, and found myself wondering if his nose had always been just a bit off the straight, or if he'd had that done for the part as well.

'Hi, Ewan,' Miles responded. He looked him up and down, then smiled. 'I knew you'd put in an appearance.' He turned to me. 'I cast this guy in *Kidnapped* and he turned up for the first meeting in highland dress.'

He glanced around the room; everyone else had turned up on time and was munching on sandwiches and drinking champagne. The conversation had stopped, though; they were all staring at the newcomer. Scott Steele was standing at my elbow. 'Fucking poser,' he muttered; he was enough of an actor to make sure that his voice carried, but Capperauld never even twitched.

'Can I have your attention, please?' Miles called out, unnecessarily. 'Dawn, Scott, you've worked with Ewan before, but let me introduce everyone else.' He went round all the cast members, one by one; the star greeted us with a nod of the head, held eye-contact for precisely two seconds, then moved on to the next.

When the 'hellos' were over he crossed to Dawn, took her hand and kissed it. 'My dear,' he murmured, 'how good to see you again.'

'I'm pleased you remember me, Ewan,' I heard her answer. I guessed she was speaking the truth, for she had told me five minutes earlier that she had never exchanged a word with Capperauld while they were making *Kidnapped*.

I hadn't been sure how Dawn would greet me, but she'd been okay. 'Have you heard from Prim?' I'd asked her.

'I saw her the day before we left.'

'Is she happy?'

'She says so; are you?'

'I think "slightly stunned" covers the way I feel. The baby is just great, but I don't have to tell you that.'

'And her mother?'

'She's great too.'

'That's good; I hope it works out for you. It's best that the pretending's over between you and my sister. Actors do enough of that in their working lives, without having to face it at home too.'

That was the most profound thing I'd ever heard Dawn say. When I met her she was just an exceptionally pretty face; now there was a lot more going on behind it.

'Okay,' Miles called again, 'attention please, everyone. There's a lot of us here, and I want everyone to know where everyone else fits in. For a start, there's the author of the book we're filming.' He pointed briefly to his left, towards a big, grizzled, middle-aged guy, with a Mediterranean tan, who was leaning against the wall, nursing a glass of champagne, which he waved vaguely, in acknowledgement. 'He isn't going to be riding shotgun on the production, but he'll be free to join us on set, any time he likes.'

He turned and beckoned towards a corner of the big room. 'Now, I want to introduce Mr Richard Ross; he's our head of security, and he's going to explain a few things to you. He's a former Edinburgh detective; I guess you could say he used to be Bob Skinner in real life.'

Ricky liked that one; I could tell as he stepped into the circle. 'Thank you, Mr Grayson,' he began, then looked around the group. He was dressed to impress, but in a different way from Ewan Capperauld. He wore razor-pressed slacks, and a double-breasted blue blazer with gold buttons, embossed with a crest, which I guessed belonged to one of Edinburgh's better golf clubs.

'I'll begin by putting you at your ease; my firm hasn't been hired because of any perceived security threat. We're here as a precaution to guard against one that comes out of the blue. Our remit is to ensure that everything goes smoothly for the production, and for its key people as individuals.' Good pitch, Ricky; I was feeling reassured already.

'I'll have a staff of five attached to the production; they're all ex-police or ex-armed forces, they're all here, and I want to introduce them now. First, Mike Reilly.' A stocky man, with light red hair and piercing blue eyes, stepped forward and nodded. 'Mike will be responsible for Mr and Mrs Grayson's welfare; round the clock.

'Next, Glen Oliver.' Big, muscular, fair-haired, late twenties, soft features, hard eyes. 'Glen will cover Mr Capperauld.

'Third, John Takei.' Oriental, a small, dark-haired package. 'He'll be looking after Mr Katayama.' The Japanese actor, a beaming man in his late fifties, nodded to his minder and bowed.

'Finally, Alan Graham and Mandy O'Farrell.' The first, early thirties, sloping shoulders, tired eyes; no obvious threat, but he wouldn't have been there if he didn't possess one. The second, late twenties, around six feet tall, blonde and tanned, angular features, long, hard-edged martial artist's hands. 'Alan and Mandy will be responsible for Mr Steele, Mr Massey, Ms Waitrose and Mr Blackstone.' Ricky looked around us all. 'They'll never be far away and you'll be given mobile phone numbers you can call if you feel under threat, or you're being harassed by a persistent member of the public.'

Rhona Waitrose grabbed my arm and squeezed. 'Hey, this is cool,' she whispered. 'I've never had my body guarded before.'

I looked down at her; in the flesh she was much shorter than she appeared on screen, but just as pretty. 'You'll have had volunteers, though,' I murmured.

'Yes,' she chuckled, 'but I find that conscripts are best.'

Ricky looked across at Liam Matthews; the wrestler was standing beside Masahi Katayama. Before the briefing had begun they had been speaking in Japanese; Liam spent a few years on their sports entertainment circuit, which can be very bloody indeed. 'I hope you don't feel left out, Mr Matthews,' he said. 'I'll give you cover while you're here if you'd like it, but I assumed you can handle your own security.'

'But, sir,' Liam replied, at his most Irish. 'Didn't Oz tell you? It's all faked.' That got a laugh, but I've seen my friend in real action; I know what he can do.

'When the crew is at work,' Ricky continued, 'our people will be there. We'll work in co-operation with the police of course, and between us we'll see to it that you can work without interruption.

'Any questions?' he asked. I stuck my hand up.

'If we are harassed by a persistent member of the public, what will your people do?'

He looked at me, dead-pan. 'Deal with it.'

'How?'

'By whatever means is appropriate, within the letter of the law.'

'Okay, suppose my sister visits me one day and has a go at me, as she often does; I'm concerned about the form of your reaction. Will you do anything without my say-so?'

'Absolutely not, Oz.'

'Thank Christ for that; you don't have enough people here to handle my sister. I wouldn't like to see any of them getting hurt.'

Ricky gave me a weak smile; Mandy O'Farrell shot me a look that said, 'I could take your sister any time.' I doubted that, but I grinned back at her.

'Okay,' said Miles, seizing the moment to move on. 'That's security; now the rest of the team.' He went on to introduce Ben Cain, the production designer, Dario de Luise, the chief cameraman, Phyllis Baxter, the unit publicist, who'd been given a reprieve after the dropped ball over the *Scotsman* story, and Gail Driver, his and Dawn's personal assistant. I knew all of them from previous projects, and so did most of the cast.

155

'The rest of the people on the team you'll meet on Sunday.' He paused and looked around us. 'Yes, folks, Sunday; that's the big day. Filming begins at seven a.m., in Advocates' Close, off the High Street. Those of you who are involved . . . that's Ewan, Dawn, and Oz . . . who don't know the layout should familiarise yourselves with it before then.

'Tomorrow, we begin rehearsals, scene by scene.'

Ewan Capperauld frowned. 'Rehearsals?' he boomed . . . without a trace of a Scottish accent. I thought of Dame Edith Evans, and handbags.

'That's what I said. That's the way I plan to do it; I've hired a first-floor auditorium in the Assembly Rooms in George Street for the purpose. I want everyone there tomorrow at nine. No excuses.

'Now enjoy the food and the fizz . . . especially the fizz. It'll be the last you see for a while. Anyone who's worked with me before will know that all my sets are dry.' As he finished he looked at our star, then, beckoning him to follow, moved towards the window, where Scott, Rhona and I were standing.

'Here,' the actress whispered. 'Have you read the script?'

'Yes,' I replied.

'What about our scene, where we get up close and intimate? That's not in the book.'

'True.'

'What'll the author think?'

'The money he's getting, he won't think a fucking thing.'

Rhona chuckled. 'I'm looking forward to it, mind. We can rehearse in private if you want.'

'Would that make me a conscript?'

'It might.'

I thought about that for a while. When I looked down again, she wasn't there; I hadn't seen any signal, but I guessed there had been one, for she was off, heading for

Dawn, Bill Massey and Masahi Katayama, leaving Miles, Ewan, Scott and me in a group.

I've never seen Miles Grayson lose his cool but that doesn't make him any sort of a soft touch. When he was younger, in his pre-acting days, he did some stuff with the Aussie special forces, and he is a very tough guy indeed.

'Listen, Ewan,' he said, very quietly, but in a way that got my attention straight away. 'We've had this argument once before; let's have it again, one last time. I do not believe in going to sleep on a grudge, far less going into a multi-million dollar project on the back of one. So if you've got something to say, spit it out.'

All three of us looked at Capperauld. He stared out of the window for a few moments, then shrugged his shoulders. 'Okay, Miles, if you insist; I believe that film should be spontaneous. I do not think that professional actors necessarily need to rehearse every minute scene before they step on to the sound stage, and I regard the suggestion that we do as mildly insulting . . .' He paused. '. . . To Steele and me, at least.'

'Hey boy!' Scott bristled, but I put my hand on his sleeve to stop him. 'Whereas for a fucking amateur like me, it's okay, yes?' I asked.

The way Ewan looked down his slightly crooked nose at me, I thought about bending it some more, to really make him look the part. 'If you put it that way, far be it from me to contradict,' he exclaimed, loud enough for Ricky Ross and Glen Oliver to look in our direction.

'Okay,' said Miles. 'Now that shit's been dumped, let's flush it away, okay. The last thing I'm going to do, Ewan, is tell you how to act, so you afford me the same courtesy. In three out of the last five years, I've directed the world's top grossing movies; that indicates, to me at least, that I know what I'm doing. So if I say we rehearse every scene, that's what we do.

'Furthermore . . .' A big word for an Aussie, I thought. '. . . I've cast every featured player in this project personally. Forget what it'll say on the credits; the agency found the bit players, that's all. You might be getting more money than anyone else, Ewan, but every member of the cast has equal status in my eyes, and . . . this is the really important bit . . . in each others' eyes as well. When we worked together before, you were in and out in a couple of days, so maybe you weren't there long enough to get to understand what I'm about. My father's a socialist politician in Australia, and that's how I was brought up. There's no class system in my life or on my sets; I've never hung a star on a dressing-room door in my life, and when it's been done for me, I've ripped them down.

'For the record, Oz is here because he's fucking good, just as everyone else is. He can play Andy Martin better than you or Scott, just as you can play your parts better than him, because you've each been chosen specifically for them.' He fixed Ewan with a steady eye. 'So, mate, this is how it is. I wouldn't have started this project if you hadn't agreed to do it. Now I'm committed, but I won't do it with a star who's disrespectful to his fellow actors, or who tries to undermine me, as producer or director.

'If you can't live with that, I'll negotiate the terms of your withdrawal with Margaret.'

I felt Scott stiffen beside me; I held my breath. I could barely believe it, but Britain's number one A-list movie actor had just been threatened with his P45.

'And who'd play Skinner?' asked Capperauld, icily. Clearly, he didn't believe it at all.

'The biggest name in movies,' Miles replied, 'Miles

Grayson. I'll make an early script change to account for the accent, and I'll do your part myself.'

I think Ewan was about to tell him that he couldn't do that, when he realised that he could. In the event he stopped himself at, 'You . . .'

We had one of those long silences, the kind in which you swear you can hear people's brains whirring and clicking. Miles stood there, straight-faced, with his back to the window. Capperauld looked at him, then through the glass, at the Scott Monument, then at Scott Steele, who can be a bit of a monument himself at times. Finally he did something that took me by surprise. He turned to me and offered his hand.

'I'm sorry, Oz,' he said; the Scottish accent was back. 'I guess I've been living in London too long; sometimes I forget myself and turn into a real fucking lovey. That was an insult, and I apologise; to you too, Miles.'

I looked at him to be sure he wasn't taking the piss; when I was, I accepted his handshake.

'I got my first job by accident,' he went on, 'as a boy, in the very early days of *Take the High Road* . . . you know, the Scottish soap. A couple of years later, I landed a film part. I've seen your first movie; you were a fucking sight better in that than I was in mine . . . and I've still never been to drama college.'

Miles patted him on the shoulder. 'That's why you don't believe in rehearsals, mate.' He flashed him a grin: the one that lights up rooms and makes him tower over everyone around him, even though he's really shorter than most of them. 'Now that's sorted, you guys get to know each other. Scott, you come with me, and meet Masahi.'

'Son,' the venerable actor beamed, 'I did a war movie with him in Malaysia, over twenty years ago, when you were still working on the docks in Sydney. You come with me, and I'll introduce you properly.'

They wandered off, leaving me alone with Ewan, half hoping that Rhona Waitrose would come back. She didn't, though, not then.

'How did your Toronto stint go?' he asked, conversationally.

'Pretty well, I think. The offers are rolling in, anyway. I'm going back to Canada after this one.'

Ewan nodded. 'The way things are headed we'll all be working there soon.'

'No. They don't do beaches.'

'They do everything. It's a big place.'

One of the catering staff who had taken over my kitchen passed by and offered us more champagne. As she was filling our glasses, another came up with a tray full of savouries. I grabbed a couple with my free hand.

'I read in the *Scotsman* that you're an old acquaintance of the woman who's been charged with doing for my late cousin,' my new friend murmured, as they moved on to the next group.

'Alison? Yes. We had a relationship a few years back.'

'Poor lass.' He chuckled. 'Not on that score, I rush to say. No, I meant, poor lass that she was mixed up with our David. Do you think she did it?'

'She's going to plead guilty to culpable homicide, as we call manslaughter in Scotland. It's on that understanding she's been charged with that and not murder.'

'Mmm, "copping a plea" as the Americans say. I hope the court goes easy on her, then. You seem to know a bit about it.'

I nodded. 'I do. I've been trying to help her; she's afraid that her business will go down the tubes, even if she doesn't go to jail. I've been trying to set it up so that it doesn't, even if she does.'

'Well, if there's anything I can do to help, you only have to ask.'

I looked at him. 'You serious?'

'Absolutely.'

'Well, if you'd agree to perform the opening ceremony at James Torrent's new corporate headquarters, you'd be helping her big-time.'

'Torrent? The office equipment man?' He frowned, furrowing his brow, thinking something over. 'Yes, I'll do that for her.'

I was slightly stunned. 'Will you? That's great. I'm seeing her this evening; I'll tell her. It'll brighten what's been a pretty traumatic day.'

'You're seeing her? In prison?'

'No, at her office; she appeared in court this morning, and the sheriff let her out on bail.'

'That's good. I hope it goes well with her.'

His concern seemed genuine. 'Alison told me you didn't like your cousin. She wasn't kidding, was she?'

'No, she was not. The little bastard made a pass at my wife, once, about ten years ago, at a family gathering. I caught him at it and I thumped him. He told his parents, my aunt and uncle, a pack of lies; he accused me of touching up his girlfriend, would you believe. My uncle tackled me about it, and I told him that his son was a lying little shit, and left it at that.

'I'd forgotten about it inside a week, but not David, though; he kept the bad feeling going. His father and my father have been at odds over it ever since. When he and Alison started in business, I thought it was a chance to heal the breach, so I called him, and offered to support them, financially and with contacts. He told me to fuck off.' He laughed and shook his head. 'What an idiot.'

He paused. 'Why did she do it, do they reckon?'

'He two-timed her, then broke off their engagement. He put the screws on her over the business after that; he was trying to force her to buy his shares for more than they were worth. At least, that's what they're saying.'

'That's typical of the little bastard. I've never met the girl, you know, but she didn't deserve him. No one did.' He frowned again, then nodded as if another decision had been made. 'I'll tell you what; when you see her, would you put a proposition to her? I'd like to renew my offer of help; if the business is saveable, and if my unlamented cousin's shares are still available, I'll buy them at an independent valuation. Obviously, I won't be actively involved, but I'll let her keep the Capperauld name above the door.'

He looked at me. 'Do you think she'd consider that?'

I whistled. 'I think she'll jump at it, Ewan; it'll be great news for her.' I couldn't help thinking that it would be great news for Susie as well. I looked him in the eye. A quarter of an hour before I'd been ready to deck him; now he'd turned out to be not such a bad guy after all.

'I'll tell her tonight. Assuming she agrees, I'll arrange for you to meet.'

'You do that. Why don't you make it here, at eight tomorrow morning?'

'That early?'

'Of course.' He chuckled. 'It wouldn't do for us to be late for Miles's bloody rehearsals.'

29

Alison's office was one stair up, in an undistinguished terrace on the south side of York Place, but I guessed that with its city centre location, it was costing her a packet in rent.

The nameplates on the street entrance and outside her glass-panelled door must have been pricey items too. I suggested as much when she let me in. 'Yes,' she said, mournfully. 'I suppose I'll have to change them now.'

'Not necessarily,' I replied. 'How did it go in court?'

She shuddered. 'It was scary. They led me up into the dock, I said "yes" when the clerk asked me if I was who I was, and again, when the sheriff asked me if I understood the charge. Otherwise, that was it; Mr Badenoch made a short speech about my unblemished character, then he asked for bail. The fiscal didn't oppose and that was it; I'm back again in six weeks, when I'll be asked to plead. I've had to surrender my passport, but there were no other conditions. I don't have to sleep with Ricky,' she snorted, 'or anything like that.'

'I don't recall that being a condition the last time,' I reminded her. 'The way I heard it, that was all your idea.'

'Well, it was a bad one,' she sniffed. 'Even if it did prick his conscience into trying to help me.'

'That prick has no conscience.'

'You can talk. Anyway, I suppose he's not that bad.' She poured me a mug of coffee from her filter, added milk,

163

without asking, and handed it to me. 'He was here half an hour ago,' she said, smoothing out her long straight skirt. She looked not half bad, in that and a sleeveless blouse.

'He told me what he'd found out about the key at David's flat, and about the fingerprints he lifted from it. It was real private eye stuff. Did you use to do that, Oz, when you were in that business?'

'You know damn well I was never in that business; I just worked for lawyers, that's all.'

'Sure. I believed that, too, until Ricky told me different. He said that you were mixed up in a murder, after you and I split up, and that for a while he thought you might have had a hand in it.'

'I think he still half believes that, but he's wrong.'

'You're mixed up in one now.'

'No. You are; he is; I'm not. I'm not involved. What else did he tell you?'

'Nothing. He asked for a list of David's friends, that was all.'

'Was it much of a list?'

She gave a short, brittle laugh, and shook her head. 'Not really. I gave him three, no, four names to be going on with, but the only really close friend among them was Don Kennedy.' She looked at me as if she expected me to know him. I looked back at her, blankly.

'Which Don Kennedy?'

'You know; the golfer.'

'Oh, that Don Kennedy.' I'd heard of him, right enough. He'd won quite a few events in Europe, and one in the States. He was a Ryder Cup player, but he wasn't exactly a household name . . . at least not in any household I'd ever had. The thought of households took me back to Susie, and our conversation that morning.

By coincidence, Alison arrived in the same vicinity at

the same time. 'What did you mean earlier,' she asked, 'when you said I wouldn't necessarily have to change the nameplates?'

'I meant,' I told her, 'that you have the most unlikely fairy godfather you could ever have imagined . . . except that I wouldn't really say he's a fairy, just a bit arch from time to time.'

I told her all about my encounter with Ewan Capperauld, in detail, piece by piece. When I got to where he agreed without a murmur to open James Torrent's building, she gasped with surprise, shouted 'Yes!' and jumped up and down. When I got to the end, and his offer to buy his cousin's stake in the business, and put his own name behind it, she looked at me in total amazement for a few seconds then threw herself at me and kissed me. She'd never done it like that in the old days. This was a real tongue-tickling-tonsils job. She didn't stop there either; there wasn't an interesting piece of her that wasn't pressed and writhing against me.

Eventually I peeled her off . . . not too soon though, for I was enjoying it, a fact of which she must have been aware. 'You are the most surprising, wonderful man,' she whispered. 'Make love to me.'

I held her away from me. 'Come on, now,' I told her. 'If you want to fuck someone to celebrate, fuck Ewan. It's only right; he's the guy making the offer.'

She smiled at me; very definitely Alison Mark Two. 'Yes, but he's not here.' She began to unbutton her blouse. Something made me stop her; Susie's face in my mind's eye . . . or maybe it was a subconscious image of her and Ricky Ross.

'Thanks again, but no thanks.'

'You really are serious about this woman in Glasgow, aren't you?'

165

I was, and it was worrying me. 'No, I just want you to be fresh for your meeting with Ewan tomorrow morning; eight o'clock at my place.'

She was still incredulous. 'He wants to meet me?'

'Of course, if you're interested in his offer.'

'If I'm what? Of course I'm interested; I'll jump at it.'

'Or for it,' I muttered, but she didn't pick it up. She was too busy planning ahead.

'Eight o'clock,' she said. 'Mmm, that's early. Oz, maybe I could stay at your place tonight. That would make sense.'

'Maybe to you, but it might not sound too sensible to me.'

She waved a hand at me. 'Don't worry about your virtue; it'll be safe with me.' I wasn't sure; I'd been in that situation before, with Susie, and it hadn't been. 'Please,' she whispered. 'Last night was awful, really, in that cell. I really don't fancy being on my own at home, not yet.'

I gave in. 'Okay,' I said. 'But I'm warning you, I'll be locking my bedroom door!' I don't think she believed me.

We did a drive-by of her place and picked up some fresh clothes for the morning, plus her toothbrush and cosmetics. I didn't notice her packing anything that looked like a nightdress, but I let that pass.

It was going on for nine when we got back to the Mound; when I showed her the spare room and dumped her bag there, Alison smiled in a way that told me she didn't regard the subject as closed. I still did; I checked my resolve, and found it holding up under the pressure. We were both hungry, but I didn't fancy cooking that late, so I called the ever reliable Pizza Hut and ordered up a double whopper stuffed crust whatever, no garlic, please, paid by credit card. There were a couple of bottles of Bollinger in the fridge, left over from the afternoon. I opened one, poured two glasses, then settled down to watch some obscure football match on Channel 5, with the sound turned down so that the awful screaming commentator didn't get on my tits.

The entry buzzer went ten minutes later. Alison jumped up; I thought she was going to answer it, but instead she headed for her room. I picked up the phone myself, and heard a female voice say, 'Pizza,' managing to make even those two syllables sound broad Edinburgh.

'Top floor,' I grunted, then pressed the buzzer and, as had become my habit, opened the front door, ready for the lift's arrival. I was looking out of the window as I heard it open, but the voice from behind still took me by surprise. 'My, who's the hungry one then?' Outside, the lift closed again and headed for the street.

I turned to see Rhona Waitrose, with a Pizza Hut carrier balanced on the tips of the fingers of her right hand, and what looked like a script held in her left. It was remarkable that I noticed these things, for she was wearing a pair of black patent shoes, a shiny raincoat, which hung open, and nothing else.

'I thought we might do a bit of early rehearsing,' she said, brightly. Then her smile faded as Alison walked back into the room. She was dressed much the same as Rhona, minus the raincoat and the shoes, and she was holding a champagne glass between breasts that did indeed seem to have grown since the last time I'd seen them.

'. . . Only I see you're auditioning this evening,' the pizza delivery girl finished. 'My mistake, sorry.'

'Hold on,' I said weakly, 'it's no mistake.'

She brightened up. 'Ah well,' the actress chuckled. 'I'm all for improvisation in my work.' She looked at Alison, who seemed slightly bewildered, but not too bothered by the newcomer. 'What do you think, dear? Does one go into two?'

'We take what we can get,' my ex replied, positively.

I thought through my options; I didn't fancy any of them. Well, that's not true; I fancied both of them, but not in the same room, at the same time. 'Can I just settle for the pizza,' I suggested, 'and let you girls sort things out for yourselves?'

They both laughed, in a tinkling harmony; then the bells stopped ringing, as the lift opened again.

'Someone left the street door open,' Susie called out, as she walked in through the open door, carrying her overnight bag. 'Surp . . .'

I've never seen a volcano erupt, but if I ever do, then like the song says, it won't impress me much. Not after seeing Susie go instantly ballistic. 'You bastard,' she screamed, as she dropped the bag, and advanced on me. 'You indescribable fucking bastard! I am mug enough to fall for you, and to think that you feel the same way about me. So I come through to bring some joy into your lonely life, and what do I find? You're waist deep in fucking whores!'

'Hey wait a minute!' Rhona protested.

Susie didn't even turn to look at her; she just threw out a hand behind her with a pointing finger on the end. 'You shut your mouth!' she commanded. Rhona obeyed. As for Alison, she just stood there; her mouth was still hanging open, but no sound was coming out.

'Love,' I pleaded with her, 'this is not what it seems.' I wondered, idly, whether going down on my knees would help, but I decided that it would only make it easier for her to punch me in the mouth.

'Well, what the fuck is it then? Which scene in your bloody movie is this?'

Behind her the door slammed shut. We all looked towards it. The tall, angular figure of Mandy O'Farrell stared back at us. I was hugely relieved to see that she was fully clothed, even if she was as astonished as the rest of us.

'Jesus Christ,' she boomed in her full, rich contralto. 'Is there no security in this bloody building?'

I took advantage of Susie's momentary distraction to seize her firmly by the arm and march her towards my bedroom. 'Mandy,' I called over my shoulder, 'get these two out of here, dressed or otherwise.

'Alison, go home, go to Ross, go wherever you bloody like, but be back here for eight tomorrow morning!

'And Rhona, leave the fucking pizza!'

I shoved Susie into my bedroom, closed the door behind us, locked it, and turned back to face her, just in time for a small bare foot to slam into my testicles, and take my mind completely off everything else that had happened that evening.

30

It took me three minutes before I could think of anything but the pain, and another two before I could even begin to croak, let alone speak. Fortunately, I'd fallen backwards against the bedroom door, making it impossible for Susie to get out.

It took me another fifteen minutes for me to get her to begin to believe me, and the best part of an hour before she was completely convinced. Even then . . .

'But if I hadn't walked in . . .'

'I'd have eaten the pizza, love, honest.'

'You can have it now, then, if those bitches haven't nicked it.' She smiled at me. 'Afterwards, if you're really lucky, you can have me.' I do not think I have ever felt more relieved in my life.

We decided to change the order of events. Later, quite a while later, I went out to check that Mandy had indeed evicted the visitors, and to recover Susie's bag from the living room. The pizza was intact, if stone cold. I squeezed it into the oven to reheat, then checked the champagne, on the kitchen counter. It was warm and flat, but it was still Bolly, so I poured us a couple of glasses and carried them back into the living room.

Susie was waiting for me, in a blue silk dressing gown, sitting on the sofa with her legs tucked under her. I handed her a glass; she sampled it and frowned. 'Were you wasting this on that cow Alison?'

'I was being hospitable,' I told her, 'that was all.'

'I take it she was the one without the raincoat, the one with the fake knockers.'

'How do you know they're fake?'

She snorted. 'At her age, if they were real they'd have started the long sad journey south . . . like mine.'

I sat beside her and nuzzled my forehead against them. 'They've got a long way to go, honey.'

'You say the nicest things; I might just stay the night.'

'Stay for good,' I suggested. 'We could move Janet and Ethel through here.'

'A nice idea, but I can't; I've still got a business to run. And anyway, I'd cramp your bloody style.'

'I don't have a style to cramp, not any more.' I looked at her. 'You scare me shitless, you know,' I told her.

'Good!' she retorted, with a grin. 'That's the way it should be. Not that I believe it, mind. I know you, Oz Blackstone; I won't catch you off-guard again.'

'I didn't mean that. I meant that the way I feel about you scares me.'

'Does it make you happy as well, though? Does it conjure up pictures of a house in the country and two point four kids?'

'Three point four, actually.'

'Be brave, then; face up to the prospect of life with me. Think how brave I'm being; I'm taking a chance on a guy who slept with someone else on his honeymoon.'

'Yeah, but it was you I slept with.'

'So?'

I left her smiling and went off to dish up the pizza; I cut it into segments and laid them on a kitchen tray, then I picked up the champagne and carried the lot through.

'Rhona Waitrose hasn't changed,' Susie said, when I got back.

I was taken by surprise. 'You know her?'

'Before she got mildly famous, she used to sing with a band in Glasgow. They played at a club I used to go to, when I was fancy free. She practically screwed the guitarist on stage, and they said that off stage she screwed the whole bloody band.

'You tell her from me that if she comes near you again, I will fix her, big time.'

'I think she may have worked that out,' I said, 'but I'll tell her, discreetly.'

'You do that. The other slut, Alison; she's the one in whose business I was going to be daft enough to invest, is she?'

'That's her. She doesn't need our help any more though.' I told her about Ewan Capperauld's unexpected Galahad act.

'Very noble,' she murmured. 'What's he like, the great man?'

'Takes a bit of getting to know, but he's all right once the ice is broken.' I told her about his run-in with Miles.

She whistled. 'Silly man, then; your friend Mr Grayson is definitely not someone I would cross. There's something lethal behind that smile.' She frowned. 'He's a bit like you in that respect.' I didn't know whether that was a compliment or not, but eventually I decided that coming from Susie, it probably was.

We finished the pizza, and Bolly, then went back to bed; I set the alarm for six-forty-five and we made love until we fell asleep.

When Darren Adam woke me next morning on Radio Forth, Susie was up and in the shower. I decided that I liked that; it felt like home. But maybe I also liked, just a wee bit, the fact that she was going back to Glasgow and leaving me to my own life . . . hell, I didn't know.

She was ready for the road by quarter to eight, having called Ethel to make sure that the baby was okay. 'When will I see you again?' she asked, as we stood waiting for the lift.

'The first chance I get,' I promised, and I meant it. Listening to Susie talk to the nanny made me realise how much I wanted to see my daughter again too. 'I'll see how today goes; if it works out, maybe I'll be able to come through tonight.

'Not tomorrow night, though; the fun starts on Sunday morning, very early.'

She smiled. 'Sometime, I'd like to come through and watch you work. Would that be okay? Could you fix it with Miles?'

'Yes, I reckon I could. Once I see the schedule, we'll set something up.' The lift arrived; I put a foot in the door, to hold it.

Her eyes narrowed, as a thought crossed her mind. 'Here,' she muttered, 'that Rhona Waitrose. Do you and she get to . . .? You know what I mean.'

'We've got a clinch later on; nothing horizontal, though, and we both get to keep our kit on.'

'Hmmph!' Susie grunted. 'That'll be a change for her.'

She patted my chest. 'Right, I'm off. Before I go, though, I'll make you a promise. No more surprises; thinking about it, I suppose I was taking a lot for granted.'

'No,' I said. 'I loved your being here . . . eventually.'

She patted my groin. 'Sorry about the kick in the balls. It didn't do any lasting damage, though; in fact . . .'

I stopped her with a kiss, and pushed her into the lift.

Ewan Capperauld arrived ten minutes later, shaved, scrubbed and still wearing that black leather coat. I gave him coffee, and offered him toast; he declined, in favour of the last wedge of cold pizza, which he spotted on the work surface. I was getting to like the man more by the day.

He was halfway through it when the buzzer sounded again. 'Package for you,' said Ricky Ross.

'Bring her up, then.'

'No, I'll put her in the lift,' he said, tersely. 'It's a bit early for me to be mopping up blood.'

I was waiting when Alison arrived, wearing the clothes she had picked out the night before. 'You'd better not be mad at me,' I warned her.

She smiled. 'I'm not; I just told Ricky I was.'

'You went to his place then?'

'I asked that Mandy girl to take me there. She phoned him first and he said it was okay. What an action woman she is, by the way . . . although nothing compared to your girlfriend. Did you calm her down?'

'Eventually, no thanks to you and that other one.'

'Yes,' Alison exclaimed. 'What a brazen cow she is!'

'Jesus!' I gave up and ushered her into the apartment. Ewan was still in the kitchen, demolishing the last of the pizza. I introduced Alison, who switched into business mode straight away. She handled it just right, I thought, letting him realise that she knew how important he was, but that she was not about to be overawed.

I went off to shower and shave; I took my time over it, leaving them alone for as long as I could.

When I got back, their deal appeared to be done, for they were shaking hands. Ewan looked at me as I came back into the room. 'What do you think the chances are of the judge going easy?' he asked me, dropping into his Skinner accent.

'Pretty good. The Crown Office is making all the right noises. Alison's lawyer's pretty confident that they won't press for a jail sentence. Your involvement will probably help too, if you're happy to have it mentioned in court, that is.'

He shrugged. 'No problem.' He glanced back at Alison. 'Who is your lawyer, by the way?'

'His name is Charles Badenoch.'

Ewan laughed, suddenly. 'What a fucking village this is,' he exclaimed. 'I was at Heriot's with Charlie. He was the classroom lawyer, even then. He used to defend guys who were accused of misdemeanours by the prefects. He got a few off, too, until he became a prefect himself, then he switched to the prosecution side.'

He glanced at his watch, then pushed himself up from the dining table, at which they had been sitting. 'Come on, Oz,' he said. 'Glen Oliver, my minder, is waiting downstairs in the car; we'll give you a lift to the Assembly Rooms, after we've dropped Alison at her office.

'Mustn't keep the director waiting; if we did that, I doubt if even Charlie could get us off.'

31

As it turned out, we made it to the Assembly Rooms a couple of minutes ahead of Miles and Dawn. The whole cast was there, in a big upstairs room with a chandelier, apart from Liam Matthews, who had so few speaking scenes that he had cut a deal with Miles, allowing him to turn up for rehearsals only a day before he was due to shoot.

Those of us who were there were each given a copy of the shooting schedule by Gail Driver. It isn't invariable that the first scene in a movie is the one that's shot first, but that was convenient in this case and so that was how it would be done.

I had thought that we might launch straight into rehearsal, but Miles began by gathering us all round, as he had done the day before in my apartment. This time, he ran through the script himself from start to finish, describing each of the locations we would use, and giving us a picture of how he saw our work developing.

That took up most of the morning; we didn't break for coffee until almost mid-day. I had just picked up a mug and a couple of biscuits when Rhona Waitrose tapped me on the shoulder. I took a quick look to see that she was respectable, then gave her a non-committal, 'Hello'.

'Too bad about last night,' she murmured.

'Too right,' I replied, maybe just a bit tersely. 'My nuts may never be the same.'

Rhona winced. 'Sorry about that.' She paused. 'That was Susie Gantry, wasn't it; from Glasgow? She's your girl-friend?' I nodded, twice. 'I remember her, when her old man was king of the city, before he had his breakdown and got put away. She had guys swarming after her like wasps, but she never gave any of them as much as a sniff. None of them pushed it too hard, either. Her father had, shall we say, a certain reputation.'

'He still has; but he's not her father. Susie's adopted.'

'Lucky girl, then, falling heir to all that.'

'Not at all; she works hard. She saved that business, after Jack's trouble.'

'Have we fucked it up between you two, me and that other girl? Who was she, anyway? The way it looked when I came in, you and she were getting ready to make the beast with two backs.'

'She was an accident, waiting to happen; as it did happen, I was getting ready for nothing but pizza. How did you get the box, anyway?'

'I saw the kid arrive, and I just asked him if it was for you, by any chance. I got lucky.'

'You won't say that if you ever meet Susie again. Since you asked, no, things are not bust between us.'

She whistled. 'You are one smooth bastard,' she said, a little too loudly for my liking, 'if you managed to talk your way out of that.' Mandy O'Farrell was on duty with the rest of the minder team. Rhona's voice must have reached her, for she looked over her shoulder and smiled at me. I excused myself to my co-star and walked across to her. She was standing between Alan Graham and Mike Reilly, but she turned away from them as I approached.

'I should thank you for last night,' I said, quietly.

She looked at me, her smile even wider, her eyes . . . very attractive blue eyes . . . sparkling. 'It's all part of the service.'

'How did you happen to turn up there, anyway?'

'I was keeping an eye on Rhona. I saw her pull her trick with the pizza delivery boy; then I saw her unbutton her raincoat. That told me the whole story. I'd have left you to it, but that other girl turned up and followed her into the building without using a key. I watched her, and I saw her get into your lift.'

'So, maybe I was planning a foursome?'

'If you had been I'd have apologised and left,' she chuckled. 'But I knew who the second woman was. With Rhona having her goodies on display, and knowing what I know about her, I guessed there could be trouble, so I used my initiative.'

'You seem to know a lot about us all.'

'I did my research; that's part of the job, too. Alison was a surprise, though.'

'That one? Every day, another surprise.'

'What's her connection with my boss?' Mandy asked.

'That's a long story. I'll let him tell you.'

'Is he trying to keep her out of the slammer or put her there?'

'I'll pass on that too.'

She looked as if she might have pressed me further, but right at that moment, Miles called us all back on parade.

In planning the project, he had decided that as much of the film as possible should be shot on location. That's the way he usually works, and given the backdrops that Edinburgh offers it would have been a shame to do otherwise on this one. For a while he had harboured a wild hope that he would have been allowed to shoot in the real police HQ building, but not even he had the clout to pull that off. Instead, he had rented part of a rambling college building on the south side of the city, and an authentic office was being set up there.

Our first stop, though, was Advocates' Close, which connects the High Street with Cockburn Street below, and which takes its name, I guess, from the fact that in old Edinburgh it was a favourite route of Scottish barristers on their way from their New Town homes to work in the Supreme Courts.

The book that we were filming opens there, with a headless body, right on page one. A little bloody, one might think, but the victim turns out to have been a lawyer, so that, as far as most people are concerned, made him fair game.

Ewan was scheduled to make his big entrance as Bob Skinner right at the start, with me hustling about as Andy Martin, and Dawn on hand as Dr Sarah Grace, the scene-of-crime examiner, who also happens to be Skinner's piece on the side. The script called for a degree of horizontal contact between Ewan and Dawn; those scenes would be filmed on a specially built part of our leased college, and were marked on the schedule as 'closed set'. That meant that only those with an absolute need to be there would get to see the producer/director's wife in the scud. I noticed that Miles had ruled himself out from that part of the movie; the scenes were to be directed by Dawn herself.

However he was involved in our first scene, and that was the one he rehearsed hardest in the Assembly Rooms that morning, and afternoon. We had to use a bit of imagination to transport the chandelier to the gloomy Advocates' Close, but he had brought along a prosthetic head, which we would use in the real thing, to give us a bit of added colour.

Eventually he was happy with the way we were playing the thing, especially with a scene in which Skinner delivers a dressing down to an over-enthusiastic young copper. The rest of the cast had been rehearsing their own opening lines and scenes in other parts of the room. Finally, he stood everyone down but us.

'Come on,' he said, to Ewan, Dawn and me, and to the supporting players. 'Let's take a run up there now, and look at the real thing. Do it today, and we can all have tomorrow off.'

With that incentive, all of us, and our minders, piled into two of the fleet of people-movers which he had hired. The city was really behind us, I guessed, when I saw that they had stickers that exempted them from the attentions of the Blue Meanies, Edinburgh's detested traffic storm-troopers.

I had walked through Advocates' Close many times before, in the years I'd lived in the capital, but I'd never really taken in the detail. As soon as we stepped into the entrance, I saw what the problems were going to be.

'This is going to take a long time,' said Miles. 'We have to do this the old-fashioned way, with a single camera, because of the narrowness of the passage. That means that many of the lines are going to have to be lit and shot individually. You guys may have to shave twice on Sunday, just for continuity's sake.'

'Where will we do that?' asked Ewan.

'They're going to close off Cockburn Street to all but essential traffic; we'll park the production trailers down there.'

Miles spent another half-hour walking us through our parts, showing Ewan how he wanted him to make his entrance, showing me how he wanted me to crouch beside the headless dummy, and taking final decisions on placing the camera. By the end of it all, we were knackered; even Dawn was getting irritable, and that's unusual. Miles got the message from her, if from nobody else. 'Okay,' he announced at last, 'that's it for today. I'll see you all back here Sunday; six-thirty. Be sharp, be rested, be good.'

32

Their departure gave me a reality jolt. Glen Oliver took Ewan away in a taxi, Miles, Dawn and Mike Reilly took one of the people-movers back to the Caledonian, and the bit players commandeered the other to go back to the Assembly Rooms.

There was I, an international movie star, left on his own in a rapidly cooling Advocates' Close. Mind you, after the day I'd had, a pint was an appealing proposition, and Deacon Brodie's Tavern was only a few yards away. Then, later, with any luck, I could escape to Glasgow, and the bosoms of my new family.

Only I wasn't alone. When I stepped out of the passage-way into the High Street, who was waiting round the corner but Ricky Ross. 'What the hell are you doing here?' I asked him.

'Waiting for you,' he told me, cheerfully. 'I thought you might fancy coming with me on a visit I have to pay on someone.'

'And why would I want to do that?'

'You're a golfer, aren't you? I thought you guys were all groupies when it comes to meeting pros. Alison gave me a list of the boy David's friends; right at the top is Don Kennedy, the golfer.

'As it happens, he's not playing on the tour event this week. He's had a couple of sponsor's days up at Murrayfield Golf Club, and I've arranged to see him there.'

I started to say that I wanted nothing to do with his games, and that I had better things to do than run around Edinburgh playing detective with some clapped out ex-copper, but then I thought about a persistent slice that had been creeping into my game.

'Okay,' I said. 'Provided it doesn't take too long.'

His car was parked round the corner in St Giles Street, beside the High Court, where, in a few weeks, Alison was due to take her chances with a man, or maybe a woman, in a wig and a red jacket. I found myself wondering how Rhona Waitrose would look in that outfit; she'd certainly done a lot for a simple raincoat.

There was a parking ticket on Ricky's Alfa Romeo. He ripped it off the windscreen and threw it away. 'These wankers will never learn,' he muttered. 'My number's on a list, and they've all got it. Whoever wrote that's in bother when he files it.'

He didn't say another word of any consequence on the journey to Murrayfield. I'd been expecting him to quiz me about Alison's unexpected appearance at his place, but he didn't. Maybe Mandy had told him the whole story, maybe she hadn't. I was fairly sure that Alison hadn't.

The traffic was light so the trip across the New Town and into Ravelston Dykes didn't take long. We pulled into the car park in front of the club-house building. I was wearing black designer jeans and a Ralph Lauren polo shirt; given the strict dress codes that operate in some of these clubs, I wondered if they'd let me in.

They might not have, but fortunately Don Kennedy was dressed in more or less the same way as I was, and also, he was waiting for us in the casual bar . . . known in some golf clubs as the 'dirty bar'.

I'd seen him maybe a hundred times on television, so I recognised him at once. He was shorter than I'd expected, but like most golfers he had shoulders that looked capable of supporting a house, and hands that were big enough to dig its foundations without a shovel. When I was in my early twenties, a bloke in St Andrews showed me what he assured me was one of Arnold Palmer's old golf gloves. God isn't all that tall either, while I'm not a little guy myself, but I swear I could have got both my hands in there.

Kennedy is not famous for smiling on the golf course, but he was affable enough as he greeted us. A weak sun was shining through the window, and glinting on his trademark copper curls. 'Mr Ross,' he began, engulfing Ricky's hand in one of his. Then he looked at me, and frowned. 'I know you, don't I,' he muttered, 'but I can't place you.'

'My face gets around,' I told him. 'Oz Blackstone; I'm a friend of David Capperauld's fiancée.'

'You're also an actor; I saw your last film. Very good, very good; no way could I do that sort of thing.'

'I could say the same about your last tee-shot. I have this terrible bloody slice.'

Kennedy smiled. 'Get your pro to work on your set-up,' he said, 'but once you start slicing, it's usually terminal.' He turned back to Ricky, as we joined him at his table. 'So, Mr Ross, you said you wanted to ask me about my poor friend David? I'm happy to talk to you, but what's the nature of this investigation?'

'Informal,' he replied, pausing as the barman appeared and took our drinks orders; two diet cokes; Ross was driving and I'd gone off the idea of a pint. 'The crown is convinced of the circumstances, and it looks as if they'll proceed on a culpable homicide charge. Assuming the judge accepts a guilty plea, the sentence will be determined by the extent to which her counsel can persuade him she was provoked.'

'What? Are you trying to prove she was out of her mind with grief when she did it?'

'Not quite, but something along those lines.'

'You'll have a problem, then. I know Alison, obviously; I knew them as a couple, although we didn't see a lot of each other latterly, since I'm touring most of the time, and my family base is in the south. To be frank, I never thought they'd make it to the altar, although I never thought, obviously, that the relationship would end like this. I thought that they were committed to their business more than to each other, and that David in particular was in it for the money.'

The golfer leaned back in his seat. 'They say you can pick your friends but not your relatives. I don't believe that; I have cousins I haven't seen since we were children, but I'm one of those guys who makes a friend for better or worse. I've known David Capperauld since first year at Edinburgh Academy juniors, and we've been chums since then. I'm not stupid, and I'm not blind; I know that he could be a cunning, ruthless little shit, and that he behaved very badly towards Alison; but he had his good side too. He was funny, he was devoted to his parents, and if you were close to him he'd always be there for you. I think part of the trouble was that he and Alison were never that close.'

I was only there as an observer, but I couldn't stop myself from picking up on him. 'You said he behaved badly towards her. Alison told me that he had broken off the engagement, or had told her as much, and that he wanted her to buy him out of the business at a value which was his estimate as much as anything else.'

Kennedy nodded. 'That's more or less the situation. The way he put it, she was trying to make him take less than market value, by threatening the stability of the company. I can see both sides of that one.'

So could I. I wondered whether Ricky and I should stop our investigation at that point, and let Alison settle for what she had.

'Do you know anything of the relationship between David and his famous cousin?' I asked.

'David hated him from way back; the whole town knew that. There were two stories about it; eventually he told me the true one. He couldn't let himself make it up with Ewan, though. It was a macho thing with him, a pride thing; every time Ewan won an award or had a hit, he got more bitter.'

'What about the woman?' Ricky's question cut right across him. 'The one he was two-timing Alison with?'

'Again,' Kennedy replied, 'that's not how he would have put it. He'd have said that the relationship had run its course and that he had moved on.' He looked at Ross; I could read the shrewdness in his eyes. 'This isn't about a plea in mitigation, is it?' he murmured, then he glanced back at me. 'You don't think she did it, do you?'

'Let's just say we'd like to be satisfied that she did,' I told him.

'But the police are, aren't they?'

'Sometimes the police are too easily satisfied.'

'I'm with you on that one.'

'So, David's other woman; who is she?'

Kennedy smiled and looked out of the window. 'Nice little girl,' he mused. 'David introduced us last time I was up in Edinburgh. She's a receptionist with a big firm out on the west side. She's a doctor's daughter; Chinese descent. Her name's Anna Chin.'

33

'You know what, Ricky,' I said, as we drove away from the golf club, 'there's truth in the old song.'

'Eh?'

'Life is indeed just a bowl of cherries.'

'What the bloody hell are you talking about?'

'Anna Chin.'

'You know her?'

'I met her the other day. She's the main hall receptionist at James Torrent's new office building.'

'You never said. When Kennedy came out with the name, you should have said.'

'Why? What difference would it have made? Kennedy isn't a suspect.'

Ross was silent for a moment or two. 'How do you know that for sure?' he asked.

'He was playing in a pro-am event in Paris when Capperauld was killed. I checked the European Tour website on my laptop.'

'Clever bastard, eh.'

'Who, me or him? Anyway, I'm telling you now. Anna Chin works for Torrent, okay. Where does that take us?'

'Nowhere of itself,' said Ricky, as he took a right at the lights, past the Roseburn Bar, 'but it's a connection. It has a pattern of a sort; there's Torrent giving Alison a hard time over Ewan Capperauld, and over money, and at the same time his receptionist's having it off with Alison's fiancé, who's also Capperauld's cousin.

'It doesn't fit right. It sticks out, a bit like that.' He took his right hand off the wheel and held it up. I looked at it and saw that his wrist was slightly deformed. 'I broke it playing rugby, just after I left school. The bones weren't fitted together properly, but no one knew until they took the plaster off. By that time it was too late, and a promising career was halted in its tracks.

'I've had that as a reminder ever since. It niggles me, and now, every time I see a set of facts that fit together like a badly healed fracture, I want to know more about them.'

'Maybe, but remember one thing. We're after the person who killed David Capperauld.'

'If it wasn't Alison . . . but what's your point?'

'Let's say it wasn't. And my point is, I'm telling you it wasn't Anna Chin either.'

'Why? Don't tell me she was playing in the pro-am with Kennedy.'

'She might as well have been. She didn't do it.'

'Let me guess. She's a wee cracker with big doe eyes, and she couldn't possibly have stuck an ice-pick in her boyfriend's nut. If I'd given up on a suspect on that basis when I was in the force, there would be at least a dozen women walking around now, instead of doing time. Listen, whoever killed Capperauld either lashed out and got completely lucky . . . or unlucky if you want to see it that way . . . or they knew exactly what they were doing.' He paused, to take a left turn on to the Western Approach Road. 'Didn't Don Kennedy say that Anna Chin's a doctor's daughter?'

'She is,' I admitted. 'She told me so herself. But she didn't kill Capperauld.'

'There you go again.' Ricky laughed.

'Yes, and I'm right. I've known people who've killed, or had the potential to do it; this girl doesn't.'

'You say; I'll make up my own mind on that when I go to see her.'

'Go easy, then. Her boss is your client, remember.'

'Don't worry, I'll just have a gentle chat with the lass.' I tried to imagine him having a gentle chat with anyone, but I let it pass. I was tired, and I wanted to get on my way to Glasgow, so much so that I took out my mobile and called Susie, to let her know I was heading her way.

We were heading up Johnston Terrace, on the other side of the castle from my apartment, when the phone rang in my pocket. I took a look at the read-out before I accepted the call. The number was mine; I'd left it on divert.

'Yup,' I answered. Best not to give too much away too soon, I always say.

'Oz, is that you? Is that you?' It was Alison, unmistakeably. Equally unmistakeably, she was terrified.

'Yes; now calm down. What is it?'

'I'm at James Torrent's office,' she wailed. 'We had a meeting. Oz, there's a girl here, and she's dead.'

My brain seemed to shut down for a few seconds. I felt numb, and weary. *Not again, Alison, not again*, I thought. I realised that Ross was staring at me, and so I forced myself back to the present.

'Is there anyone else there?'

'Not as far as I can see. Oz, I'm scared.'

'If you're on your own, how did you get in?'

'By the side door, it opens into the hall.'

'Have you touched anything?'

'No.'

'Then get out of there, now.'

'What?'

'You heard me. Get off your mark, as fast as you bloody can!'

As I ended the call, Ricky pulled the Alfa to a halt, just down from the Ensign Ewart pub. 'What was all that about?' he asked.

I stared back at him, hard. 'As far as you're concerned, until I tell you different it was a hoax call. Now turn around and head for Torrent's place.'

'Why?'

'You're his head of security, right? Well, I'm reporting an incident. Now shift!'

34

Ricky quizzed me all the way out to Edinburgh Park, but I told him nothing other than that I'd had a call from someone reporting an emergency at the Torrent group corporate headquarters.

'But why you?' he demanded.

'I don't know!' I yelled at him. I don't shout very often; when I do, it usually has an effect. He dropped the subject and drove, while I phoned Susie and told her that I'd been delayed.

What I did know from the start was that I didn't want him, or anyone else, to find out any sooner than necessary that Alison had been there, not until we found out ourselves exactly what had happened and to whom . . . not that I was in any doubt about that. Ricky's badly healed fracture was sticking out like an elbow in my mind.

The building was locked and unlit when we pulled up outside, but the big red T on its pole, was glowing. As I looked at it, it occurred to me that it was shaped, more or less, like a cherry.

Ross jumped out and ran up the steps to the main entrance. It was locked and brass gates had been locked across the glass doors. He knew his way around, though; he headed straight round the side of the building, with me at his heels, until he came to a fire exit.

'Open,' he muttered, then pushed it, sending it swinging

violently on its hinges. I followed him into a short passage-way, which ended with another door; we burst out into the main entrance hall.

It was just before eight-thirty and it was a bright evening, so there was still enough natural light coming down from the atrium for us to see what had brought us there.

No more than twelve feet from us, the body of a young woman was sprawled across the reception desk. She was on her back, gazing sightless at the glass roof above. On the floor, all around us, lay ripe red cherries spilled from the wooden bowl in which her head now rested. I saw that several of them were squashed flat.

Ricky tried to hold me back, but I shook his hand off and made my way through them carefully, up to the desk.

I looked down at the dead girl; she was still wearing her plastic name tag, but I knew who she was, anyway. I had guessed as soon as I had taken Alison's frantic call. 'Anna Chin,' I said, quietly, as if I was trying not to disturb her. She looked peaceful; the only odd thing about her was the angle of her broken neck. Apart from that there was not a mark on her.

I looked over my shoulder at Ricky and saw that he was brandishing his twisted wrist. 'What did I tell you?' he exclaimed. 'That was Alison who called you, right?'

'Yes. Now tell me what else doesn't fit.'

'What do you mean?'

The words had barely escaped his lips, when we heard the siren outside. 'No, it's okay,' I told him. 'That's what was missing. Listen, when they get in here, ask them when they got the call.'

He frowned at me. 'Why?'

'Just do it.' I glanced at my watch. 'It's about twenty minutes since I had that phone call. I'll bet you the police were delayed by about that length of time; I'll bet they should have been here sooner, so they could catch her on the premises.'

Ricky isn't at all dumb. He saw the same picture I was looking at. 'Okay,' he said. 'Don't tell me any more.'

Just at that moment, two uniformed constables burst through the side door; one was a youngster, but the other was a veteran, grey hair showing at his temples.

'Where the fuck have you been?' Ross barked.

The older copper glared at him for about half a second, until he recognised him, then changed his expression, instantly. 'I'm sorry, sir,' he said. 'We're the second car. The one that was supposed to respond was in an accident at the Barnton traffic lights; the driver went through on the red and a lorry smashed his side in. I got the call after that, and I'd to come from Granton.'

'Okay. Were the other guys hurt?'

'I don't think so, sir.'

'The lorry driver?'

'No.'

'That's a relief; if he was there'd have been hell to pay.'

The veteran nodded; he was only relieved that he hadn't been in the other car. 'What about CID?' Ricky asked him.

'I don't know about that, sir.'

'Well, call them in pronto, and a doctor . . . not that there's any helping this poor lass.'

'What'll I call it, sir?'

Slowly and deliberately, Ross walked round the desk; he didn't look down as far as I could see, but I heard more cherries squash under his feet as he walked. 'Tell them it's a suspicious death, and that they should send a full scene-of-crime team. You two wait here and don't touch anything. We'll be outside.'

I got the message and followed him along the corridor, to the fire exit. I hadn't noticed before, but there were red marks on the floor that could have been made by the juice of crushed cherries. As he walked, outside and round to the main entrance, Ricky's shoes, and mine by that time, made even more.

'You're right,' he said as we stood waiting at the top of the steps, speaking quietly as if there was someone around who might have heard. 'This was a set-up. Whoever killed that girl knew that Alison was coming here and arranged it so that she would find her.

'I guess they watched her then called the police, expecting them to arrive with her still at the scene.'

He took a deep breath, then looked at me. 'You did the right thing, Oz, telling her to vanish. First she finds her fiancé's body, then she's caught standing over the girl he's been having it off with. It would have been all over for her; she'd have gone down for twenty years.'

'She might still. They're bound to find out she was here.'

'I don't know that; you never told me that.'

'What if they trace the call to my mobile?'

'What call? You never had a call, and you were with me all night.'

'Why did we turn up at the scene, then?'

'There's a sign on the gate saying that these premises are protected by Ross Security; my phone number's on it. I had an anonymous call at around the same time as the police, telling me that there had been an incident at Torrent. I came straight here, bringing you along for the ride since you were with me at the time.'

'What if they check to make sure there was a call to you?'

He gave me an offended look. 'They won't: most of the CID in this division used to be under my command. Their boss is my brother Mason, and so are some of them.'

'If it's that cut and dried, can I get out of here?'

'As soon as the CID arrive, yes; take my car and leave it at the Mound when you go to Glasgow. But before you do any of that, I want you to find Alison. Call her mobile, and tell her everything's under control. If she isn't waiting there already, tell her to go home, as normal. You meet her there, get her calmed down and settled in and, most important of all, take the shoes she was wearing and scrub the soles; make sure they're spotless. Tell her to sit tight and wait for me; I'd better stay at her place tonight.'

'You think she's actually in danger?'

He gave me a 'Be patient, he's an idiot' look. 'Someone's tried to frame her for two murders, and failed twice. What will they do next? Of course she's in fucking danger!'

35

That's how it went. The CID arrived . . . two detective sergeants. They both knew ex-Superintendent Ross, called him 'sir', and accepted his story without question. They didn't even talk to me.

Ricky gave me his spare keys to the Alfa, and I headed off back into town; as soon as I was out of sight, I called Alison's mobile number. She answered on the fifth ring, as if it had taken her that long to decide to take the call. She was at home, but she still sounded terrified.

I drove straight there. She was in her dressing gown when she let me in; her hair was wet, straight from the shower.

'That girl, Oz,' she whispered.

When I told her who Anna Chin was, and what they had in common, she slumped down into an armchair. After a few seconds she began to cry. 'Someone's got it in for me, Oz,' she moaned, 'and I haven't a clue why.'

'Maybe not, but you've got the good guys on your side. We'll find out and put a stop to it.'

The soles of her shoes were still stained dark red with cherry juice. I went to work with bleach and a nailbrush, until they were spotless.

She had stopped crying by the time I was finished. I thought about questioning her, but decided that already I was way more involved that I'd planned.

So I gave her a big drink, drove the Alfa back to the

Mound, picked up some overnight kit, and headed for Glasgow.

It was midnight, but Susie was still pleased to see me; no more, though, than I was pleased to see her.

'My God,' she said, looking at me in the doorway. 'You look dead beat; you must have had a hard day at the office.'

'I have,' I said, and then I picked her up and hugged her, for quite some time.

When I woke there was a strange, middle-aged lady leaning over the bed . . . only when I could focus, I realised that she wasn't strange at all. It was only Ethel; she had been trying to put a mug of tea on the table by my head without disturbing me. I don't know why she thought I'd like to wake up to a mug of cold tea, but that appeared to be the game plan.

'Morning,' I mumbled.

'Sorry, Oz,' she said, with the bright morning voice of the professional nurse, 'I was trying not to wake you. This isn't part of the service either,' she added, almost as an afterthought, 'but Susie's feeding baby Janet and she asked me if I would bring your tea in.'

I mumbled again as she left, then checked the bedside clock. It told me in big red liquid crystal numbers that I'd slept for almost ten hours. I pulled myself up in bed and used a remote to switch on the television in the corner, but all I could find was cartoons, kids making a noise, and that blonde girl with the tattoo on her bum who does the Saturday morning football programme.

I gave them all up and settled for Radio Clyde One, just as Susie came into the bedroom with wee Jan still attached. Maybe it was all the stuff that had been happening over the last few days, but my heart and my eyes just seemed to fill up at the same time.

'Come here,' I said, barely able to see them. 'Come into bed and let's be a family.'

We did that, we just lay there, did Susie and I, for about half an hour, with our child between us, talking mostly nonsense. I told her about Ewan and Alison having done their deal, I told her about the rehearsal and the scene set visit to Advocates' Close, and I told her about meeting Don Kennedy, the famous golfer, and his gloomy prognosis for my slice. But I did not tell her about Anna Chin; that sort of stuff has no business invading a moment like that.

Eventually we got up, and each of us, while the other showered, took turns at playing with the smiling Janet. Some people say it's only wind at that age, not a real smile, but that is sheer nonsense . . . I have two nephews and a daughter; I know these things.

It was Ethel's hard-earned weekend off; she muttered something about going to see her sister in Roseneath and headed off in her all-silver Ford Ka. 'Right,' Susie declared. 'Janet's fed, now what about us?'

'Saturday morning,' I replied. 'Glasgow. I'll go for the rolls and the papers, like any other bloke. You start the fry-up, and get the tea on, like any other woman.'

'Bloody chauvinist! But I don't fancy going out looking like an unmade bed . . .' See? Stereotypical behaviour; with her red hair tousled, and her freckled face fresh from the shower, she looked absolutely stunning. '. . . So we'll do it your way.' She took the door keys from the kitchen table and tossed them to me.

The flat is in a building near the top of Woodside Terrace, so I cut along to Lynedoch Street, and down to Woodlands Road, where I could take my pick of grocer newsagents, each one just like my friend Ali's place. I went into the nearest, bought four morning rolls, baked that day, the *Daily Record* and the *Scotsman*. The woman behind the counter gave me a knowing look, probably marking me as an out-of-towner, because I hadn't taken the *Herald*. I had a reason for picking the Edinburgh daily, though.

I sprinted across the street, and stopped on the other side, turning to glare over my shoulder at a taxi-driver who had blown his horn at me. As I did so, I caught a figure at the edge of my vision, turning away from me. Of itself, there was nothing unusual in it, but something clicked in my head, all the same.

I looked after the bloke, but he was heading briskly off towards Charing Cross . . . yes, Glasgow has one of them too. *Paranoia, Blackstone; not everyone is out to get you*. I forgot about it and opened my *Scotsman*. The death was worth a paragraph on page one, and a longer story on page three. That told me that the police had launched a full-scale murder investigation after the body of a twenty-five-year-old woman had been found in the new headquarters building of the Torrent group. The victim, Anna Chin, a doctor's daughter from Barnton . . . *If she had been a waiter's daughter from Leith, would they have mentioned that?* I wondered . . . was in the habit of working late on Fridays to take week-end returns from the field sales team. Detectives were working on the theory that she had disturbed an intruder.

Fine, I thought. *Ricky's put them off the trail, for now at least*. I knew that it was a matter of time before they tumbled to the David Capperauld connection, but hopefully by that time there would be nothing that would tie Alison to the scene.

I took out my mobile and called Ricky on his, ship to ship, as a pal of mine used to say. 'How is she?' I asked him.

'Okay,' he replied, in a quiet voice. There was a pause: I guessed he was still with Alison and that he might be going somewhere she couldn't hear him. Knowing her better by now than I ever had before, I guessed that he was probably getting out of bed.

I heard the sound of a closing door; Ricky was probably in the toilet. 'She's calm now,' he said, more clearly.

'Did she tell you anything else?'

'Only what we guessed; someone called her and told her that Torrent wanted to see her at the office.'

'Who?'

'She doesn't have a clue. She said that the voice wasn't clear; the caller said he was passing on a message from Natalie Morgan, that Torrent wanted a quick meeting that evening.'

'What about Torrent? Do we know where he was?'

'The records in his office showed that he signed out at three, with Natalie. The police tried to get hold of him last night; eventually they found them both at a dinner at Gleneagles Hotel. I called someone I know there afterwards. They checked in at four-fifteen.'

'Separate suites?'

'Of course, she's his niece.'

I couldn't help laughing; there are some things that coppers can't contemplate. 'Cynical bastard, Blackstone,' he muttered. 'Even if they were, they still wouldn't just take one suite.'

He had a point; I wasn't as smart as I thought. No need to let him know that, though. 'It could still have been Natalie who made the call,' I pointed out.

'Sure. I'm betting it was.'

'She couldn't have killed Anna, though,' I said. 'She must have been alive when the last person signed out.'

'She could. She could have checked in, driven back, done the girl and been up there again for dinner.'

'And why would she want to do that?'

'That's a question I'd love to ask her, but I can't risk it.'

'Then get one of your tame policemen to ask.'

'I can't do that either; they're off chasing intruders, remember.'

Yes, I remembered. We were boxed in, good and proper. Or at least, Ricky was; I had to remind myself that this investigation had nothing to do with me.

I had almost put it out of my mind by the time I got back home to the family. I had got the best of the deal all round; Susie's a much better breakfast cook than me, and she always uses olive oil when she's frying. I'll use anything.

We stuffed the four rolls with fillet steak and egg . . . decadent, eh . . . and ate them in front of the telly. The tasty bird with the tattoo on her bum had finished, and we were into previews from around the grounds.

'That's enough of that,' said Susie, once we were finished. She grabbed the remote and switched off. 'We are taking our daughter out for an airing.'

'Where?'

'I thought that Kelvingrove would be nice. We could walk there.'

That sounded good to me. 'Okay,' I agreed, 'if I can do the Transport Museum as well.'

Susie got the baby dressed for the outdoors, we did the same, and we headed out into the bright autumn day. We walked Janet, in her pram . . . a sort of multi-purpose vehicle for kids . . . down Elderslie Street, and turned into Sauchiehall Street, the most famous thoroughfare in Glasgow, if not the nicest. We strolled along at no great pace, but it didn't take us long to come to the old Kelvin Hall, which houses the city's museum of transport. When I had lived in Glasgow, before, and Jonny and Colin, my nephews, came to visit, they always made me take them there. I took no persuading; I love those old Glasgow trams and I'd love to have ridden on one for real. My Dad did, on a visit to Glasgow as a child, and he still talks about it. The city was all the poorer when they were replaced by giant electric trolleybuses; Whispering Death, they became known as, as they came rolling silently up behind a number of unwary Glaswegian drunks who had chosen exactly the wrong moment to step off the pavement.

Wee Janet was a bit young for the trams, and Susie's an unromantic Weegie, so we didn't stay there long. We had just left the building and turned into Argyle Street, heading for the crossing to Kelvingrove Museum and Art Gallery, when I saw a man step swiftly back into Blantyre Street, on the far side of Kelvin Hall. He was in my line of vision for less than a second, but I was dead certain that it was the same bloke I'd seen earlier, in Woodlands Road. I saw a little bit of face this time, or at least a flash of beard, and the glint of the sun reflected from dark glasses.

For a moment, I almost set off after him, but that would have alarmed Susie, so I held myself back. Instead, we crossed the road and, carrying the pram, mounted the steps to the entrance to the big, baroque building.

At the top, I glanced over my shoulder, quickly, while Susie was looking the other way, but I saw nothing out of the ordinary.

Inside, seats were laid out in rows, and a man was playing the big pipe organ, above the central hall. 'Sit there for a minute,' I told Susie, as wee Janet stirred in her MPV pram. 'I'm going to the gents.' I found a sign showing the two matchstick people, one legs apart, the other legs together . . . Shouldn't they be the other way around? Ah, never mind . . . and followed it.

I wasn't sure I'd get a mobile signal in the toilet, in the great sandstone building, but I did. When Ricky answered, I could hear the unmistakeable sound of domesticity in the background. 'Have you got someone following me?' I asked him.

He hesitated. 'Yes,' he admitted at last. 'Alan Graham's looking out for you. I had to, Oz, it's in the contract. If you have an emergency, someone has to be on hand to respond. You shouldn't have seen him though; I warned him not to disturb you.'

'This isn't him; this is someone else.' I told him about the man I had now seen twice in a few hours. 'Tell Alan to stop looking out for me, and concentrate on him. I want to know who this guy is and what he wants. If he comes near Susie and the baby, I'll bloody well kill him, and I'm not joking.' I must have been shouting, because a guy standing at a urinal looked over his shoulder at me, with a degree of alarm. I glared at him and he went about his business.

'Okay, Oz, calm down,' said Ricky, in his reassuring voice. 'I'm on to it. If I have to I'll send someone else through as back-up, plus I'll leave Alan on Susie when you come back to Edinburgh, at least until this man is identified and eliminated as a threat, if he is one. Give me a description.'

'Tallish, long hair, dark beard, age . . . I didn't get a good enough look to tell; wearing jeans and a bomber jacket, and shades.'

'Okay, that'll do; I'll get after him. But please, and I mean this; if he does confront you, do not touch him yourself, leave him to my people. When you said that just now, I really did believe you.'

36

There were no more sightings of the stalker, if such he was. A couple of times people tapped me on the shoulder and asked me if I was me, then asked for my autograph, but they didn't bother me. I had a hunch that the watcher knew bloody well who I was.

Susie hadn't a clue what was going on, of course, so she sat and listened happily to the organ recital for a while, then she and I walked around the museum . . . the art gallery side is without a highlight now, since they moved the Dali.

I tried to stay a pace behind her all the time, because it was easier than keeping up an unconcerned appearance. It didn't fool her, though, even if she did get the wrong idea.

We were hardly back in the flat, and I had hardly finished changing wee Jan . . . it was my turn . . . before Susie punched me lightly in the ribs. 'Go on,' she said. 'Away you go back to your movie. You've been like a cat on hot bricks all afternoon.'

She really did take me by surprise; I thought I'd been pretty cool about the thing.

'No, I haven't.'

'Yes you have.'

'Well, okay, maybe I have; but I get a bit jumpy in public places, especially today, when I was trying to have a normal family day out.'

She laughed. 'All you wanted to see were your trams. You couldn't wait to get home after that.'

She was right, even if she didn't know why.

'I'll tell you what,' I said. 'Why don't we take hospitality boxes at Ibrox and Celtic Park? We could go to each one on alternate Saturdays, and teach our daughter true ecumenicism.'

Susie frowned. 'What are you talking about? I've got boxes at Celtic and Rangers, through the company. My managers use them every week for clients and suppliers. You can go any time you like. You're a director, remember? Just don't expect me to join in, and don't expect to expose our daughter to the sort of language those crowds use.'

She tugged my sleeve gently, drawing me towards her on the couch. I was holding the baby, so I sat down carefully. 'Speaking of religion, loosely,' she said, 'how do you feel about having the baby christened?'

Belief was a subject I'd never discussed with Susie; it's a subject I don't discuss with anyone as a rule. I was an atheist pure and simple until my mother died, then things changed, but I've never gone in for denominations or such stuff. As far as I'm concerned they're only another excuse for people to fight.

'I feel she should make up her own mind, when she's old enough.'

'So do I. Let's just try to set her a good example, okay.'

I leaned across and kissed her; not a let's-go-to-bed kiss, just a simple show of affection. Then I picked up the remote and switched on Gillette Soccer Saturday on Sky Sports. 'Yes,' I said, 'let's.'

We watched as the pundits described the games from television monitors, and as the final scores began to appear on a ribbon at the foot of the screen. Eventually the East

Fife score came up, a four-nil home gubbing by East Stirlingshire, and my Saturday afternoon was over.

While Susie fed the baby again I made supper for the two of us. I found all the ingredients for a very nice stir-fry; onions, chillies, shitake mushrooms, bean sprouts and chicken breast. I cooked them all up in a mix of olive oil, soy sauce and Lea and Perrins, and right at the end, I cracked in a couple of large eggs and beat them in firmly, to help bind the lot together.

Nobody taught me to do that, but ever since I heard a dodgy comedian claim on telly that whatever blokes cooked, no matter what they called it, it was always bloody stew, I've made a point of being able to do other things. Who knows? Maybe if I'd liked that comedian, rather than being annoyed by the smug sod, the world would have lost a great stir-fry chef.

'This is great,' said Susie, as she tucked into a small mountain of the stuff. She looked at me, appraisingly, across the table. 'I think you're hired.'

I couldn't think of something to say, so I just shrugged my shoulders. The thing was, I wasn't one hundred per cent sure that I'd applied for the job.

I stayed for as long as I could, but given my flying start next morning, and a growing streak of professionalism which demands that I'm at my best when going to work, I announced around eight-thirty that I'd better hit the road.

I thought about telling her that she had a minder, but I decided against it. If I'd done that, I'd have had to tell her why, and I reckoned that would have scared her . . . not for herself, but for the baby. Besides, the first time I'd seen the guy he'd been following me alone; as I saw it, they were probably safer with me out of the way.

I had confidence in Ricky's people, but I was half hoping that my friend would have a go at me. Okay, maybe he was no more than a fan trying to get close, but he'd interfered with my family time and I didn't like that.

I found myself thinking about him for most of the way back to Edinburgh and I didn't like that either. I was starting work on my most important movie in the morning . . . it's like football, but you're only as good as your next game, rather than your last . . . and here I was having to force myself to concentrate on it. No, I was annoyed, and given half a chance, the cause of it would pay.

When I got back to the Mound, I thought about calling Ricky, but he'd know where I was, and I knew that if he'd anything to tell me, he'd have been in touch. So I parked the Mercedes and walked up the slope to the tall grey building. I let myself into the apartment, and went straight to my bedroom, flicking on the light when I got there, dropping my bag on the floor, and heading straight for the shower, ripping off clothes as I went.

I must have stayed in there for a good ten minutes, trying to wash that man right out of my hair, I suppose. Eventually I succeeded; I towelled myself dry, brushed my teeth and headed for bed, focused fully on next morning.

I stepped out of the bathroom into darkness. At first I thought the bulb had blown, but then I sensed movement on my right. I spun towards it . . . then felt my world turn upside-down.

I call myself a wrestler. I mean, I've been trained, I know proper holds and throws and everything; the real stuff. I hadn't a chance: my legs were kicked out from under me, and a slim but very strong arm went across my chest in the same instant, driving me down. I landed on my back, hard enough to wind me for an instant. My arms spread out wide as I fell. As I hit the ground, I felt them pinned down, and a weight pressing on me.

There wasn't much moon but a little light was creeping in

206

from the outside, through the slatted blinds. I could see . . . and feel . . . that my attacker was naked, and at the same moment I could feel . . . and just about see . . . that she was female. She was straddling me, trapping my upper arms with her feet, pressing my thighs to the ground with strong arms.

My eyes grew more accustomed to the light; I couldn't believe what they were seeing, close up. Then I felt something else, and I heard a voice that was more of a loud mumble. 'Lie still,' Mandy O'Farrell ordered, 'or I may bite.'

I flexed my biceps and used my leg strength to lift her clear of the ground and to pull the part of her that was nearest to me even closer still. 'I could say the same to you,' I pointed out. In the end, we called it a draw.

The apartment was warm; we were both covered in sweat from our brief struggle when she rolled off me, and swung herself round. She was grinning. 'Think you're so tough, eh?' She was right; half an hour before I had been thinking about filling in my stalker.

'Do you realise', I asked her, 'that I could have you fired?'

She gave me a look of pure innocence. 'But Mr Ross,' she exclaimed in a girlie voice unlike her own, 'I was only obeying your orders.'

I stared at her in what must have been amazement, for she laughed out loud. 'Ricky told me that you were heading back to Edinburgh on your own, and that I was to get here and stay as close to you as I could. Couldn't do better than that, eh?'

'So how did you get in?'

'I told you, this building has no security . . . well, actually, it has but I'm rather good at that sort of thing. I'm good at all sorts of things, as you know by now.'

I have to move out of here, I thought. *It's bad luck; I keep getting beaten up by women.*

I could feel an incipient carpet burn on my bum, so I pushed myself up from the ground and slid into the king-size-plus bed. Mandy followed me under the duvet. In the circumstances I couldn't be bothered protesting. I caught another flash of her in the moonlight, as she stood. With her long powerful limbs, high breasts, and genuine blonde hair, she made me think of a silver wolf.

'Is this the way you usually go about your job?' I asked her.

'Not very often; in fact, hardly ever. Sometimes clients expect it; they think it's part of the service. Those ones really have no chance. You'd think Arabs might be the worst for that, by the way, but they're not. No, it's the Americans you have to watch out for.'

'I'd have thought they'd have to watch out for you.' She laughed. 'Those who tried it on, that is.'

She ran a hand across my chest. 'I'm glad you're one of the nice types,' she said. 'You're a strong boy; I don't know how I'd handle you if you got rough.' My self-esteem was restored.

'Very carefully,' I suggested. She took me at my word, and moved across me; I found myself looking up into her smiling eyes. 'Mandy,' I told her, 'fidelity has never come easy to me, and you're making it more difficult by the second.'

'I can feel that,' she remarked.

'So please . . . and don't be offended, because I'm having trouble asking this . . . go and sleep in the spare room.'

'No,' she said. 'I've got my orders.'

37

I don't know how I did it, but I made it to Advocates' Close at the appointed hour next morning, looking reasonably fresh-faced, and feeling fit and ready for work. When the alarm woke me, at six on the dot, Mandy was up and dressed. She offered to make breakfast while I showered but I knew that the caterers would be taking care of that in the production trailers in Cockburn Street.

The location was so near at hand that I was able to walk there in only a couple of minutes.

The book says that it's dark and raining when they find the body, but Miles had taken a liberty with that as well. If we'd shot in darkness we'd have had to spread it over at least two nights, and the cost would have shot up. As I said, the man knows the value of a pound.

Advocates' Close was blocked off when Mandy and I got there, guarded by policemen, who were actually extras in uniform. The High Street was open to traffic, though, and a small crowd of on-lookers had gathered at the barrier; some, but not all of them, were on the payroll. Once the cameras started rolling, though, all the punters would be cleared away. Continuity is everything in film; if the faces in the background changed from shot to shot, it would stick out like a sore thumb.

Speaking of which, as I eased my way through the crowd, I saw Ricky Ross standing inside the alleyway. I walked up to him, and Mandy strolled off to join the other minders. 'She picked you up, then?' he asked, nodding after her.

'She never left my side,' I told him, 'as per your orders.'

'You should be so lucky,' he muttered, sarcastically. 'The Ice Maiden's above the likes of you, son. Her job's to collect you from your flat and get you here on time, and that's that, so don't you get any ideas.'

'As if I would.' I changed the subject, fast; if Mandy's visit had been extra-curricular, I didn't want him to get more of a sniff of it than I'd given him already. 'Have your people spotted the guy who was following me?' I asked him.

'Sorry. There hasn't been a trace. You are sure about him, are you?'

'Of course I'm fucking sure!'

'Okay, okay, keep your hair on. You've probably spooked him. Chances are he was just an idiot punter and you'll never see him again, but we'll keep looking, and I'll keep the cover on Susie.'

'Thanks.'

For the first time, I wondered about his presence there. 'Where's Alison?' I asked.

'Still at home. I've got someone watching her too, though.'

'Do you really think she's at risk?'

'I'm not taking any chances,' he said, curtly.

I caught something in his voice. 'Here, Ricky,' I challenged, 'are you getting keen on her?'

He glared at me. 'I like the girl, okay?'

'Christ, it's thanks to you she could be going to the slammer!'

'I don't need reminding about that, thanks. Anyway, she won't; I've seen who the judge is likely to be. He and I were at school together; if I speak on her behalf she'll get probation, okay.'

I laughed loud enough to turn the heads of the minders, who were gathered in a group at the foot of the Close. 'Is there anything in this bloody city,' I asked him, 'that can't be fixed by the power of the old school tie?'

'Cancer,' he said, cheerfully, 'but that's about all.'

'You won't be so sure of yourself if the police tie her to Anna Chin.'

'They won't. I've had word; they've got a new lead. They haven't given up on the intruder theory, but they're off following the scent of Anna's boyfriend now.'

That got my attention. 'Her boyfriend? But that'll lead them straight to David Capperauld, and Alison.'

He shook his head. 'Not him. He must have been on the side. She had an official boyfriend, a corporal in the Parachute Regiment. He's on leave just now; Anna's father told the CID they had a blazing row a few days ago.'

'Sure, about Capperauld.'

'No. That's not what the father said, and it's not what the soldier's saying. Their story is that he was pressing her to give up her job and go south to live with him, and that she refused, point blank.'

'Because she was having it off with David.'

'I'm telling you; his name hasn't come up.'

'For now,' I said, gloomily.

Behind me I heard a buzz among the punters in the crowd of onlookers. I turned, just in time to see them part, as Glen Oliver led Ewan Capperauld on to the set. I checked my watch; dead on time.

'Okay,' came a voice from the foot of the Close. 'Actors to make-up,' Miles commanded. 'Let's make a movie.'

38

The wardrobe mistress gave me a brown leather jerkin for my first scene; it fitted pretty well. As far as I'd been able to tell from the book, Andy Martin rarely wore anything else. She handed me a pair of black Levi's as well; they were my size and had been washed several times to give them a worn look. I tried to tell her that the pair I was wearing would do fine, but she pointed out that a middle-ranking Edinburgh detective would be unlikely to turn up at a murder scene wearing Gucci.

The production trailers, great articulated things, stretched halfway up Cockburn Street; two of them were split into reasonably spacious dressing rooms. I had my own on this project; a first for me, since I'd had to share with other cast members before. As Miles had promised, there were no stars on any of the doors, only our names.

Make-up didn't take too long; all they had to do with me was to damp down what was left of my California tan, and replace it with a more authentic Edinburgh pallor. I'll never like wearing slap, but it's a small sacrifice for the money, and the stuff they use now is non-allergenic, unlike the make-up Jan and I wore in our drama club days, which brought me out in spots . . . or maybe that was just my age.

By the time we were ready, so was the crew. Miles led Ewan, Dawn and me back up the Close. The truncated dummy and the scary false head were in place, and pretty soon, so were we. The first shot was Ewan, in his Skinner coat, steel-grey hair tousled, expression grim; the camera focused tight on his eyes, then panned out, to take in the rest of the scene. I was crouching by the side of the body, and Dawn was a few feet away.

The first line of the movie was down to me, as I stood to greet him, a tired-sounding, 'Morning, boss.' It was hardly deathless prose, but I did it in one take. That was it; Miles called 'Cut', as directors do, and we moved on to scene two.

As we'd been warned, most of the time was taken up by changing the camera positions; we had a lot of standing around to do, but we did it patiently. Ewan turned out to be a football fan, or at least a Falkirk supporter, the poor sad bastard. He lamented his club's weekend defeat, and its continuing failure to build itself a ground worthy of the name.

'Why don't you build it for them?' I suggested.

He raised an eyebrow, creasing his make-up. 'Not all followers of the Bairns are completely stupid,' he replied.

Eventually, around mid-morning, Miles called a refreshment break. The weather was holding up, so there were no continuity worries on that score. I stopped in at the canteen truck, picked up a mug of coffee and a couple of BLT rolls, loaded them on to a tray, and headed back to my dressing room . . . if you've got it, flaunt it.

Awkwardly, I unlocked the door with my left hand, stepped up and inside and let it swing shut behind me, then went to set the tray down on the table, against the wall.

I only saw the thing because of the mirror, and even then, it only caught a corner of my eye. I couldn't see what it was, but it hadn't been there earlier, of that I was sure. At first I thought it was a leaflet, but when I slid the tray to one side, I saw that it was a photograph, an A4 computer print-out, lying face up on the table-top.

I picked it up and looked at it, and as I did I felt the blood racing to my head. It was a picture of Susie, and me, pushing Janet in her pram, taken, I guessed from the steps of the Kelvingrove Museum, as we approached the Kelvin Hall.

It was my turn to go ballistic. I jerked the door open again and yelled out into Cockburn Street. 'Ricky!'

It was Mandy who responded; she jumped out of the canteen wagon and ran up the hill. 'He's gone back to his office, Oz,' she said, barely out of breath. 'What is it?'

'What sort of a fucking operation is this?' I snarled at her. Dawn's dressing-room door opened as I spoke and she looked out, puzzled and curious. I grabbed Mandy by the arm and hauled her inside.

I waved the photo in her face. 'Someone's been in here,' I told her, making a conscious effort not to shout. 'He's left me a calling card. You people are supposed to be trying to trace this guy, you're all over here, and yet he walked into this closed street, broke into my locked room and left this, and nobody stopped him.'

'Oz, I'm sorry,' she said, her face as pale as mine in my make-up. 'I don't know anything about this. What do you want me to do?'

'I want you to interrogate everyone on this crew, and I mean everyone, until you find someone who saw this guy getting in here. Then I want you to circulate his description to every one of your people. Then I want you to find the bastard and bring him to me, so that I can find out what his fucking problem is with me and my family.

'And while you're at it, you tell that boss of yours that if this is how he protects me, then I'm starting to get seriously worried about Alison.'

I shoved the picture into her hand and stepped into the street to cool down. Miles was waiting outside. 'What's the problem, mate?' he asked.

'I've got a stalker,' I replied, then told him the whole story. His face grew more and more serious as I spoke. Through my still-open door I could hear Mandy on the phone to her boss.

'Don't worry,' he said, eventually in that quiet, dangerous tone he has. 'We'll find this guy, even if I have to bring in Mark Kravitz to do it.' He slapped me on the shoulder. 'Come on, let's go down to the canteen truck and chill out.'

I followed him down the street and climbed up the steps that led into our travelling canteen. When he got to the top, he stopped in his tracks, and I heard him gasp. I stepped up beside him, and gasped just as he had. Facing us was my soon-to-be-ex-wife Primavera, and her new lover, Nicky Johnson.

'Hi,' she said, without a trace of uncertainty. 'We're passing through, on the way to Auchterarder for Nick to meet Mum and Dad.'

'Yeah,' said the former hot-dog vendor, with a greasy smile. 'I couldn't be here and not call in to wish you luck with the new movie.'

I'd never actually met the man before; I'd heard of him, seen a couple of his movies, and we'd spoken that one time, but I'd never encountered him in Los Angeles. I knew right there and then that if I had I wouldn't have liked him, whatever the circumstances. As it was, given what had just happened in my dressing room, he couldn't have picked a worse moment to introduce himself.

I took a pace towards him, winding up the great big left hook that I've honed to perfection on the heavy punching bag, and with the serious intention of knocking his head clean off his shoulders. Then I felt Miles grip my arm, hard. 'No!' he shouted, stopping me in mid-stride. Nicky and the catering staff all sighed with relief; especially Nicky, who had gone pale all of a sudden.

What happened next was just a blur. Miles took half a pace forward and hit Prim's new stud with the fastest right-hander I have ever seen in my life. Johnson's quite a beefy bloke, but still the force of the punch spun him half round and lifted him right up on his toes. He held that position for a second, almost like a footballer going up for a header, then pitched forward, face down, raising a small cloud of dust from the floor as he landed.

'Sorry, mate,' said Miles, over his shoulder. 'I know the son-of-a-bitch was trying to rub your nose in it, but I couldn't let you hit him. If you'd broken your hand, the delay while it healed would have cost us a fucking fortune.'

39

Nicky Johnson started crying when he came round. He was dazed and confused, and somewhere at the back of his mind, he may have realised that he had done something very stupid, which would, given Miles's wallop, figuratively as well as fistically, have a bad effect on his career in the long run.

Prim knelt beside him as he stirred on the floor; he was only out cold for a few seconds, and soon she had him in a sitting position with his back against the trailer wall. He looked like a big dummy sitting there, dazed, not quite knowing where he was, with two big tears tracking down his cheeks.

It put a damper on Prim's show of outrage, as she glared up at Miles and me. 'You're a couple of thugs,' she snapped. 'I should call the police.'

'What did you expect?' I told her. 'Whose idea was it to come here, yours or the boy's?'

'We thought of it together,' she said. 'We were in Edinburgh and it seemed the right thing to do. Dawn's my sister, remember, and Miles is my brother-in-law. Why shouldn't I come to visit them? It's got nothing to do with you. You're nothing to me now.'

I looked down at her, and I could see in her eyes that she was economising with the truth. If Susie Gantry's taught me one thing, it's that I've usually been more in love with myself than with anyone else. There have been a few exceptions to that, but Prim wasn't one of them. I think what bound us together was luck, more than anything else. There's no doubt about it; my life changed irrevocably from the moment we met. She was like a lucky charm to me; when she was around, at first at least, everything we touched turned to money.

We believed that we cared for each other, and we probably did, but looking back it was superficial. As a basis for a shared life, lust alone doesn't last. We fucked a lot, Premier-League class sometimes, but we never talked about anything worth talking about. Before too long, each of us was cheating on the other and justifying it in our own minds, until eventually, for one of the few times in my life, I got honest with myself, and went back to Jan. Even without Prim, my good-luck streak seemed to carry on, until the night when it turned very bad.

Afterwards, I turned to Prim again, maybe in the subconscious hope of restoring it . . . that possibility hadn't occurred to me until that moment in the trailer, but yes, maybe I did. If that was the case, it didn't work out. Sure, the money kept rolling in, but it was offset by black moments too. Even our wedding day had its crisis. Come to think of it, our short-lived marriage was one big crisis. As for our honeymoon . . . but that's another story.

All that said, though, flawed, selfish, cynical, and ultimately doomed as a couple as we may have been, we never were ordinary. The bond that tied us might not have been true love, but whatever it was, its fabric was strong, and conductive. Sparks did fly between us, and sometimes, bolts of lightning.

That's how it was as we looked at each other in the canteen trailer. 'I'm nothing to you, am I?' I challenged her. 'So why are you looking at me that way? You don't know whether you want to stab me or shag me, do you?'

She jumped to her feet. 'Given the choice I bloody well do!' she shouted. 'Do you think I've forgiven you for Susie Gantry? Or forgiven her, for that matter?'

'You think I've forgiven you for yours?' I heard myself snap back. Actually, I thought I had, but old Oz had been lying to himself again. 'Do you want me to run through the list? Or the age range of the guys you had? Half a century wouldn't cover it.' We glared at each other. She had forgotten Nicky; I had forgotten everyone else. 'So don't go telling me I mean nothing. I mean plenty, otherwise you wouldn't have set up that poor sap there to see what I would do to him.' A twitch of her right eye told me I'd hit the mark. 'I bet you got your jollies off him being flattened, didn't you? I'll bet you're all moist now.'

She slapped me, hard, across the cheek. I laughed at her. Then I heard a shout from the door. 'You two stop it! Stop it at once!' It was the first time I'd ever heard Dawn speak sharply to anyone, other than on the screen. 'If you're going to scream at each other, do it in private.'

'Yeah,' said Miles, quietly, his calmness contrasting with his wife's anger. 'That's a good idea. There are things you two need to get out of your system; without knocking ten bells out of each other, of course. Oz, you aren't in the next couple of shots. Take time out and we'll see you back after the lunch break.'

'I've got nothing to say to this bastard,' Prim hissed.

I had cooled off. 'Well, I've got things to say to you. Let's go up the hill to my dressing room.'

Nicky Johnson was still sitting on the floor, against the wall. He made a small sound, of protest, perhaps, but everyone ignored him. My wife glared at me again, but nodded. 'Okay.'

She followed me up the hill to my trailer and stepped inside; I locked the door behind us to make sure we weren't interrupted. 'No more yelling now,' I warned her. 'You don't want to disturb Ewan Capperauld, if you haven't already.'

'Don't you bet on it,' she snorted. 'After what you just said.'

I felt my cheek; it was still stinging. 'I was right, then; Nicky getting belted over you did give you a wee thrill.'

'No it did not!'

'Then why did you bring him here? You must have known it was on the cards.'

'You promised me you wouldn't touch him.'

'Since when did you and I start keeping promises to each other? You just wanted to see what would happen, didn't you?'

'What sort of a bloody nerve have you got?' she gasped.

Time for a change of tack, Osbert. 'Sorry,' I murmured. She blinked. 'I said. "What . . ." '

'I heard you the first time, and I said "Sorry". I want to apologise properly for what happened with Susie. I've never really done that, and I should.'

'Apology noted,' she murmured, 'even if I can't accept it, in the circumstances. And I'm not apologising, for any of what I did; I was more than entitled.'

'Not quite,' I pointed out. 'Not even in the eyes of today's liberal matrimonial courts do two wrongs make a right. Plus, when you decided to get even with me for Susie, you did it with a married bloke. So neither of us is innocent.'

'So, are you just doing it to ease your conscience; telling me that you're sorry you slept with Susie?'

'I don't have a conscience over that.'

'Your cock certainly doesn't have one.'

'True, and I should have got my terminology right too; apologising doesn't always mean you're sorry. I'd have wound up sleeping with Susie sooner or later, so I'm not sorry about that. It's just that my timing was a bit off; that was wrong.'

'That's about as clumsy as you can get, but at least it's more honest than usual.' She ventured a grim smile.

'I'm trying, really. You should, too.'

'What do you mean?'

'I mean you and that lump of nothing back there, that Nicky. What the hell are you doing with him?'

'I'm in lo . . .' she began, until my exploding laugh cut her short.

'Stop. Don't be daft. You're no more in love with him than you were with me, in fact probably less; he's a prat and he's not worth your time. You know that. Come on, honest up; you got involved with him because you weren't finished punishing me. Yes or no.'

She pursed her lips. 'Maybe,' she muttered.

'From you, that's a yes. Tell me, did you expect me to come flying down to Mexico, bop the boy there, and take you back with me?'

She looked at me again; her eyes widened, then narrowed as if she was about to start shouting again, then went back to normal. 'If I did, then I was a bloody fool, wasn't I,' she said, grimly.

'You didn't know then that Susie was pregnant, though, did you?'

I've seen Prim in many states, but I don't think I've ever seen her look as totally stunned as she did then. Her mouth fell open and she gasped, then she sat down hard on the chair by my table, and started to cry. 'Oh hell,' I heard myself whisper. 'You never knew at all, did you?'

I put my hands on her shoulder, raised her to her feet, and held her to me. 'Oh, love, I really am sorry about that,' I murmured into her ear. 'I assumed that Dawn would have told you.'

I felt her shake her head against my chest. 'No, she didn't,' she mumbled. Then she pushed herself away from me. 'But you should have told me.'

'Primavera, I can't remember when we stopped telling each other things; maybe we never started. I didn't tell you because I didn't know what to do about Susie, even though she wasn't making any demands of me. When you ran off with Johnson, that helped me make my mind up.'

'And the baby?' she asked. 'Is it born yet?'

'We have a daughter.'

She sniffled. 'I really messed up with Nicky, then, didn't I.'

'Both times. I should feel sorry for him, but he's such a creep . . . and he's a fucking awful actor as well.'

Her face was blotchy and a bit crumpled; yet it gave her smile a fetching, vulnerable quality that I'd never seen before. 'You're so great, are you?' she teased.

'Better than him. If I wasn't I'd go back to the investigating business.'

'Maybe you should. Maybe all this isn't really for you; maybe you should go back to being the old Oz Blackstone.'

'Whoever the hell he was?' I grunted. 'No, make no mistake, love. On balance I like being rich and famous; I admit I'd settle for being just rich, but if I have to I'll take both.'

'But it's made you different.'

'What's wrong with different?'

'You were never scary before; you were always nice.'

'I've told you before; nice was a front. Anyway, you were always nice too; if what you say is true, you've changed as much as me. When I met you I thought you were Mother Teresa; then you started acting like the village slapper.'

'That's the effect you have on a girl when you dump her, my love. Anyway, I wasn't that bad . . .' She chuckled. 'Not all of the time.'

There was a box of tissues on the table. I pulled a couple

out and dried the tears from her face. 'What are you going to do about that poor sod down there?' I asked her.

'God, I don't know.'

'Tell me the truth now. Whose idea was it to come over here? Yours or his?'

She smiled again; this time she looked like a kid who'd been caught doing something naughty. 'Mine,' she admitted. 'I booked the trip to Perthshire. When I suggested to Nicky that we should call in here to wish the new movie luck, he jumped at the chance. I reckon he thought it would get him back into Miles's good books.'

'Well he knows different now. Come on, Prim, you can't take that guy to meet your folks; he's worse than Steve Miller, that car salesman you had it off with.'

When she snorted, cute wee laugh lines that I'd never noticed before creased up around her eyes. 'No, he's not,' she protested. 'No one was worse than him! But you're right; I've been going off Nicky for a while. I only brought him over here to flaunt him in front of you. I didn't think you would hit him, though . . . and I expected even less that Miles would do it for you.'

'That's what friends are for.'

'You and Miles are two of the biggest chauvinist pigs I've ever met.'

'Oink,' I said. 'But admit it, you love us for it.'

She looked up at me; her eyes were clear again. 'I don't know what to call it; you are an infuriating bastard and I should hate you till the day I die, but you do have an effect on me.' She slid her arms around my waist. 'What am I going to do, Oz?'

'About Nicky? Own up, tell him you don't love him any more and put him on a plane back to the States.'

'I'd worked that out for myself. No, what am I going to do about me?'

'Go and see your folks for a while. Get your head together, then decide. Whatever you want to do, you can. Money's no object.'

'I can't go back to Los Angeles. I hate the place; I felt safer when I worked in Africa, and there was a war on there.'

'So go back there. Or be Mother Teresa again; go to Calcutta and work with the poor.'

'I'm no saint; besides, I prefer the rich.'

'Go to the south of France then; go back to Spain.'

'Come with me?' She said it tentatively.

'Now that would be crazy.' In spite of myself, I felt sparks begin to fly. 'There's no such thing as third time lucky. We'd end up killing each other.'

'I'd behave.'

'I wouldn't.'

'What if I withdraw from our divorce agreement?'

'Now I know you're joking. Even you must realise that whatever else we're good at, we're lousy at marriage.'

She ran her hand up inside my shirt; I felt its warmth on my chest. 'There is one thing we're very good at.' She pulled my head down and kissed me; I kissed her back . . . out of sheer habit, of course.

'Yes, but . . .' I said when we came up for air.

'What?'

'Susie.'

'She did it to me; I'd do it to her in a minute.' When she grinned at me, and those extra sparks flew, I thought I'd had it. 'Although, I'd really take much longer than that.'

There was a sofa thing against the far wall of the dressing room; it was well long enough for us. I looked at it and saw us there; so did she, and pulled me towards it. Then all the lies and deceit, mine and hers, that had driven us apart, came back to me. And something else too.

224

'I can't,' I said. 'I'm sorry, but I can't. There's someone else involved now.'

'Who?' she asked. 'Let me guess; that big blonde goddess who let us into the canteen truck and who went running when you shouted.'

'Close, but no cigar. No, her name's Janet, and she's two weeks old. She changes everything.'

She took her arms from around me. 'I see. So that's what I should have done to keep us together, is it? Had a baby with you?'

'No. What we should have done was build a relationship on the rocks of truth, not the sands of deceit.' I tried to smile as I said it, but fell short.

'Jesus,' Prim exclaimed, 'have you got a scriptwriter now?'

'No, that trite double metaphor was all my own.'

'Thank God; I'd hate to think a professional came up with it. So what are you telling me; that you and Susie are building your thing on the basis of a kid? Because there are millions of examples to show that that doesn't work.'

'I don't know what I'm telling you. I don't know, period. I think I do, and then something will happen to make me uncertain again.'

'Like me turning up out of the blue?'

'Yes. No. Fuck.'

She smiled at me again; but with real warmth this time. I couldn't remember the last time she'd looked at me that way. 'My darling, those three words encompass your entire approach to life, and mine. Susie's wrong for you; she's much too complicated.'

I sat on the couch and pulled her down beside me; all of a sudden I was dead tired. She put her head on my shoulder. 'You may be right, Prim; you may well be. But you've got to let me work that out for myself, not try to persuade me.

'Last time you came back into my life it led to all sorts of disasters for us both. Having you do it again scares me a wee bit . . . no, scares me a lot. So please, you do what you have to do to get rid of lover-boy, go see your Mum and Dad, and let me get on with making my movie and with sorting myself out.'

She nodded. 'Okay,' she whispered, then she drew me round and kissed me; again, I kissed her back, but not out of habit this time.

Finally, she stood. 'I'd better leave now,' she murmured.

'Yeah,' I said. 'But before you go . . .'

She looked at me with a mixture of surprise and expectation. 'Yes?'

'You'd better take some of those tissues and wipe my make-up off your face, otherwise People Will Talk, even more than they're going to already.'

40

I was bugger all use for the rest of the day; I fluffed a couple of simple lines and tried even Miles's patience, but somehow or other I got through it without too much embarrassment.

Mandy was waiting outside my dressing room when I got back down to Cockburn Street at the end of it all. 'It's not like you to let a locked door bother you,' I said grimly. 'Come to think of it, it's not like anyone around here.'

'Shh!' she whispered, urgently. 'Ricky's back. He's in the catering van and the door's open; he might hear you.'

'I might tell him all the same,' I grunted, but I didn't mean it. It had been a bad enough day as it was and if I dropped Mandy in it by telling her boss about her surprise visit, I'd just make myself look even dafter, not to mention getting her fired. As I opened the door, her look told me she didn't believe my threat anyway.

'Has my wife gone?' I asked her.

Her mouth fell open and stayed like that, for a good few seconds. 'Your wife?' she exclaimed, at last.

'Primavera. The woman who visited the set at the lunch break.'

'She told me she was Dawn's sister.'

'She is; she's also my wife. But we're getting divorced.'

'I'm not surprised.' she said, with a snorting laugh. 'I thought I'd been fully briefed about you, but Ricky left that bit out.'

'It wasn't relevant. Has she gone, do you know?'

Mandy nodded. 'Yes, about half an hour ago.'

'What about the guy she was with?'

'Nicky Johnson?' She surprised me by looking star-struck; there she was working with three of the biggest name actors in the world in Miles, Dawn and Ewan, but it took his name to make her eyes go dreamy. No accounting for tastes, is there? Just as well she hadn't been there when Miles decked him; she might have leapt to his defence. 'He left before her. They had a big argument, and I heard Gail Driver booking him on the next London flight.' She shook her head. 'More fool your missus.'

'You don't know the half of it,' I muttered. 'But she's well shot of that clown.'

Mandy looked at me as a nun might have looked at a heretic.

'Come on,' I said, 'back to business. What have you got to tell me about the guy who left that photo for me?'

'Nothing much. I did find a catering worker who saw a man near this van, but she didn't see him break in or anything. He was just standing there, leaning against the wall smoking a cigarette.'

'Description?'

'He was wearing a hard hat and an orange donkey jacket. There's a shop being refurbished up the road; they're working seven days a week and that's what the builders wear. He was probably just a joiner having a smoke.'

'Nevertheless, did she notice anything else?'

'He was around six feet tall, he had a beard, and he was wearing flashy wrap-round sunglasses.'

'A joiner in Raybans? Did anyone think to go and see if any of the guys working on the site fit that description?'

Mandy gave her lip a quick nibble. 'No,' she murmured.

'We'll do it tomorrow; they'll have knocked off for the day by now.'

'A waste of time,' said a voice from the door; I turned to see Ricky climbing into my room. 'If that was your guy, he's not going to be back. If it wasn't . . . so bloody what?'

He had a point. 'So what's he up to?' I asked. 'Why pull a stunt like that?'

'I don't know, Oz. It could just be a nutter; that's the likeliest explanation, in fact.'

'But what if it isn't? In my experience the likeliest explanation hardly ever turns out to be right.'

Ross took a deep breath. 'Mine too,' he admitted. 'In that case, this could be leading up to an extortion attempt. You might get a letter, threatening Susie and the baby, and demanding a pay-off. The photo, the way it was taken and the way it was planted, could all be an attempt to scare you into paying up.'

'What about a kidnap attempt?'

'Not a chance; the guy would have done that already, or tried it, if it was on his agenda. Let's assume he isn't a nutter and he isn't stupid; he'll know that Susie's protected.'

'I want that stepped up.'

'Don't worry, it has been. You'll need to tell her what's happening, though. I don't want her picking up the phone and getting any nasty surprises.'

I agreed with that. 'I'll call her right away,' I said.

'I've talked to Mr Grayson,' Ricky continued, 'and we both think I should step up your cover as well. We should make it more obvious; you should have someone full-time, like him and Mrs Grayson and Ewan Capperauld. It could be that he's picked you because you're the most vulnerable. I thought Mandy could do that for you; she's well capable and you've got spare rooms up there in your apartment. You okay with that?'

I risked a quick glance at my lady minder; she was deadpan. 'Attractive as that suggestion is,' I replied, 'I don't want that. One; I've promised a bedroom to Liam Matthews whenever the schedule brings him to town; he's all the minder I'll ever need. Two; I have another plan for Mandy. Three; I don't want to scare this guy away. I want to meet him. In fact, if he does send a demand for money, I plan to deliver it in person.'

230

41

Did that make Ricky's day? Not by a long way. He tried everything to talk me round; he even got Miles in on the act. But I wasn't having any of it, and eventually they came to terms with it. Most of all, of course, what I wasn't having was Mandy O'Farrell in my spare room.

I did phone Susie, though, as I'd agreed, as soon as I got home. I told her the real reason for my jumpiness the day before and I told her about the photograph. I didn't expect her to sound frightened, and she wasn't. I did expect her to sound angry, and she was. But not just at the mischief-maker; she turned the heat on me as well. 'Why the hell are you only telling me this now?' she demanded. 'Do you think I'm some sort of a bloody wimp? If this guy's threatening anyone he's threatening our daughter, and I had a right to know that from the start.' She paused, for emphasis, I guessed. 'Now tell me what you're doing about it . . . and I'd better be impressed, or I'll make my own arrangements.' I didn't like to think what they might be. Lord Provost Jack Gantry had had connections with some euphemistically named security firms around Glasgow, and the survivors were still around.

'You've had cover since last night,' I told her. 'One of Ricky's guys has had you in his sight ever since. I plan to step that up. There's a woman on his staff; you met her, briefly, the other night. I plan to move her in with you, until this guy's nailed.'

'That big blonde Amazon?' she exclaimed. 'The one you called Mandy?'

'That's the one.'

'Can she handle herself?'

'Oh yes. She wouldn't be working for Ross if she couldn't.' I was taking a chance that she could also keep her mouth shut . . . something she hadn't been able to do the night before . . . but I wanted Susie and Janet to have effective close protection and I couldn't think of anyone who was better equipped to do the job.

'Okay,' she agreed, just a touch grudgingly. 'I'll give her a try. But the best solution is to catch this guy. Have you reported it to the police?'

'Ricky's briefed his contacts; they know what's happened, but they're keeping it under wraps.'

'So what the hell are you and Ross actually doing, apart from giving me a house-guest and sitting on your arses?'

'The only thing we can, love. We're waiting for his next move.'

42

I had hoped that my day was done, but no such luck. I had just finished speaking to Susie when the phone rang again. 'I need to see you,' said Ricky. 'There's been a development on the Anna Chin investigation.'

We agreed to meet half-an-hour later, in the Oxford Bar, where real detectives are supposed to hang out. Ten minutes after that, I knew that it never rains but it pours. Ricky told me that the police had released Corporal Adam Cruikshank, Anna Chin's paratrooper boyfriend, pending further investigation.

'He's got a petrol transaction slip from a filling station in Canonmills,' he said. 'The time on it doesn't prove absolutely that he couldn't have killed Anna, but he'd have had to be some driver. They still like him for it, but there's absolutely no evidence to place him at the scene, so until they find some, they've had to let him go.'

'Mmm.' I muttered. 'Still, it keeps them away from Alison.'

'Aye, but . . .' said Ricky, ominously. 'There's something else. Even if this lad had found out about his girl and David Capperauld, he couldn't have killed him. I made some enquiries of a close-mouthed military source of mine. When the boy David was done, Corporal Cruikshank was jumping out of a plane on a training exercise in the Middle East.

'Only we know about that connection. Only we know about the attempts to set up Alison. They still mean that the same person committed both murders. The police are barking up the wrong tree with the soldier. I can't tell them that, but sooner or later they're going to find out.'

The guy with the beard had become my big concern, but he wasn't my only one; as much as I wanted to, I couldn't forget about Alison. I had hoped that the corporal was the end of our troubles on that score; now he had been hit on the head as a likely suspect, and she was still a thorn in my flesh.

It wasn't that I was too worried about her, though. Hell no, I had my own position to think of. After all, Ricky and I had messed up the crime scene and we had hidden information from the police that would have led them straight to the most obvious suspect.

Yes, we had done it for the best of motives . . . we believed that Alison was innocent . . . and I was cool about that. We had also done it very well, so there was no reason why anyone should ever find out; unless, of course, . . . and this was my one niggling doubt . . . the police found out about David and Anna and put the thumbscrews on Alison herself.

Ricky had told her to deny everything and say nothing else, if it came to that, but still, she was flaky under pressure.

All in all, I reckoned, and I said as much to Ricky, the sooner the real killer was caught the better it would be for everyone.

'That depends who it is,' he muttered darkly. The Oxford was busy, as always, but we had wedged ourselves into a quiet corner.

'What the hell do you mean by that?' I demanded.

'The real killer's got it in for Alison, Oz. He's done two people and tried to frame her for both of them. To all intents and purposes he succeeded the first time, and if it hadn't been for a police car being in a traffic accident, she'd be remanded in prison right now, and wouldn't be coming out again until she was past fifty.

'Whoever's done that had a bloody good reason for it; when we find out what it is, we might not like it.'

'Have you asked her about it? I know you two have been pillow-talking, after all.'

'Yes, I've asked her, as directly as I could. She swears she hasn't a clue who or what could be behind it.'

'And do you believe her?'

He looked down into his beer and nodded.

'If that was me talking,' I said, 'you'd bloody laugh at me. You'd go on about the power of the furry purse to blind you to the obvious, and in the end I'd agree with you. Jesus Christ, for years I thought Prim was Mary Fucking Poppins.'

Ricky chuckled. 'Aye, and that you were Bert the chimney sweep, I suppose. You're right, though; that's exactly what I have told myself. And I still believe her. So do you, come to that. You never thought she killed Capperauld, and you know she didn't kill Anna Chin, because someone set her up to be caught.'

'Sure, but believing that she doesn't have a clue why all this has happened, that's something else.'

'Nonetheless, I do.' He finished his pint, went up to the bar and ordered two more. 'You're right about something else too,' he said, when he returned. 'Two correct in one night; that's good going for you.'

'Thanks. What is it?'

'We do need to catch this character. He knows about the connection between David and Anna; clearly he does, because he's killed them both. At the moment, as far as we're aware, he's the only one who does, but if the police don't tie in Alison in the next few days, then, sooner rather than later, he's going to find a way to let them in on the secret.

'If we allow that to happen, my famous friend, for all I've told Alison to act wide-eyed and innocent, chances are we are all waist-deep in the shit.'

'So where do we begin to look for him?'

'Stick a pin in a map of the city. That's as good a way as any in the circumstances. Do you have any bright ideas?'

'What connects the two killings?'

'It's a triangle. That's what we're meant to think. Maybe it is. Maybe Alison knew about it from the start. Maybe we're just a pair of saps and she is just playing us along. Maybe she made those anonymous phone calls to herself . . .'

'And maybe she fixed that accident to the police car?'

'Yes. At the end of it all, that's the one lucky break she's had, and that's why I believe all the rest of it. So to come back to your question, what connects the two killings?'

'Torrent.'

'What do you mean?'

'He was a client of Alison and David's; he was Anna Chin's employer; he was putting pressure on Alison when all this happened. And he's dodgy in business, as we know from Susie. Yet when I spoke to him, he was as nice as nine euros, handing out treats like he was Scrooge on Christmas Day.'

'But so what?'

'But so it's all we've fucking got! We need . . . bugger it, you need to get in there and see what you can find. You're his security consultant; start a complete review in the wake of Anna's murder, and while you're at it, look for anything that might help us here.

'Otherwise, we're not just waist-deep in the shit. Any minute now the tea-break'll be over and it'll be back to standing on our heads.'

236

43

Actually I was in it already, as I found out when I left the Oxford. I had switched off my mobile while I was talking to Ricky; when I turned it on again, outside in Young Street, it flashed at me impatiently to tell me that I had a voice message.

It was Susie, terse and to the point. 'Call me back.'

I obeyed, trying her mobile first, since its ringing was less likely to disturb Janet. 'You might have warned me,' she said, as soon as she answered.

'I thought I had,' I protested, not knowing what the hell she was on about. 'Is Mandy there with you?'

'Yes,' she replied, 'and that made it worse, having her in the house. She knew who she was, when the buzzer went and she answered it.'

The third pint of lager had fogged my brain. 'Who?' I mumbled.

'Prim, you idiot, who else? Your wife came to see me and our daughter. You might have bloody well warned me she was around.'

'But she only turned up this afternoon,' I heard myself protest, lamely. 'And when she left I thought she was going up to Perthshire to see her folks. I'd no idea she'd go to see you, or I'd have told her not to.'

'Fat chance she'd have listened,' said Susie, scornfully.

'So what did she say? Did Mandy have to referee?'

'Mandy wasn't there; I sent her into the kitchen while we had our chat.'

'And?'

'And she was as nice as only Primavera can be when she puts her mind to it. She asked if she could see the baby, and when I showed her to her she got all misty-eyed. She'd even stopped in at a shopping centre and bought her a present.

'Then she said that the way things had worked out were probably for the best. She hoped that you and I would be very happy together and she wished us both luck. What do you make of that?'

'What should I make of it?' I replied. 'I'm relieved, I suppose. She didn't know about Janet until she turned up in Edinburgh this afternoon. It came as a real shock to her. I'm pleased that she's taken the news so well.'

'She didn't know? She told you that? And you believed her?'

'Yes.'

'Oh, you poor, gullible lad; she's a better actor than you are . . . not that it would be hard.'

'Come on, Susie,' I protested, stung by her critical review, 'what's your problem with all this?'

'I know her,' she shot back. 'Her turning up like this was not spur of the moment, and as for her best wishes, they were a declaration of war. I was always wary of Prim at the best of times; as things are now, I wouldn't trust her an inch.'

'Ah, come on. Sometimes you have to take people at face value.'

'She isn't people! She's your wife, and she's got the biggest down on me any woman could possibly have on another. So when she swans into my house, goes gooey over my baby, and wishes me long life and happiness, no way will I believe a bloody word she's saying!'

'Well I do, okay?'

'Sure you do, like you believed her in the past, when she was having it off with half of Spain in your absence.'

'She didn't really lie to me, though. I just assumed. Anyway, all that time was none of my business.'

'Yeah? And what about her and Mike? When she was with you and he was with me? What about that?'

Young Street grew blurred all around me; I held the phone away from my ear and looked at it until my eyes focused. 'What did you just say?' I asked her, when I could find the words.

'Nothing I ever planned to,' she replied. 'I never intended to tell you, but the two of them had an affair, in Glasgow.'

'Prim and Dylan? You're making that up; you have to be.'

'I wish I was, but I'm not. After he died, I found a letter she wrote him; the daft bastard kept it, inside the birthday card it came in. It was wishing him many happy returns, in more ways than one.'

'So,' I said slowly, 'when you turned up in Spain, and we got it together, you were getting your own back too?'

Susie fell silent. 'No,' she answered eventually. 'I didn't plan it that way. But it made it a hell of a lot easier, I can tell you.'

'So why didn't you tell me about her and Dylan until now?'

'I don't know. I didn't see the need, I suppose. You liked him and he's gone. What was the point of telling you?'

'And did you tell Prim you knew?'

'No. I'm keeping that in reserve for when I need it.'

'And when will that be?'

'When she tries to get you back, as she will.'

'She won't; she knows better.'

'I know better; she will, believe me. Maybe she's started already.'

I thought about our encounter that afternoon, and Prim's willingness to put the couch to good use. Susie latched on to my silence. 'She has, hasn't she!' she exclaimed, almost triumphantly.

'Well if she did, she failed. And when she saw that she had she went to see you and wished you all the best.'

I heard her laugh. 'In your dreams, big boy. Tell me something. This man who's been following you, the guy who took our picture and planted it in your room; has it ever occurred to you that he might be working for your wife? Did it never occur to you that she was being far too compliant over the divorce?'

No, it had not; never, until that moment. I told Susie as much. 'Well maybe you should give it some thought. You're trying to make a movie, which she knows all about because her sister's in it. Out of the blue, dodgy things happen. Why shouldn't she be behind them? Why shouldn't she be behind all of them?'

44

I thought about what Susie had said for the rest of the night. I started thinking about it again, as soon as I was wakened next morning by the sound of the door buzzer.

I checked my watch as I answered; it was five to nine. I'd overslept and Liam Matthews was at the door, ready to begin rehearsals for his big week of being a movie star. Having shot the beginning of the movie the day before, we were scheduled to film one of the climactic scenes, a complicated shoot-out in Edinburgh University's McEwan Graduating Hall, which had been made available to us for a full week.

As I waited for the lift to come up from the street, I ran through what Susie had said. Could Prim have sent the stalker? Could she have planted that photo herself? She'd had the chance. Sure, if she had she'd put on a terrific act when I'd told her about the baby, but she'd put on some A-list performances for me in the past . . . not least keeping me totally in the dark about her having it off with Mike Dylan, God rot his bones.

Yes, I told myself, as I listened to the whoosh behind the sliding steel door, *she could be behind the man who followed me. I wouldn't put that past her. But to be behind all of it . . .*

Then the lift opened, and there he was, the GWA World Heavyweight Champion, a true superstar of wrestling. I half expected him to have the big leather and gold title belt slung over his shoulder but, thankfully, he was out of character for the week.

When I first met Liam, I took an instant dislike to him. He was pushy, arrogant, playing all the stuff in his ring persona in real life, pissing off just about everyone around him, and surviving in his job only because of his exceptional physical gifts, his technical skills . . . he was a world championship medallist as an amateur . . . and his natural acrobatic talent. Pound for pound, because he's much smaller than most of his enormous colleagues, Liam is as good a sports entertainer . . . wrestler, that is . . . as the world has ever seen. Happily, he's also worked his way though his difficult period, found himself a nice girl, and let the nice guy within him work his way to the surface.

He filled a void in my life when Dylan's death left me short of a best pal; given what I'd learned in the last twelve hours or so, was I glad to see him right then.

He looked me up and down. 'Jesus, boy, what have you been up to? You look frazzled. You've got eyes on you like piss-holes in the snow.'

'I'd a few beers last night, then I didn't sleep very well. I've had a disturbing weekend.' I heard myself give a slightly hysterical laugh. 'Weekend? Fuck, since I came back to Edinburgh, the whole place has been growing crazier and crazier.' I dumped Liam's bag in the spare bedroom off the living area, took him into the kitchen and made him coffee, then led him through to my suite. He sipped quietly as I shaved then showered, and as I told him, stage by stage, about everything that had happened to me over the last few weeks, from Prim's walk-out in California, to her reappearance on the shoot and her visit to Susie in Glasgow. 'You think I look frazzled, do you?' I asked him, as I buckled my belt. 'Is it any bloody wonder?'

'No,' Liam conceded. 'I don't suppose it is.' He looked at me, appraising me once again. 'You know what's the most dangerous thing in the sports entertainment business?' he asked, in his light Dublin brogue.

'Tell me.'

'Aggression. It's when a wrestler goes into the ring in an aggressive frame of mind that someone gets hurt. You're so full of it right now that if you came across this guy who's been following you, the good Lord alone knows how far you'd go. What you need, Oz, is to take that aggression out on someone who can absorb it.'

'Who? You?'

Liam laughed; it was loud and refreshing and I felt a bit better right away. 'Don't be so fucking stupid. I'd damage you. No, you need to take it out on yourself. What's our timetable for today?'

'We meet up for lunch at the rehearsal room in George Street; one o'clock sharp.'

'Fine. Have you sorted yourself out a gym in this town?'

'Yes. Not far from here.'

'Then that's where you and I are going to spend the morning. We'll get you healed there.'

My friend was as good as his word. We headed down to the Edinburgh Club, where Liam put me through his own training routine. While he's small for a wrestler, around my height, he's maybe fifteen pounds heavier than my one-ninety-five, and fast and exceptionally strong with it. He worked each piece of apparatus flat out and he made me keep up his pace all the way. He made me press weights I'd never even attempted before, with my arms and legs, until I screamed out loud with the effort. When we were done with that, he made me put on the gloves and held the heavy punch-bag while I hit it, harder and harder, combinations at first, then single punches, big booming shots, every one of

243

them aimed at a bearded guy, wearing shades. Finally, I nailed the red leather bag with a huge right-hander that broke Liam's grip on it and sent him rolling over backwards. 'Jesus,' he grinned as he got to his feet, 'I'm glad that was between me and you.'

To wind up, he took me on the judo mat and showed me some new moves, and other stuff he had been working on himself, not necessarily for use in the ring, more the type of throws and holds that had won him his world championship medal. When we were done with that, he sat down in the middle of the mat, and told me to do the same.

'Close your eyes,' he instructed, 'cleanse your mind of all but the most peaceful thoughts. Take the biggest lungful of air you can, and release it slowly, then breathe shallow, quietly, so you can't even feel it. Then find what's dearest to your heart and focus on that alone.'

I did as he said. As I exhaled I had a vision, behind my closed eyes, of Jan, my dead soul-mate. She'd come to me before in times of need and she did so again, wordlessly this time. I could hear nothing but the sound of my own heart, its beat slow and steady. As I concentrated on the picture in my mind I seemed to close in on its centre on something within her. It grew and became clearer until two figures formed; Susie and the baby.

I sat there motionless for I know not how long, looking at my child and her mother, aware only of them and of the violence draining out of me. I'd probably have stayed in my trance all day, had not Liam broken it by touching me gently on the shoulder.

'Okay, boy,' he said. 'Time to be moving.'

As I took my second shower of the day, I felt cleansed in every sense. As I towelled myself dry and dressed, I realised just how strung out I had been, and how close to the edge I'd come. I took a look in the mirror, and couldn't see a trace of the guy who'd been there a few hours before.

'You have to master yourself, Oz,' Liam said to me, quietly, as I drove back to the apartment on the Mound. 'There's something dangerous about you; it needs to be driven out and kept out. What we did this morning should be your standard work-out from now on, but the most important part of it is the part at the end. If you can't do anything else, none of the physical stuff, at the very least you should commune with the peaceful side of your nature every day in life.'

Since then, I've taken that advice to heart and followed it, religiously; it works, most of the time. I still find it strange to think of the GWA champion as a man wholly cleansed of aggression, but I understand completely why that has to be. These people are trained professionals, kids; don't try their stuff at home.

We were dropping our gym gear at home . . . straight into the washing machine . . . when my hard-won serenity was put to its first test. I had missed my morning check of my e-mail, so in the few minutes that were left before we had to head for George Street, I switched on my laptop, plugged in my modem, and set up an AOL flash-session.

Even if there's mail, normally it takes seconds to run, unless there's an attachment to download; this time there was, an untitled JPEG file. It took just under a minute until it was complete and Joanna's voice said 'Goodbye'. I opened my off-line filing cabinet and looked at the 'incoming' folder. There were two new messages; one was a cheery 'hello' from Susie, saying sorry that she'd given me a hard time the night before, and assuring me that everything was okay in Glasgow.

The second was from a source I didn't recognise; it was on Hotmail, untitled, and the sender address was no more than a jumble of letters, 'mzrimnmeal92'. I opened it, thinking that it was junk mail, expecting someone to be offering me free insurance, promising me a bride from St Petersburg, or trying to sell me a magic pill that would make my dick three inches longer . . . I've had all of those and more in my mailbox in my time.

This one was different, though; the message was two words, that's all. 'Hello, Oz.' At the foot of the screen, an icon indicated an attachment.

I have my computer set up so that all my downloads go straight to my desktop. I clicked three times, and the folder was open. I found it, easily; 'u' for 'untitled' with the JPEG symbol. I opened it and watched as it unrolled on the screen.

It was another photograph of Susie and the baby from our Saturday outing, this time taken inside the Kelvingrove Art Gallery. So much for my powers of observation; I'd been wise to the man yet he'd still been able to follow us inside and take the second photograph. *Stupid, Oz, rushing off to the gents like that to play detective. You could have come out and they could have been gone.*

But they weren't, I answered myself, *which means, surely, that the man's intentions aren't violent.*

Don't be daft. The next e-mail will ask for money.

'What's up?' Liam asked.

I showed him the screen. 'The guy's been playing silly buggers again.' Inside, I was strangely pleased with myself. I didn't feel a trace of anger.

I picked up the phone, called Ricky, and told him what had happened. 'Give me the sender address,' he said; I read it out letter by letter, number by number. 'I'll try it on Mark Kravitz. He has contacts with the thought police. Mind you, given that it's Hotmail, they might be able to tell you where it was sent from, but as for identifying the sender, there'll be little or no chance of that.'

'Maybe he sent it from his home phone?'

'Nah. He'll have used a public internet access for sure.'

'Have faith, Richard,' I told him, 'in the inherent stupidity of your fellow man. This guy's been daft enough to stalk two of the most protected people on the planet. Maybe he's been daft enough to lead us to him.'

'He'd have signed his fucking name if he was going to do that.'

'Maybe so. Anyway, he's letting us know he's still there; that's the main thing.'

'Yeah,' said Ross sourly, 'look on the bright side; make my fucking day.'

'What's up with you?'

'I get like this when I lose a client.'

'Who?'

'Torrent. The fat bastard called me into his office this morning and fired me. He blames me for leaving Anna Chin open to attack. I pointed out to him that it was his niece who instituted the Friday evening call-in system for the reps, and that it was the two of them who left her vulnerable by fucking off to Gleneagles for the weekend, when normally at least one of them would still have been there when she finished.

'Didn't do any good, though; Ross Security's contract is terminated from this date for dereliction of duty.'

'I'm sorry about that, Ricky.'

'He may be too; I may sue the fat fucker.'

'You do that. But it won't help us catch our killer, will it?'

'Ah, but I've made progress on that. I was in there through the night. I made photocopies of all the Health and Safety sign-in sheets. I know everyone who's been in there since the company moved into that building five months ago. I also took what I could from Anna's desk.

'You never know, the killer might have signed his fucking name too.' He gave a short bitter laugh. 'Oh, by the way, Torrent's been really busy this morning. He called your co-director, Alison, in too.'

'Is she at work?'

'She insisted. Don't worry, she's covered.'

'Did he fire her too?'

'No, nothing like that; but he did ask her to draft a letter to Ewan Capperauld, putting his invitation on hold. In the light of Anna's death, he feels that it wouldn't be appropriate to proceed at this stage with something that might be seen as a celebration.'

'That's unusually sensitive of him.'

'Maybe, but he's still postponed it, indefinitely.'

'He'll get his reward in heaven.'

'Soon, I hope. While we're waiting, I'm off to look at those lists.'

He hung up and I turned back to my computer. 'Yes, pal,' I said to the screen, as I reached for the track-pad to begin the close-down process, 'pity you didn't sign your name, isn't it.' I looked at the address . . . and my hand froze.

All at once, I couldn't see anything but those letters and numbers . . . mzrimnmeal92. I focused on them, totally, as if I was back on the mat, meditating. They seemed to swim before my eyes as I rearranged them in my mind. And all of a sudden, I knew who my stalker was . . . the stupid bastard really had signed his name.

I just couldn't make myself believe it, that's all.

45

I carried the name in my mind all through lunch and into the afternoon rehearsal. The scenes which we were shooting were relatively easy for me; all I had to do was look alert, shout a few words and fire a pistol convincingly.

Any other director in the world would have hired an ex-soldier to teach the gun-toting members of the cast how to use them in an authentic way. Not Miles; he was an ex-soldier, and in his young days in the Aussie army he had learned the true marksman technique himself . . . along with a few other things which would not be needed in this project.

We could have used empty magazines, and dubbed the gunfire noises on to the soundtrack, but Miles had decided that we would fire blanks, so that the weapons would react properly in our hands when we pulled their triggers. So he spent a good part of that afternoon teaching us individually . . . Ewan, me, Bill Massey, Liam, and a few bit players . . . how to handle the weapons we'd be using, and letting us feel for ourselves how it felt when they were fired, almost for real. Mine was a big heavy Colt automatic, and I was really glad that there was no business end on the cartridges; the thing was so clumsy that I'd have blown out half the lights on the chandelier by the time I was through.

While I've never fired a gun in anger myself, I've seen it done close up; I understand the power of the things, physical and psychological, and I've seen their after-effects. I do not like firearms, not at all, and I'm glad that in my country at least, their ownership is restricted.

By the time we'd finished for the day, my earlier conviction that I knew my follower had gone more than a bit hazy. It was a coincidence, sure, but that's all it was; it had to be. Strange, though; when we left the rehearsal room to walk back to the Mound, I didn't feel threatened any more. I knew that he was still there, and I guessed that he and I would come face to face pretty soon now. I was looking forward to it; not for what I was going to do to him, for Liam had pounded most of that out of me, but because actually I wanted to meet him.

Miles and Dawn had invited Liam and me to join them for dinner at the Caledonian that evening. I found myself looking forward to that too; I had trouble remembering the last time I had sat down to a formal meal. Grazing had become my norm.

By the time we had checked the news and were ready to go, time was getting a bit tight, so we took a taxi down to the hotel. As we hailed it, I had a fleeting thought that the driver might be my stalker and that he might flood the back of the cab with gas, then whisk us off to parts unknown. As it happened, he was an old bloke with a flat cap and a hacking cough; he did try to whisk us off on a convoluted route to the Caley, but I was wise to that and made him drive straight down the hill and along Princes Street.

Miles had a couple of surprises in store for us when we were shown into the private dining room he had booked; we weren't his only guests. Ewan Capperauld was there too, with a pleasant, dark-haired, bright-faced lady; I wouldn't have known her from Eve, but he introduced her as his wife, Margaret. She was about his age, tall, athletic . . . from the back of my mind, I dredged up an old piece of showbiz trivia I'd read once; in her teens she'd been an Olympic

250

gymnast . . . and very attractive in an understated way. I could understand why young David had made a pass at her ten years back.

The Capperaulds' fame as a couple was based on their privacy, rather than their public face. They were never to be found in the pages of *Hello* or *OK*, and they seldom attended film events together. Having got to know Ewan, I had come to understand that he viewed his wife as his business partner. She handled all the stuff off-screen and off-stage, and he did everything else. I thought of the two agents I'd employed in my short career; they were all right, but I wouldn't have wanted to sleep with either of them.

The second surprise arrived a couple of minutes after we did. It was Susie; there was a light in her eye, and she was dressed to kill. 'Wow,' murmured Liam, as she walked into the room. 'If I didn't know whose girl she was . . . ' Even Ewan's head turned, and he's seen more than a few glamour queens in his time.

She walked right up to me and took my arm, stood on tip-toe and kissed me. I felt myself smiling awkwardly, and I knew why. Susie and I, having dinner with my sister-in-law and her husband; I looked at Dawn, checking for any frost in her expression, but I saw none.

Miles read my mind; he walked over to us. 'After yesterday,' he said, 'we thought we should make it clear where we stand as far as you two are concerned.' He took Susie's hand and kissed it. 'Welcome,' he murmured. 'You're among friends.'

She gleamed with delight; I smiled a bit myself. Why wouldn't I? There I was with a partner who was the brightest light in a room full of movie stars and their consorts. I'd made the jump from a bad marriage to a new relationship with a ready-made family. So why did I feel just a wee bit boxed in?

Ewan and his wife came across and I made the introductions. 'You're Susan Gantry?' Margaret exclaimed. 'I've read a lot about you. I can't tell you how much I admire what you've done with your business.' That was it; the ice wasn't just broken, it was shattered.

'How did you get here?' I asked Susie quietly, when eventually we were seated at the rectangular table.

'Mandy drove me through.'

'You going straight back after dinner?'

She shook her head and grinned. 'Ethel's given me an overnight pass. We'll go back in the morning.'

'Any scares through there?'

'I was never scared; but no, it's been all quiet. What about you?'

I told her about the second photograph, via e-mail; I did not tell her about my wild flight of fancy about the sender. No way did I tell her that.

That dinner party was the best night I'd had, we'd had, since Janet was born. Susie was treated not as a newcomer, but as a member of the cast. As for Liam, his girlfriend is an air steward, and she was en route for Miami, but even on his own, he fitted in; he's like that. I noticed that Miles was watching him from time to time, and I guessed that if he handled his not-too-taxing part reasonably well, it might not be his last.

Looking back, one of the reasons for the evening's success was that there was no centre of attraction. Miles was the perfect host; he said very little all night, letting the rest of us chat as we liked about whatever we liked. The only thing that was off limits was our current project . . . and quite right too.

More and more, I found myself watching the Capperaulds. Apart from my parents, I'd never seen a couple who complemented each other so well and who were as relaxed and confident in each other's company. I like to think that Jan and I would have turned out that way. Round that table I found myself thinking that maybe Susie Gantry and I would. Maybe.

The evening was over too soon; Miles ordered a round of liqueurs for those who wanted them, and that was that. As we broke up, Susie asked Miles, Dawn, Ewan, Margaret and Liam to sign her menu; she surprised me slightly, but I supposed that even the most confident among us can be a punter at heart. I was slightly huffed that she didn't ask me to add my name, but she told me that she had something else in mind for me to sign.

'What?' I asked.

'You'll find out soon enough.'

Liam was just a bit awkward about being in the spare room with Susie in the apartment; he even volunteered to move into a hotel.

'Don't be daft,' she told him. 'Just you think of yourself as a nanny. We're used to them; you can be a big Irish version.'

'We could always call Mandy on her mobile,' I suggested, 'and ask her to sleep over, for added security.'

He grinned at my jest. 'Sure. And I could teach her some new holds, yes?'

I almost retorted, 'No, she could teach you some.' Good sense made me put the brakes on the words, right on the edge of my tongue. I had got away with murder once with Susie; I didn't fancy pushing my luck any further.

46

There is a myth that movie-making is all early starts and late finishes and that the other side of the coin for guys like me is that we earn our vast sacks of gold by being dumped in arduous locations for weeks and months on end and are then screamed at from six a.m. till midnight by neurotic directors who are overly jealous because we can act and therefore are recognisably famous while they can't and therefore aren't.

I believe that's true on occasion, but it's never happened to me yet. My experience is of filming in attractive cities and countryside, under the guidance of a mentor who explains how he wants a scene to look and sound once it's shot, rehearses until he's happy it's going to turn out that way, then completes in a minimum of takes and with no histrionics at all.

But then, so far, I've only worked with Miles Grayson.

No, as I've come to appreciate, the people who really work hard on movie projects are those behind the cameras . . . and there are a hell of a lot of them. Every one seems to look after his or her own bit of the business, and most of them seem to have exotic titles. For example, there's someone called a focus puller; I assume that her job is to pull focuses, but how she pulls them, and with what, is and always will be completely beyond me.

The crew's first day at the McEwan Graduating Hall was

scheduled to begin at six-thirty. For the cast, it began at mid-day.

Susie had a flying start; she had asked Mandy to pick her up at seven-thirty, and she was up and ready. We had a coffee and toast breakfast, I took some in to Liam, and then we headed for the Mound.

'Thanks,' I said as the lift wound quietly down to the ground floor.

'What for?' she laughed. 'Coming through for a posh dinner at the Caley, sat beside Ewan Capperauld and across from Miles Grayson, then getting to sleep with you? That was not a chore, my darling, I promise.'

'No. I mean thanks for putting up with me and all the shit I have brought into your life; having a minder at home, surprise visits from Prim, and all that crap.'

She patted my chest. 'Listen, all of that is offset by the incredible good you've brought into it. There wouldn't have been a Janet without you.'

'Which begs . . . no screams . . . the question,' I told her, 'that has been gnawing at me. I know you've said you love me, and you keep on showing it, but is that only because we've made a family together? A family's something you've never had, not properly. So, without Janet, would there still be a me?'

The lift doors opened and we stepped out; the entrance hall was empty.

'Funny you should ask that,' Susie whispered, 'because just occasionally, when I brush the stardust out of my eyes, and look at the real world, I ask myself that very same question about you.'

'What's your answer?'

'I'll tell you. Remember the signature I want from you, the one we joked about last night? I want it on our marriage forms.'

255

I whistled; as in whistling in the dark, perhaps. 'Jesus! You've taken my breath away. I mean, no one's ever proposed to me before. You sure about it?'

'I'm in business, Oz. I wouldn't propose a merger if I didn't think it was absolutely right for my company. The same principle applies in my life. I know how I feel and I know what I want. Now, how about you?'

'I know how I feel too. For a while I believed that there was no goodness in the world any more. But you and Janet changed that. I love you and our daughter and I will always be around for you. I don't need to tell you that, I hope. But remember, I've stood before the anvil twice, and twice I've been burned by the heat of the forge.

'Christ, the ink isn't even *wet* on my divorce, never mind dry. On top of that, am I a guy you can trust?'

'I think so. If I can trust you after what I walked in on the other night, for God's sake . . .' Her eyes were laughing; they made me want to say, 'Yes, yes, yes,' right there and then. But it wasn't as easy as that.

'Let me think about this, Susie. There are things I have to sort out.'

'Such as? Whether or not you really love me?'

'No. The past; that's all.'

The light went out of her eyes in an instant. 'Prim got to you, didn't she? You're having second thoughts about the divorce?'

I shook my head. 'Not one.'

'Well she is, in that case.'

'I wouldn't let her. No, that's a done deal, honest; even if she did try to back out, it's done. I'd use her fling with Johnson as grounds.'

'She might counter-sue.'

'Tough.'

'Well, what is it that you have to sort out?'

'Everything. Me. Jan. Everything.'

Her eyes were full of doubt now. I had hurt her and I knew it, but if I told her the real reason for my hesitancy, the mad idea which was still there at the back of my mind, that would hurt her a lot more. The devil alone knew what it would do to her.

47

Liam and I hit the gym again at eight-thirty; we hit it bloody hard. We did an hour flat out, going through the same routine as the day before, ending with ten minutes of meditation.

We had taken our shaving gear down with us; I was just wiping off the remnants of the gel when my mobile phone sounded. 'Where are you?' Ricky asked. He was using his crisis voice; I leapt straight to the worst conclusion imaginable. The police had found the link between David Capperauld and Anna Chin; they were after Alison, and us.

'I'm at the gym.'

'Wait there. I'll pick you up. Gimme the address.'

I did; I handed Liam my car keys and told him that if I didn't see him back at the apartment, I'd head straight for the McEwan Hall. Privately, I hoped that I'd make it anywhere other than the cells at Gayfield police station.

Ricky's Alfa pulled up outside the club in less than ten minutes. He looked as grim as he'd sounded, and that made me feel no better. 'Where's the fire?' I asked him. He answered with a savage grunt. 'Ah, I see,' I muttered. 'It's at your house.'

He headed up towards the city centre, swung round Picardy Place, and then along York Place. When he didn't stop outside Alison's office, I began to feel a bit easier. He didn't say a word as he drove along Queen Street, then out across the Dean Bridge towards the west of the city.

'I don't know why I'm taking you here,' he muttered, eventually. 'But you've been arriving at disaster scenes since you got back to Edinburgh, so you might as well pitch up at another.'

'Where are we going?'

'You'll see.'

We drove, in renewed silence, out through Blackhall, until he took a right turn just past the library. I still hadn't a clue where we were going, until, after another couple of twists and turns, he swung in to Gamekeeper's Road and into the driveway of one of the big villas that line it.

Three police cars and an ambulance were lined up in front of the house. The doors of the ambulance were open, but no one was hurrying; I knew what that meant.

I still hadn't a bloody clue. Then I looked at the garage to the side of the sandstone mansion. The wide door was open and I could read the personalised plates on the Roller and the Mercedes that were parked inside.

'James Torrent,' I heard myself gasp. 'This is James Torrent's place?'

'Was,' said Ricky, tersely. 'Now it belongs to his estate.'

My head went all over the place again, as I realised what he had said. 'Very sad,' I managed, 'but why are we here?'

'Ronnie Morrow didn't know I'd been fired as security consultant. He phoned me.'

He'd filled that gap in his knowledge, though. He was standing in the doorway as we crunched up the drive; he was dressed in a white crime-scene tunic.

'You might have told me, sir,' he said, reproachfully. 'I found this on his desk.'

I peered at the copy letter as he held it up by a corner; I couldn't read it all, but I could see that it was addressed to Ross Security and I could guess what it said.

'As far as I'm concerned we still have a contract,' Ricky snapped back.

'Okay.' He nodded to me. 'But why bring him?'

'He was with me when you called. I didn't have time to drop him off. What happened?'

'Come and have a look.' He gave us each a tunic like his, from a pile by the door, and waited till we put them on. Then he led us into the house and up a big wide staircase; it reminded me of the place in Spain that I was in the process of selling to Scott Steele. At the top we turned left; a heavy panelled door lay open and we could see the people bustling inside.

We could also see James Torrent. He was behind a big wooden desk, in a chair that looked like the twin of the one in his penthouse office. He was reclining, his little piggy eyes staring at the ceiling, his great mouth hanging open, slackly.

'Don't go beyond the doorway,' said Morrow. 'You can see enough from here.'

'How?' asked Ricky.

'Stabbed. Right through the heart.'

'When?'

'Just after midnight, the ME reckoned.'

'Weapon?'

From one of the cavernous pockets of his tunic, Morrow produced a knife, encased in a clear plastic evidence envelope. A sound like a police siren went off in my head. I recognised it; when we were together, I'd once given Alison a fancy desk set for her office. It had included a paper knife with a long thin gilt blade and a fancy tooled handle, just like the one Morrow was holding. Okay, it wasn't a one-off piece, but after the last couple of weeks . . .

'We're going to have to speak to Alison Goodchild again,' the detective sergeant announced, as if he'd been reading my thoughts.

'Why?' I blurted out; I was startled and couldn't disguise it.

'When he was killed, Mr Torrent appears to have been

signing his day's correspondence. The letter I showed Mr Ross was at the top of the pile he'd done, but there was another folder in his briefcase with more, not signed yet. One of them was to her, terminating her contract.'

'Aw come on, Ronnie,' Ricky protested. 'You might as well list me as a suspect!'

'Don't take it like that, sir. You and she aren't the only people getting bad news in those letters. We'll have to talk to everybody; you know that.'

Ross was mollified. 'I suppose so.'

I tapped him on the shoulder. 'Listen, I need to go. I have to be on set at eleven-thirty and it's five past now.'

'Okay. I'll take you.'

Morrow led the way back to the front door; we stripped off the tunics and dumped them on a pile of discard just outside, in the pathway.

'I won't bother to interview you, sir,' said the sergeant.

'Thanks for the courtesy,' Ross shot back, as we walked towards his car.

'You might have told me you'd such a tight deadline,' he grumbled as we climbed in.

'I don't.' I told him about the knife.

'Oh fuck,' he whispered, when I was finished.

'But it's a plant. You know that.'

'Sure.'

'And she's got an alibi, hasn't she?'

'Sure. She was in my bed. And I've got a grudge against Torrent as well as her! Some alibi. That knife'll have her prints on it. Sure, I'll say she was with me, that we're in a relationship. All of a sudden she's got an accomplice. Do you know what? They'll wind up arresting us both.

'Worse than that; they'll assume we've been having it off since before her fiancé was murdered. Chances are they'll do us both for that as well.'

261

48

I'd never seen Ricky Ross panic before; it was not a pretty sight. It was all I could do to stop him picking up Alison and making a run for it. He saw sense at last, though, on the drive back to the city centre.

'We have got to concentrate on what we started on Sunday, man,' I told him. 'We have to find the killer before it goes pear-shaped for us all.'

'You think it isn't already?' he retorted, as we drove across the George IV Bridge. 'But you're right. We've got some time yet; even if Alison's prints are on that knife, it'll take them a while to lift them and match them. If she goes away on a business trip, even if it's only for a couple of days, that'll buy us more.'

'So how are you getting on checking the lists you took from Torrent?'

He swung the car round, past Bristo Square, into George Street, and stopped on a yellow line. 'I've been through them all; wee Anna was efficient. Everyone who came into that building printed and signed their name.'

He chuckled. 'All the well-known ones signed her own wee book, too . . . even you, flash bastard that you are. Must have been a great job for an autograph hunter; they came to her. Every signature in there matched a signature on the list, bar one.'

'Whose was that?'

'Haven't a fucking clue. The thing was completely illegible; just a straight line with squiggles in it, that's all.'

'I know the one. Like an ECG chart?'

'That's it. It's nowhere on the Health and Safety lists. Some pop star probably; she'll have taken it with her to a concert.'

'So where does it take us?'

He threw me a gloomy look. 'Nowhere, pal. If you were making a western here I'd say I could hear the sound of the sheriff's posse closing in on me. As it is, I can almost feel Mr Skinner's hand on my collar.'

I could see that his earlier panic was still pretty close to the surface. I'd never imagined him like this before, never thought it possible that he, super-cop, super-Mason, super-connected, could lose it. If he was scared surely I should be too, I told myself. And then, as if in answer, a strange feeling of certainty swept over me; it told me, beyond doubt, that everything would be all right.

I smiled at him. 'You're forgetting one thing, Ricky.'

'What's that?' he grunted.

'You're sat next to the luckiest bastard on the planet.' I held up my right hand. 'Grab that, and some of it will rub off on you.'

He looked at me as if I was a lunatic. Maybe he's right; maybe I am. I only have my own word that I'm not. But then, he took his white-knuckled fist off the steering wheel and grasped mine. 'At this moment,' he said, 'I'll try anything.'

49

The set-up in the McEwan Hall was still not complete when I walked in. Everything else was ready though, including the production trucks, which were lined up on the Bristo Square car park. The cafeteria van was nearest the hall, with the others in ranks behind it. My dressing room was out of sight, but that was fine; that was the way I liked it.

I had told Miles as we were leaving the Caley the night before that I wanted the minders pulled off me altogether. Mandy should stay with Susie, but I was to be left alone. He hadn't been too keen on the idea, but I had insisted. I knew that something else was going to happen; I wasn't certain what it would be, but I didn't want anyone around when it did.

I picked up my Andy Martin costume from the wardrobe department and headed along to the truck to change. When I was in my screen clothes, I locked my watch, wallet and wedding ring in the safe, which was set in the floor, and went to make-up. I didn't even bother to lock the door as I left.

Liam was on set as I walked into the hall, big grin, teeth sparkling, looking like Mario McGuire to the life. He had his jacket slung over his shoulder; I couldn't see any of the wiring associated with a blood capsule, so I guessed from that alone that we weren't going for a take that day.

I said as much to Miles and he nodded. 'We're barely ready in the hall yet. We've had to make modifications to the seating and the carpenters still have a couple of things to do. So I've sent all the non-essential extras home for the day. The key players can run through the scene though; the crucial part, with Bill and the video camera, that's got to work for real, and I want to see that it does.'

'You could fake it, though. It wouldn't show'

'Yeah, but I'd know it. Besides, faking it costs.'

That's typical Miles. The dinner in the Caley the night before must have cost the earth, but in terms of his personal cash it was small change. But the production budget is the investors' money, and it's a matter of personal pride with him never to waste that.

'The guns are here, though,' he added. 'They're paid for anyway.' He had cut a deal with the army; they were providing all the necessary firearms, plus an armourer, for a flat fee.

There were men in black uniforms and balaclavas too, extras cast as SAS soldiers. I've seen a couple of these people in real life, and our version looked pretty authentic to me. I asked Miles whether he'd hired the uniforms from the military as well. He put a finger to his lips and went, 'Sshhh.'

We spent the afternoon doing rehearsals of all the scenes in the hall, up to and including the big gunfight at the end. Miles concentrated on Liam, who was a bit like a schoolboy when the action began and tended to overplay his hand. Acting was not new to him; all wrestlers play parts these days, assuming characters good and evil, some of them quite complex, all of them far-fetched. Some of the performers, for example Everett Davis, the main man of the GWA, are pretty good on microphone. Some, like my other friend Jerry Gradi, the Behemoth, aren't good at all, so they're given very little to say. Most of them, though, have a little of the ham about them.

Liam is one of the best, but even he has a tendency to overact, and it showed as soon as we got under way. In the final scene, which involved us . . . the good guys . . . confronting an assassin armed with an Uzi . . . the bad guy . . . his character . . . Mario . . . was meant to take two in the chest as he leapt heroically between the gunman and his target. The script had Ewan . . . Skinner . . . leaning over him, giving him a few encouraging words before they carted him off to ER in the Royal Infirmary.

He didn't have a word to say; all the script called for him to do was look up at Ewan with a plea for reassurance in his eyes. His problem was that, while he was fine on his feet, acting horizontally was a new experience for him. He couldn't get the hang of doing everything with his eyes. Eventually Miles broke into the third rehearsal, laughing in spite of himself. He could see the joke; the big cameras weren't running, only video, so it wasn't chewing into the production budget.

'Mr Matthews,' he said. 'We are not doing the death of Nelson here. The way you're approaching this, I'm up here expecting you to ask Ewan to kiss you. If you're like this when you have your bedroom scene with the lady sergeant, we're all in trouble.'

'I'm sorry, Miles,' the wrestler replied, propping himself up on an elbow. 'I guess it's because all my stuff's fake, and we have to give the audience a hint that it is.'

'I understand. So let's start from the ground up. Don't show any emotion; just lie there and think of Ireland.'

'Sure, and if I do that I'll start to cry.'

We might have had a problem there, if I hadn't saved the day. 'Hey, Liam,' I called out, cutting across Miles's response. 'Remember that time down in Newcastle when a prop broke and you got a metal shaft through your side?'

He grimaced. 'Remember it? Will I ever forget it?'

'Okay, put yourself back there, and just act exactly as you reacted then.'

He had no trouble after that, none at all; when that incident had happened he had been hurt just as badly as his character was meant to be.

When we wrapped up for the day, we were all happy with the way things had gone. I was even whistling a wee tune as I walked back to my dressing room to change out of my gear, and to retrieve my watch, wallet and keys from the safe.

I wasn't surprised when I saw the parcel on the table. I felt this sense of unreality, sure, but I wasn't surprised. I let it lie there while I changed into my own clothes, replaced my Andy outfit on its hangers and took it back to the wardrobe caravan.

I thought about it as I wandered into the cafeteria truck to grab a coffee and chew the fat with Liam, Bill Massey and some of the crew. But I was in no hurry to open it. Somehow I felt that I was in control of the game now. As everyone began to drift away, Liam said that he fancied a Chinese that evening. I told him that was fine by me, but that I had a couple of things to do first, so I gave him the keys to the apartment and headed back to the dressing-room truck.

The parcel was still there, wrapped in bright blue fancy paper, with wee white horses on it. I looked at it, and smiled; it could wait a bit longer. I took out my cellphone and called Susie, just to say hello.

'How's your sorting out going?' she asked me.

'It was interrupted.' I told her about James Torrent; I was surprised she hadn't heard about it already.

'Jeez,' she hissed. 'I've been working all day; I haven't had the radio or the telly on. There'll be a long list of candidates for that one, from business rivals, to pissed-off suppliers, to unhappy customers with a big-money grievance. Have the police got any specific leads?'

'They've got one that's going to take them straight to Alison Goodchild.'

'I thought you told me that Ricky Ross was looking after her.'

'He is; the trouble is, he's on that long list you were talking about.'

'Oh dear. Let me try to summon up some sympathy for them both.'

I didn't tell her that I might need some as well. Instead, I said hello to Janet over the phone, listened to her gurgle, then said goodnight to them both.

Finally, I was ready for the parcel. I guessed that whatever was in it had been wrapped in the shop where it was bought. It didn't occur to me for a moment that it might be something sinister. There was a nice silver bow on top, and letter-bombs generally don't come in fancy wrappers.

I opened it, carefully, again not because I was worried, but because I felt it merited the same care with which it had been put together. (Plus, I'm a Fifer; you never know when you're going to need a sheet of wrapping paper.)

The tape adhesive wasn't exactly superglue; it came away easily and the paper lifted clear in a piece, without tearing. Nice one, Oz.

Inside was a large packet of Pampers, two Babygros, age six to nine months, one pink, one yellow, and a teething ring. I picked them up, one by one, looking for a card, but I didn't expect to find one. I sat there for a while, smiling to myself, looking at my daughter's presents and wondering what to make of them.

I wasn't thinking about what I should do next . . . I knew that already . . . I was just thinking.

Eventually I stood up, slipped on my red Lacoste wind-cheater, and stepped out of the truck. This time, I locked the door behind me.

At a leisurely pace, I walked across the car park, crossed the road at the lights and made my way down past the mosque, to the Pear Tree. We were just short of the start of the university year, otherwise the old pub would have been heaving with students, adding to their loan debts. (Ask yourself, as I do, often; what sort of country is it that doesn't invest in its brightest and best young people?) It wasn't quiet, but there was space at the bar for me to order a pint of Eighty . . . (How do British publicans get away with their attitudes to their customers? Virtually everywhere else in the world, you pay for what you've had when you leave. In Britain they're not far short of seeing your money before you see their watery overpriced product.) . . . and a spare table in the beer garden for me to sit.

I sipped my beer and looked around me; some of the production team were gathered around a table in the corner of the garden. I waved to them but didn't join them; instead I popped open my packet of crisps . . . salt and vinegar, I can't stand any other kind . . . and gazed back across the square, taking time to admire the late Victorian grandeur of Atkinson's McEwan Hall. Parts of Edinburgh are an architectural dream, others, like the St James Shopping Centre and office block, are a nightmare.

I sat and I wondered and I waited. Eventually I found myself pondering upon the wisdom of two pints of Eighty before a Chinese. It was an easy decision to make; I was on the point of rising to go back to the bar, when, as if by magic, another was placed on the table beside me.

'Thanks,' I said, without looking up, or round.

He set down his lager, then settled on the bench, facing me. There were flecks of grey in his hair, which came down almost to his shoulders, and in his heavy beard. The sun was long gone, but he still wore his shades. I couldn't see his eyes, but I knew that he was staring at me, wondering, maybe, why I hadn't shit myself.

'Hello,' I said, evenly. Then I reached across the table, almost lazily, and punched him in the mouth. A girl at the next table looked across and gasped, then looked away again, quickly.

His sunglasses went skew-wiff; he put them back in place then wiped blood from his lip with the back of his hand. 'What was that for?' he asked.

'You know fucking well what it was for. Glasgow . . . not last weekend; a while back.'

'Oh,' he said, 'I see. You found out.' He took a drink, swilled it around in his mouth as if he was washing away more blood, and swallowed. 'You were expecting me?' he asked.

'Of course I was expecting you; I was meant to. Fucking stupid e-mail address.'

'I thought it was quite clever,' he said, his crest a little fallen.

'It was too clever by half; just typical of you . . . mzrimnmeal92.' I mumbled the jumble, as if the Eighty had got to me already. 'An anagram of Zimmerman; give me a bit of credit, I'd have got that eventually. But to add in the numbers as well; I was almost insulted by that.

'Zimmerman is Dylan's real name; now I might be fucking famous these days, but I can't imagine Mystic Bob wanting to get in touch with me. Apart from him, and the dead poet, I only know of one Dylan.'

'You're forgetting Bob Willis.'

'You're right; I'm forgetting him. Who is he?'

'The cricketer; he took Dylan as his middle name.'

'Big deal. Anyway, even from the anagram I'd have got the link, but you had to put the icing on it by adding the numbers; another anagram, of the day and month Mike Dylan was shot in Amsterdam.'

270

'How did you know for sure it was me and not someone pretending?'

'Two reasons. The first and most obvious was that you knew my e-mail address. The second was the gifts you left for Janet. An impostor wouldn't have done that.'

He tilted his head back; I could just see that behind the shades his eyes were closed. 'How did I know that's what the two of you would call her?' he murmured.

'Because,' I hissed, 'you're a clever bastard . . . too clever by half, remember. So fucking clever it got you killed . . . remember? You're dead, Mike. I know you're dead, because I was there. I saw you get shot, I saw you die.'

He shook his head. 'You saw me cough up a lot of blood and start to choke, then you saw me pass out. Then they got you the hell out of there. What you didn't see was when they whipped me out of there to the emergency room.

'If the man they sent had been trying to kill me he'd have blown my brains out. He didn't; he shot me through the right side of the chest. It got a bit hairy, because he hit my lung, but that served to convince you, didn't it? They wanted the other guy dead, but not me.'

'Why not? You were a rogue policeman, and Special Branch at that. Surely they wanted you even deader than him?'

'No. They wanted the names in my head; I'd never been debriefed before I did my runner. I knew what the guy they killed knew, namely some key links in the chain of drug imports, not just to Scotland, but to the whole of Western Europe and beyond. When I began to recover, they gave me a choice . . .'

'Who were "they"?'

'Our security services, the Dutch and the American DEA; heavy hitters all of them. They scared the shite out of me, I can tell you. I gave them the names I had, but they said that wasn't enough, that the list didn't go far enough. They gave me a new identity and they told me to contact some of the guys I'd been told about, to infiltrate the network, and to stay in until I had the whole chain and could deliver them.

'I tried to tell them to get fucked. They offered to dump me in the North Sea.'

'So did you do everything they told you?'

He sighed. 'Yes. Two months ago there was an international operation starting in Burma and Thailand, and winding up in London, Glasgow, Amsterdam and New York. All sorts of people were taken down; some of them were taken out completely . . . like me, for example, I'm dead again.'

'What do you mean?'

'I mean they did again what they did in Amsterdam, but in Bangkok this time.'

'What? They shot you?'

He grinned. 'Right in the head; but not with a bullet, with a special cartridge filled with blood, like you guys use in the movies. There were witnesses, a couple of the middle-ranking people who were being arrested. The idea was that when they got to jail they would spread the word that I'd been bumped.'

'Did it work?'

'As far as I know; but these dealers have tipsters everywhere on the inside. I should know, I used to be one.'

'So who are you now?'

'I can't tell you that. But you're right, I have a third identity now; I was set up with that, and with a chunk of money. The deal was that I'd go to Portugal and never go near the drugs business again.'

'As easy as that?'

He gave a grim smile; it was less than a couple of years since he'd gone tits up at Schiphol, but his eyes looked twenty years older. I wondered what they'd seen since then. Of course, he'd been dead twice; that must have an effect on a bloke. 'Not quite as easy,' he replied. 'They told me that they know where I am, and who I am. They may have a use for me in the future.'

'So what the fuck are you doing here? Why haven't you got yourself yet another false passport and gone somewhere out of their reach? Why have you been following Susie and me?'

'I'm taking a chance, that's what I'm doing . . . and there is nowhere out of their reach. No, I was ready to split for Portugal, when I picked up a Scottish paper in London and who did I see on an inside page, but you and Susie, and your new baby.

'You might have been surprised when I turned up . . . think how I felt when I saw that. What the hell happened, Oz? What happened to Prim?'

I looked at him, hard; for all his adventures he didn't scare me, not a bit. It was the other way round and he knew it. By coming back, he'd put his life in my hands. 'You know what the punch in the mouth was for. Didn't it even occur to you that Susie might have spilled the beans about you and her?'

He winced. 'I left a letter behind, didn't I?'

I nodded. 'Some secret operative; you couldn't even cover your tracks with your best pal's fiancée.'

'I'm sorry, Oz, it was just . . .'

'. . . one of those things? Spare me, please. So was Susie and I at first. The fact is I didn't know about you and Prim till a couple of days ago. Susie only told me when she showed up at her place.'

'Her place? I thought . . .'

'She bought it from me. Before we . . . Anyway, back to your story; you saw us and you were gob-smacked.'

'Yes. I bailed out. I told my minder I was going and I split. He took me to the airport, but I lost him, went back into London and caught a train to Glasgow. It took me a while to pin you down, but when I did, I started to follow you.

'I wanted to see you, man, to see the two of you, to see how you had turned out. That's all. I'm sorry if I spooked you . . .'

'Lying bastard! You're not sorry at all.'

'I am if Susie got worried; honest.'

'I'll take your word for it. So, now that you've seen us, what do you think?'

He drained his glass and gave me a long look. 'I think you're all right. You look like a family, you know. I really hope you stick it.' He gave a big sigh. 'You know, I always thought that we had the wrong women, you and I; I always thought that Susie was more your type and Prim was more mine.'

'What do you mean by that?'

'I mean that you two are basically straight, while she and I are basically bent.'

I laughed. 'That has to be a compliment, coming from you.'

He grunted. 'Here,' he said, suddenly, 'what are you doing hanging out with my old boss, Ricky Ross? He was your mortal enemy for a while.'

'Aye, and you were my best friend.'

'Touché.'

'Ricky's head of security on the movie,' I told him. 'That's all.'

'Mmm. You going to get more beer in?'

I raised an eyebrow. 'Like hell! You are. You owe me, pal.'

He gave me a grin and disappeared to the bar, returning after a couple of minutes with two more.

'So what's next?' I asked him.

'I'm going to turn up in Portugal, as planned. I've seen what I came to see, and I'm content.'

I leaned across the table. 'That's good,' I murmured, 'for you have to know one thing. Susie is never to learn about this, or about you. If you ever show up near us again, if you ever try to contact her . . .' I paused. 'You've changed, I've changed. If you ever do that then I promise you . . . you will be dead again, and it will be for real this time.'

I looked him in the face and gave him time to think about it. 'Do you believe me?'

'I reckon I do. There was always a hard bastard under your surface, wasn't there. But don't worry; I'm too fond of Susie . . . and of you . . . ever to threaten either of you. The only thing is . . .' He hesitated, then took off the shades and stared at me.

'I've got no one, Oz. I'm cut off from everyone I've ever known in the life I had before all this; they've fucking buried me. You've no idea how lonely it is, being dead.'

I heard what he was saying, loud and clear. 'You've got my e-mail address,' I told him. 'If the need really arises . . . and it had better be more than going for a pint, mind . . . that's how you can reach me. Use the same stupid name and I'll know.'

'Thanks.' He drained his lager in a one-er, and stood up. 'So long.'

The guy who had once been Mike Dylan turned on his heel, and walked out of the Pear Tree, into whatever kind of a future might await him.

50

It had been a while since I had drunk Eighty at all, let alone shifting three pints of the stuff in under an hour, so my brain was even fuzzier than it had been after the Oxford when I got back to the apartment and pushed the entry button.

'Whozzat?' Liam asked, through the speaker.

'Santa Fucking Claus.'

'You can come in down the chimney, then.' But he pushed the button, anyway; just as well, by that time my bladder was feeling the pressure.

He gave me an appraising look when I re-emerged from the bathroom. 'Where the hell have you been then?' he enquired. It's a funny thing about mates, is it not; when you share a flat with them, they can be worse than wives in some ways.

'Thinking,' I told him.

'Thinking about how fast you can get to the bottom of the glass?'

'That, among other things. Come on, superstar of wrestling, let's go get that Chinese.'

We grabbed a cab on the hill outside; by chance, it was the legendary white taxi, the one with the tartan-lined interior, and Jock and Roll music playing from the moment you step in until the moment you close the door behind you. It is to Edinburghers what the great white buffalo is to Native Americans. There is a theory that the driver is long dead, and that it is but his shade that cruises the city

276

streets bringing eternal delight to tourists. Whatever the truth of it, he took us straight to the Kwei Linn.

The crispy duck was as I remembered it from a few years back, and so was the chicken in black bean sauce. We walloped them down, with a beef dish and a mild prawn curry. I stuck to fizzy water . . . Okay, I admit it. We shared a bottle of Lambrusco, but it's much the same . . . and by the time we got to the coffee stage, I could see clearly again.

'You back in the land of the fully conscious, then?' Liam asked. I nodded.

'Where did you go tonight?' He was still doing the 'pal as old woman' routine. It's instinctive with blokes; we can't help it.

'I had to meet someone.'

'Male or female?'

'Male. Someone I hadn't seen in a long time.'

'Let me guess. You found the guy who's been stalking you.'

'No. I let him find me.'

'And?'

'And nothing. We had a talk and he's gone.'

He frowned. 'Oz, you didn't hurt him, did you?'

I laughed, quietly. 'Nah. All that communing with my peaceful side's done me good. I only hit him once, and not very hard at that.'

'So what did he want?'

'He only wanted to say hello. He came a long way to do it, and had a funny way of working up to it, but he got to it eventually.'

'You sure that's it?'

'Absolutely. We won't see him again.'

He looked at me for a while, then grinned. 'Thanks for helping me out this afternoon. I was having trouble until you came up with that suggestion. You got any more tips for the bedroom scene with the lady detective sergeant?'

'Yeah. All the time, as she's getting her togs off, keep a picture of Tony Blair in your mind. No way can you think of him and still get a hard-on.'

Liam laughed out loud. A quartet of women, who'd recognised us when we came in, looked back in our direction. 'That's quite an occupational hazard, when you think about it. In my game, you worry about your knees, or your back, or springing a rib cartilage. It's odd to think of getting a boner as a workplace accident.'

'Don't worry about it,' I said, leaning back in my chair so the women across the restaurant could hear. 'Like I said, there's the stuff they put in your tea as well. It hardly has any after-effects.'

He gasped, and held the pose . . . long enough for the girls at the other table to latch on to his surprise. A natural actor, indeed.

We got talking to them after that; it turned out that they were a hen party, from the Standard Life office in Lothian Road. One of them, a pretty brunette called Serena, was being married on the following Saturday. Funnily enough, she was the one who made the biggest eyes at Liam . . . so, why should women be any different from men? A couple of years before, he'd have been right in there, but since he found his air stewardess, he's flown straight as an arrow.

The taxi that picked us up was one of the ordinary black kind . . . or it would have been if it hadn't been painted like a mobile phone. It dropped us back at the Mound at around eleven-thirty. There's a pub beside the door to the apartment block. We thought about going in, but were hit by a double blast of self-discipline, being due on set at eight-thirty next morning. Plus, I reckoned that if I had any more to drink I might start to think of Dylan again, and I didn't want to do that.

So instead, we went straight up to the penthouse, where I got myself a bottle of still water from the fridge and headed straight for bed, I was almost ready to crash, when my eye was caught by something on the dressing table. At first I thought it was a postcard, or a piece of junk mail . . . that stuff gets everywhere . . . until I realised it was Susie's menu, the one she'd had signed the night before by everyone at the table, bar me.

'Daft bat.' I smiled as I picked it up. 'Forget your head next.' I glanced at the signatures on the white card. 'Miles Grayson', clear and confident; 'Dawn Phillips', scrawled and spidery, but legible; 'Margaret Capperauld', traditional primary-school style, joined-up writing; 'Liam Matthews', as quirky and flamboyant as the man himself; and one other.

I couldn't read it; not a snowball's chance in hell of that. It didn't look like a signature at all; more like an ECG printout. It was more than familiar, though; it was an exact match of the unidentified scrawl in Anna Chin's notebook. And now, by a simple process of elimination, I knew that it was the autograph of Ewan Capperauld.

All of a sudden I wasn't tired any more. All of a sudden I didn't care what time it was. I grabbed the bedside telephone, found Ricky Ross's home number from his business card, and called him.

'Oz,' he moaned. He sounded slightly breathless. 'Do you know what fucking . . .'

'No, but I can guess who. This is your lucky bastard calling. I need to see you, now.'

'So come out to my place.'

'I've had a drink; you come here. And bring Anna's autograph book with you.'

'But what about Alison? I can't leave her.'

'Bring her. There's a fair chance we might need her anyway.'

51

My urgency must have got through to Ricky. I had expected him to take half an hour to get to me, but the entry buzzer sounded in just over fifteen minutes.

He stepped out of the lift, wearing jeans and a heavy sweater and needing a shave. Alison followed behind, dressed almost identically to him; she was completely without make-up and her hair was pulled back in a pony-tail.

I led them through to the kitchen. Liam was asleep directly off the living area, and I didn't want to disturb him.

'So why the alarm call?' said Ross, tersely, as I poured two mugs of coffee from the filter jug. Susie's menu card was lying on the work-surface. I picked it up and handed it to him. He looked at it, then his eye hit on the cardiac squiggle.

'Jesus,' he murmured. 'Whose?'

'Ewan Capperauld.'

'What!' The word came out in an astonished half-shout. I worried that it might waken Liam, and signalled him to be quiet. 'But Capperauld's never been to the Torrent building,' he said.

'In that case he's the only person in Anna's book who hasn't. That's remarkable, isn't it? But she told me that was where she'd collected all her autographs, so he must have been. Yet James Torrent clearly didn't know it. He told me so himself, almost in so many words. "*It would be good to have someone as eminent as Ewan Capperauld visit this building.*" That's what he said to me, when I saw him in his office.' I turned to Alison. 'Did he ever say or imply to you that Capperauld had been there?'

'No,' she replied. 'The opposite in fact; he told me that he wanted every eminent Scot to visit his new headquarters, and that Ewan was at the top of that list.'

I nodded. 'And yet when I saw him there, he wasn't all that bothered. Something happened between him giving you that instruction and my visiting him, to make him change his mind, or at least go soft on the idea.'

'Something,' said Ricky. 'Like what?'

'Like maybe he found out that Capperauld had already been to his building.'

'It's a pity we can't ask him.'

'Or Anna,' I added. 'But there's someone we can ask.'

'Who?'

'Come on; waken up. Ewan himself.'

Ross looked at me as if he had a wrestling hold on something in his brain. 'Easier said than done. Capperauld's a big name; he's also Miles Grayson's star attraction, and Miles is my client. I can't just go interrogating him.'

'Okay, I'll do it. Call his minder and have him brought here.'

'Are you crazy? Talk to him in the morning, if you must.'

'Have you got that much time, Ricky? Has Alison?'

'I'll take that chance.'

'Nice of you to take it for Alison.'

He glared at me but said nothing.

We had been drinking our coffee in silence for almost five minutes when the mobile in Ross's pocket sounded. He scowled and answered the call. I wouldn't have thought his face could have got any grimmer, but as he spoke, it did.

'You're kidding,' I heard him snap. 'How would I?' He flashed gimlet eyes in my direction. 'Do your own fucking job, son!' he growled into the phone at last, and jabbed the red button to end the call.

He told me what I'd guessed already. 'That was Ronnie Morrow. They've matched some of the prints on the knife.' He looked at Alison. 'He's looking for you, love. You've just gone top of the list of people he wants to question. He said he's been to your flat, but you're not there. Surprise. Then he tried to say that technically you're still bailed into my custody so I should help him find you. You heard what I told him.'

'Sure,' I said. 'That'll keep him at bay for a long time, and it's probably put you second on his list. Now I don't want to be third, so get that bloody phone out again and call Ewan's minder.'

Ricky was well beaten. This time he did as he was told. It took Glen Oliver less than a minute to answer; quickly his boss gave him his orders. 'What do you tell him?' Ross exclaimed, suddenly. He looked at me, as if for an answer.

'Tell him,' I said, 'that it's a very important matter involving his cousin's murder, and that if he doesn't get here pronto there's every chance it'll be all over the red-tops by the weekend.' He repeated what I had said, almost word for word. After that, there was nothing to do but wait. I tried to imagine what we were going to say to Ewan. I could manage that okay, but when I tried to guess what he might say to us, I came up short; the Case of the Baffled Detective.

It was fifteen minutes short of one when the buzzer sounded again; this time it did wake Liam. He appeared in the bedroom doorway, bollock-naked, drowsy, growling, 'What does an Irishman have to do to get some sleep around here?' Then he saw Alison, who had come out of the kitchen. 'Fuck,' he said, 'we could have pulled in the restaurant.

Why change your mind now?' At that point he remembered his state of undress, and dived back behind the door.

Ewan came storming out of the lift; I could see that he was in full Skinner mode, locked and loaded, ready for a fight. He blinked when he saw Alison, but his expression stayed hard. I led him through to the kitchen, where Ricky was waiting, and closed the door on Oliver, leaving him in the living room.

'Okay,' Capperauld boomed. 'This had better be the story of a lifetime, Ross, or your security career will be over.'

His anger was so impressive that for that important moment Ricky was struck dumb. I wasn't, though; I had seen him act before. 'Come here,' I said, beckoning him over to the work-surface, and pointing towards what lay on it.

'This is the menu you signed for Susie last night.'

'So?'

I took the book from my back pocket, opening it at the place I had marked and laid it beside the card. 'And this is Anna Chin's autograph book. Let me tell you about Anna. She was James Torrent's front office receptionist, and she had a harmless hobby. Every time a celebrity signed into the building, she asked them to sign her autograph book as well. Nearly all of them did. Every signature in that book is matched by a signature on the Torrent registration sheets . . . every one except yours, that is.

'Let me tell you two more things about Anna. Maybe they're new to you, maybe they're not. First, she was having it away with your late cousin David; she's one reason he dumped Alison. Second, last Friday night someone killed Anna in the office, at her desk, and tried to set it up so that the police would find Alison there.'

I looked at Ewan. 'That's appalling, Oz,' he said, 'but how does it justify you hauling me out of my bed in the middle of the night? It's just as well Margaret's gone back to London, by the way, or there would have been an explosion bigger than you can imagine.'

'Have you heard any news bulletins today?' I asked him.

'No. Should I?'

'I reckon so. If you had, you'd have heard that James Torrent was stabbed to death in his home overnight. The murder weapon was a paperknife which someone stole from Alison's office. The police are looking for her now, and in the morning, Ricky's going to have to take her in. He's got no choice, or he's in the crapper too.

'When he does, he's going to take that card and that book with him. He's going to tell the police about James Torrent suddenly going all coy about your opening his building, when a couple of weeks before only the Greatest Living Scotsman would do.

'Torrent thought you had never been in his building, yet if you look at the dates of the signatures after yours in Anna's books, it appears that even when he gave Alison an ultimatum to get you there, you had been. We just want to know why, Ewan, that's all.'

'Then you can get stuffed.' The anger was gone from his voice, though. He was playing a scene he hadn't rehearsed.

'Fine. Then we'll go to the police, and they will interview you, for sure; discreetly, I would imagine. You'll maybe tell them that Anna stopped you in the street, and they'll leave it at that. If you'd told me that rather than telling me to get stuffed, I might just have believed you myself.

'But you didn't, so this is what's going to happen. As soon as the police call you in for a chat, or even call on you, I'm going to tip off the tabloids, all of them, that you've been detained for questioning in connection with the murders of your cousin, Anna Chin and James Torrent.

'I don't know who or what you're trying to protect here,

Ewan, but you are not going to do it at Alison's expense, or Ricky's, or mine. You might think you can keep this under wraps, but I promise you, you do not have a fucking chance.'

I leaned back on the work-surface and looked at him, letting what I'd said sink in, staring hard in the hope that he'd know I wasn't bluffing . . . because I wasn't. Alison and Ricky stood there silent beside me.

The wait seemed as long as any I'd ever known. The seconds seemed to be stretched like thick elastic as they passed. He opened his mouth as if to speak, and his teeth snapped together, but then he closed it again, and another elongated minute began. Looking at him, I knew what 'he was doing; the guy was rehearsing, mentally. The next thing he said was going to be very important, so he could not afford to falter over a single line.

Finally, he gathered himself, and nodded, as if he was a director satisfied with his own performance. He looked at Ricky, then at me, and finally at Alison.

'Do you know what sort of a little shit your late fiancé was, my dear?' He didn't wait for an answer. 'He was the worst kind I know; a blackmailer.'

His delivery and timing were perfect. He held her eyes for a few seconds then turned back to me. 'You've had a colourful career with the ladies, Oz; I know that much about you.' (Spot on, Ewan; you've got my attention. That deals with the why; I could guess the who, but it wouldn't be right. You're on stage; you're in the spotlight.)

'It all began at a dinner party in Edinburgh, about six months ago. My private investments are handled by one of the oldest partnerships in town. They invited me to be their guest one night, along with a few other key clients. I went alone; Margaret was detained in London on business. As it happened, James Torrent, another of their important investors, was out of town that night too. He sent his niece,

Natalie, in his place.' (Of course he did. Who else in that set-up had the class to have pulled Capperauld?)

'I was fascinated by her. You've met her, Oz . . you must have, when you visited Torrent . . . so you'll understand when I say that there's more depth to her than any woman I've ever known.' He smiled, summoning up some classic wistfulness. 'It was instant and it was mutual. It was faintly ludicrous, too; here we were, surrounded by elderly fund managers, people more staid than you could ever imagine, with lightning shooting between us. You have to understand, Oz, that this was not normal behaviour from me. I love my wife, and I'd never been unfaithful to her before, although it goes without saying that in our business one has plenty of opportunities.' (Too right there, mate; I'd have been sorted with at least one of the four in the Kwei Linn if I'd fancied it.)

'We left there as soon as we could and took a taxi to the Balmoral. I wasn't staying with my parents on that trip; I had a suite there. We drank a little champagne, talked into the small hours and then went to bed.

'The affair was in earnest from then on. That's all it was, though; a fling, for her as well as me. We were very discreet. We conducted it either in Edinburgh, at her place, or on neutral ground; in Paris, once, when I had a premiere; in Madrid on another occasion, when I had a meeting with a producer. Natalie confided in no one, and naturally neither did I.'

He paused. I opened the fridge, took out a bottle of water and gave it to him. 'Thank you,' he said, and took a drink.

'Then,' he continued, 'I made my only mistake. We had an assignation in Edinburgh, one Friday evening. I flew in on the shuttle and took a cab from the airport. I called Natalie on my mobile, to let her know that I'd arrived. Her car was being serviced, so she asked me to pick her up from the office.

'It was six-thirty when I arrived. Anna Chin was still there. I told her I'd come for Miss Morgan, and she paged her. Then she produced her autograph book, and I signed it. Technically, of course, I was never in the building, so I didn't sign anything else.'

He gave a beautifully wry smile. 'How was I to know that the girl . . . the poor sad girl . . . was my cousin's lover, or that she wouldn't be able to resist telling him who had called for Miss Morgan and whom she had kissed in the hallway, before they left? How was I to know?'

Then his eyes narrowed, and his mouth tightened. 'I found out, though; as soon as I got back to London, I found out. David called me on the following Sunday evening. There was no preamble; he told me that he knew and that he wanted money, or he'd tell Margaret. He asked for a quarter of a million.'

'Did you pay him?' Ricky asked.

Ewan looked at him as if he were a heckler. He ignored his question altogether; no ad libs in this performance. 'I called Natalie immediately, to warn her. Her first reaction was to declare that Anna was fired. I asked her not to do that; it could only have raised questions. I said that I would pay him what he asked, in the hope that it would be his last demand . . . a hope more than an expectation, I admit. Natalie wouldn't hear of it. She's a very powerful woman and formidable when she's angered. She told me that her uncle had a business relationship with David's firm. She said that she would speak to Torrent and that he would take care of the matter.

'I trusted her to do that. I heard no more from David; and then I heard of his death. When I did, I assumed that Alison had indeed killed him. I haven't heard from Natalie since then either. When all this blew up we decided that we should cool things, for a while at least, although really, as far as I'm concerned, it's all over.'

He sighed, heavily, loud enough to be heard in the back stalls. 'So that's the story, Oz. I will tell that to the police, happily, but I will expect from them, and from you, a little discretion.'

'You'll take what you fucking get,' I told him, cheerfully. 'So Natalie thought that Uncle James could lean on David and that would be it. But what she didn't know was that he was effectively out of the firm, and that Torrent had no leverage over him at all.'

'So he got really heavy,' said Ricky. 'He took care of the problem in the old-fashioned way. But who?' He sighed. 'Ah fuck, who cares. With luck, Natalie Morgan will back up Mr Capperauld's story, and Alison'll be off the hook. Maybe she can tell the police who did the dirty work for her uncle.'

'And will she tell them why he was killed, do you think?'

He looked at me. So did Ewan. So did Alison. 'Well?' I demanded. 'So Torrent has criminal connections and he puts a contract out on the two of them? The business gets done, and he pays the money. So who killed him, and why? Did he welsh on payment?'

'Unlikely,' said Ricky. 'People like that want paid in advance.'

'Okay, why knock him off? Also, if it was a straight-forward contract job, why go to all that trouble to frame Alison? Come on, man, what's wrong with this picture?'

'Yes.' He nodded. 'I take your point. So what are you thinking?'

'I'm thinking that the person Torrent told to take care of the problem was someone he knew. Let's suppose that after the second killing, Torrent panicked; he became a threat to the killer himself, so he had to go. So who was that close to Torrent?'

'Natalie?'

288

'No. If she was going to do them both herself, why tell her uncle at all?'

'Maybe he found out?'

'No!' Ewan shouted; at last, there was some spontaneity in his performance. 'Natalie did not do those things.'

'How do you know?' I asked him.

'Could Susie do such a thing?' he asked.

'No,' I answered.

'How do you know?'

He had me. 'I just do, that's all.'

'Very well. Trust me on this in the same way. It wasn't her.'

'In that case,' Ricky murmured, 'who?'

'There's only one person left to ask,' I told him. 'Natalie.' And then I paused. 'There's only one person left who knows about this . . . or so the killer thinks.'

'Oh Jesus!' Ewan moaned.

'Do you have her phone number?'

'No. I had, but I tore it up when I stopped seeing her.'

'I have,' said Alison. She picked up the shoulder bag that she had dropped on the kitchen floor and dug out a personal organiser. She flicked through it, stopped, then read out, 'Natalie Morgan, home; 261 3641.'

I put the kitchen phone on to speaker mode and dialled, carefully. The number didn't ring out at all; instead it went straight on to the answering service. Natalie had a personalised message; 'Hi, this is Nat,' her chocolate voice announced to all of us in the kitchen. 'I'm either out, on the bog, or on the phone. Please leave a message.'

I pointed at Ewan. He nodded, and moved closer to the phone. 'Natalie,' he said, 'it's me. I need to speak to you urgently, please call my mobile.'

I clicked the line shut. 'The answerphone picked up right away,' Alison pointed out. 'That means she's either on another call . . .'

I gave her both raised eyebrows.

'. . . or the phone's off the hook.'

'Where does she live?' asked Ricky.

'Ravelston,' Ewan answered. 'Near Mary Erskine's School, in a flat; it's a top floor like this, but I can't remember the number. I never even knew it; I never wrote to her, or even noticed it on the door when I was there. The police will know.'

'The first thing the police will do,' Ross barked, 'is come here and arrest us. Come on, you're taking us there. Make sure your mobile's on, just in case Natalie calls back.'

52

Four of us headed for the door; Ewan, Ricky, Glen Oliver and me. Okay. I could have stayed behind, but no way was I going to, not after everything.

'You can't leave me here,' Alison wailed.

'Too right we can.' I told her. 'If you get frightened, get in beside Liam.'

The lift was getting close, when a thought came to me from nowhere. 'Hold on a minute,' I said and went back inside.

'Alison,' I asked her, 'those calls you had, the one that got you out the night David was killed and the one that took you to the Torrent building last Friday; can you remember anything about the caller?'

'No. The voice was indistinct both times; I had trouble hearing what was being said.'

'It was a man, though?'

'I can't even tell you that for certain.'

'Okay.' I headed back to the other three. Ewan was holding the door. The script was done; we were on to the impromptu stuff now, and he had stage fright, bad.

Glen drove us out of the city centre and towards Ravelston Dykes. It was dry but cloudy; there was no moon to compete with the orange glow from the street lights. Ewan gave directions from the front passenger street; eventually he called for a right turn; the lighting was less bright off the main road but still we could see in front of us the dim outline of a block of flats. 'That's it ahead,' the actor whispered . . . though I couldn't think why he did. Maybe he didn't want the audience to hear.

'I know that building,' Ricky exclaimed. 'It's got good security; I know that because we renewed it two years ago, and we look after it on a contract. Every flat's alarmed and there are video cameras on all floors.'

'My building's supposed to have good security too,' I grumbled. 'Only it doesn't.'

'Should I call her again?' Ewan asked.

I nodded and handed him the number; I'd noted it on a piece of kitchen roll. I watched, as he waited. 'Answering service again,' he announced at last. 'But the phone seems to be back on the hook. Maybe she's asleep,' he added, hopefully.

'Sure,' Ricky grunted.

Oliver drew the car up a hundred yards away from the block. I tapped Ricky on the shoulder and motioned him to get out and follow me. He looked puzzled, a little annoyed even, but he did it. I had a good reason; I didn't want Glen to hear what I was going to say.

'I want to ask you something,' I told him, in a whisper not unlike Ewan's stage version. 'Suppose you were Torrent, and you had a problem that you wanted to go away. We've already considered underworld contacts. So who else would you ask?'

'My lawyer, I suppose.'

'Not that sort of problem; you can't interdict a blackmailer, for Christ's sake.'

'Okay, so who, then?'

'How about your security officer?'

He gaped at me and his eyes widened. 'Hey wait a minute! He never said a word to me.'

'No, but do you handle all your accounts in person? Don't you ever delegate?'

'Of course. Every client has someone in charge.'

'So who ran Torrent?'

He sucked in a long breath; it sounded like a moan of foreboding. 'Mandy O'Farrell, but . . .'

'Tell me, honestly. Have you ever suspected that Mandy might have given Torrent a bit of extra service?'

'Not that way. She's protective of her clients, but that's all.'

'How protective?'

'Aw, come on, Oz,' Ricky protested.

'Yes, come on. Suppose Torrent told Mandy about the problem, and told her no more than that he wanted it to go away? Suppose she took it to extremes? Capperauld dies, and Alison's arrested, fine. But then Anna's murdered, right in his office. He knows the connection and so does Natalie, but it can't be her, because they're off to Gleneagles when it happens. No one else knows, though, other than Mandy.'

He shook his head, in firm denial. 'No.'

'What was the first thing Torrent did after Anna's death? He tried to distance himself from your firm, that's what. He fired you, to put space between him and Mandy. That scared her; she saw herself being dropped in it. Where was she last night, when Torrent was killed?'

'In Glasgow, minding Susie.'

'No, she fucking wasn't! Susie was with me, getting Ewan's autograph on her menu. Mandy was off watch, in Edinburgh.'

Ross looked up at the penthouse. 'Okay, so where is she now?'

'There's one good way to find out.' I took out my phone and keyed in Susie's mobile number. It took her a few seconds to answer; when she did she was pissed off. 'Sorry, love,' I said, 'but it's important. Is Mandy with you?'

'What are you talking about?' she asked me, wearily. 'You know she's not. She's gone back to Edinburgh. She told me that they'd found the stalker. You mean they haven't?' She sighed with exasperation. 'Ah who cares! Good night.' The phone went silent.

So Mandy said they'd found the stalker. *Where did she hear that?* I wondered. Only three of us knew about that. I hadn't told her, Liam hadn't, and I was damn sure Mike Dylan hadn't either.

I looked back at Ross. 'We may have a problem.'

He nodded towards the building. 'You're wrong,' he said, 'but best get up there.'

53

Ewan wanted to come with us, but that idea got short shrift; he was emotionally involved up there. Also, given the outside chance that things might get a bit physical, he was too valuable for us to run the risk of him getting hurt. There was a third consideration. What we were about to do was probably illegal; I was pushing my own luck, and as Miles's friend I just couldn't let his star be part of it.

Ricky wasn't even keen on letting me go with him and Glen, but I squashed that notion. 'You need me up there, pal,' I told him. 'I'm your independent witness; I'm not an employee of Ross Security.'

Ewan still couldn't recall the number of Natalie's apartment, but when we got to the door that turned out not to be a problem; her name was on a label next to the top buzzer, number 10a.

Ricky pressed it. There was no sound. 'We should have heard that feed back from the other end,' he said. 'That's funny.'

'No it's bloody not! How do we get in?'

'With difficulty, if no one will open up for us. Of course if I'd known we were coming here, I could have brought a pass key.'

It had been a bad news day all round, so I tried one more. 'Which of your operatives is responsible for this?' I asked him. Glen Oliver was on his other side; I spoke quietly, hoping that he didn't hear.

I could see his face fall. 'Mandy O'Farrell,' he whispered.

'Terrific. Now tell me this. Suppose we get the hubcap lever from Glen's car and use it to jimmy the lock on the door, what happens?'

'An alarm goes off.'

I stood back and looked at the entrance; there was a single door, half-glazed, with glass panels on either side. 'Suppose we break one of those panels? Are they alarmed?'

'No, but the glass is toughened.'

'So am I.' I looked around. The communal gardens around the block had a rockery in one corner. I walked across and looked at the big stones, embedded in the ground. I tried one; it was set firm, but eventually I managed to work it loose. It was heavy, but after all the gym work I'd been doing it was no problem.

I carried it across to the doorway. 'Give me your jacket, Glen,' I said. He was wearing a big black leather jerkin. He nodded and slipped it off. I laid it on the ground, put the stone on top and zipped it up around it. Then I took the arms, tied them together and picked it up. I swung it experimentally, a few times. The boulder stayed in place; I had myself a club.

The glass panel wasn't just strong, it was laminated; two toughened layers with a clear plastic lining between them. I hit the panel three heavy swinging blows; each one made a thumping noise, but there as no smashing of glass. After the third whack, the panel was hanging loosely; it was opaque now, with shattered crystals clinging to the lining, and there was no way I was going to be able to club through that.

Glen Oliver may be a man of few, indeed, of no words, but he can rise to the occasion. He reached into his trouser pocket and produced the biggest Swiss Army knife I have ever seen . . . more like a Swiss Army bayonet, in fact . . . and handed it to me. I folded out the main blade, which was so sharp I could have shaved with it, and sliced through the laminate, side to side, top to bottom.

I had been working as quickly as I could, and as quietly, in the circumstances, in the hope that there were no insomniacs in the flats above us. It seemed, as we stepped inside through our newly made door, that we'd got lucky.

'Let's walk up,' said Ricky.

'Don't be daft,' I told him. 'What's wrong with the lift?'

'You might hear the mechanism from the penthouse.'

'In that case, we run up.' I led the way towards the stairway.

There were ten storeys in the block; ground, one to nine, and then the top floor. Ricky was breathing hard when we got to the top, but Glen and I still had our wind left.

There were two apartments on the penthouse floor, one on either side of the stairway door; number 10a was on the right. Ricky moved towards it, but I signalled him to stop. I unholstered my cellphone and dialled Natalie's number yet again. We could hear it ring inside, eight times, until the message clicked in. I hit the red button but it played itself out.

'Maybe she's a really deep sleeper,' Ross muttered. 'Maybe she is on the bog.'

'Maybe she should try Immodium,' I suggested.

I looked at him in the green landing light. 'Are we going in, or what?'

He nodded. 'Glen,' he said, 'your moment has come.'

'Try ringing the bell just once?' I suggested.

'What's another fucking door? Glen.'

Ewan's minder stepped forward, raised his right leg and opened Natalie Morgan's apartment with a single kick.

The night breeze met us as we stepped inside. I looked

across the open-plan living room and saw wide glass doors, leading to a west-facing terrace. They were open. There was something piled on the tiled floor outside, but I couldn't make out what it was.

The flat was absolutely silent; we stood there, unwilling to switch on a light, looking around us for the prospective horrors that had drawn us there.

And then in a door to the left, a figure appeared. All we could see was a silhouette; around medium height, slim, wearing a one-piece, head-to-foot garment strikingly similar to that I had seen worn by the SAS extras in the McEwan Hall. I'd seen Mandy in the dark before; naked, or clothed like this, the shape was the same.

A whisper came from Ricky. 'Glen.' The minder and the black figure moved towards each other. He carried himself loosely, a bit like a wrestler, looking to restrain, then detain.

He never had a chance. The figure seemed to leap straight off the ground, then hit him with a left-footed jab to the midriff, and a right-footed kick behind the ear. Oliver moaned quietly, and sagged to the floor like a sack of potatoes.

Ross started to moved forward, but I held him back. 'You block the door,' I told him. 'There's a fire extinguisher on the landing outside. If this character gets past me, put it to good use.'

The figure stood there, waiting for another of us to have a go. I obliged, by inching forward; in the dim light I could see teeth gleaming in the centre of the tunic's black balaclava-type helmet. I edged sideways, round Oliver's motionless form, until I bumped into a wooden-framed swivel chair, positioned in the middle of the room.

'Okay, Mandy,' I said quietly. 'Round two.' I feinted a move with my left foot. She bought it and launched into a spinning, right-footed counter-kick. I ducked under it, and as I did, grabbed the chair one-handed, and threw it at her. Its wooden edge caught her flush on the knee-cap. She almost fell, but recovered her balance. Too late though; I had closed in by then. I whipped the feet from under her with the Russian leg sweep that Liam had taught me, and followed up as she went down, driving my knee hard into the midsection of the black tunic. It was all over then, but I had seen and experienced enough to take no chances, so I hit her, once, hard, with my right fist in the middle of the forehead. I could see her eyes now; they glazed over as she went out, cold.

'Find a light, Ricky,' I shouted, as I pushed myself up from the motionless figure and headed for the door through which she had come. I fumbled for a switch on the inside of the door but found none. Then for the first time I became aware of a soft splashing sound. It was a bathroom; I found the switch on the outside and flicked it on.

I didn't see Natalie Morgan at first, but I heard her quickly enough. Her bath was a big old Victorian thing, big enough to accommodate a five-a-side football team. She was in it . . . on her own.

The tub was full almost to overflow point. Natalie was beneath the surface. A big strip of gaffer tape had been slapped over her mouth, her arms were bent behind her and her legs were doubled beneath her. Her wrists were lashed tight to her ankles, and lying on her back as she was, she was helpless. She was also on the point of drowning, she was moving, but only slightly, and I couldn't see any bubbles coming up.

I plunged my arms into the bath . . . the water was no more than tepid . . . and lifted her out, then laid her on her side, in the middle of the floor. She had been tied with a satin cord, which might have been the sash of a dressing gown. Whatever it was, it was sodden and the knot would not budge. Luckly, I still had Oliver's big clasp knife in my pocket. I produced it and cut her free, then I ripped the tape from her mouth.

She had stopped moving altogether, and her lips had a bluish tinge to them. I rolled her on to her back, and was about to begin mouth to mouth, when she coughed, and spluttered. Quickly, I turned her over . . . and jumped clear as she vomited all over the tiled floor. As I did, I saw an empty vodka bottle, and a glass, on the floor by the bath.

'Do we need a medic?' Ricky was in the doorway.

'I'll tell you in a minute,' I replied. 'How's Glen?'

'He thinks it's Christmas. I told him that if it is, the fairy on top of the tree just kicked the shit out of him. He's okay, though.'

'And how about Mandy?'

He surprised me; he laughed. 'Come and see,' he said.

We left the naked Natalie to puke in private, and I followed him into the living room. It was lit by a fancy, modern, five-bulb halogen arrangement. The figure on the floor was still out; although as I looked down, her right leg twitched, involuntarily, as if she was dreaming about kicking some bloke in the head.

Ricky had ripped off her helmet. I looked down, and whistled, as I realised why he had been laughing. 'I think we'd better get Ewan up here,' I told him. 'Mrs Capperauld's got some explaining to do.'

54

We paid Margaret Capperauld plenty of respect; when she came round a couple of minutes later, she was tied into the swivel chair with the same cord she had used to bind her would-be victim.

Natalie herself was sitting on the couch, wrapped in a towelling robe, shivering with a mixture of cold, fright, and alcohol. She must have drunk all that vodka; she was completely pissed.

Ricky had vetoed the idea of Ewan coming up; correctly, when I thought about it. He'd have wigged out. Instead he had sent Glen Oliver down to sit with him in the car, and to call Ronnie Morrow's home number and dig him out of bed. There would be credit going, he had pointed out, and he wanted his protégé to get it.

It took another minute or so, but, eventually, Margaret's eyes were fully focused. When she realised where she was, she strained against her binding for a moment, then gave up.

'Olympic gymnast, eh,' I murmured. 'And them some.'

'And free-style climber,' she replied, 'and martial arts student.'

'. . . And vengeful wife?' I suggested. She glared at me.

I had already worked out the climbing part; on the terrace outside I'd found a coil of rope and a heavy hard rubber grappling hook. She'd got up to Natalie's penthouse by scaling the whole damn block, floor by floor, taking the stairway balconies one by one.

'David spilled the beans, didn't he?'

She looked at me again, as archly as her husband might have, then she winced in pain from the big lump that had sprouted about an inch above her nose. 'What did you hit me with?' I held up my right fist. 'That's no way to treat a lady,' she murmured.

Then she nodded. 'Yes, he did. He came to see me in London and told me the whole story. He said that he had asked Ewan for money to forget about his adventure with Natalie, and that all he had got was a threatening phone call from her uncle.

'He told me that he guessed I would do anything to protect Ewan's reputation and his career, so he proposed that I pay the money instead.'

'And did you confront Ewan?'

'Absolutely not!' she snapped. 'I love him. He can have all the bimbos he wants . . . not that he has before, to my knowledge . . . and I'll overlook them, as long as he comes back to me. No, I confronted this bitch here. First I told her that if she ever looked at my husband again, I would kill her, and then I told her that I would take care of the problem myself.'

She frowned; it made her wince again. 'David was right, you see. I would go to any lengths to protect Ewan.'

'So when you went to see him, that Wednesday, he thought you were going to pay him off?'

Margaret gave a cold smile. 'That he did . . . and that I did.'

'But why implicate Alison?'

'I needed someone to take the blame quickly, to avoid any chance of the police looking in our direction. She was the obvious person . . . and anyway, I was sure, I still am sure, that she was in on the blackmail attempt.'

302

I waved a finger at her. 'No she was not, but we'll let that pass. Okay, so you killed David, then Natalie, here . . .' on the couch, the drunk rolled her eyes at the mention of her name, '. . . let you into the office so you could kill Anna Chin, and have Alison caught red-handed, as it were. Only the last part didn't quite work, thanks to a random accident.

'But why Torrent? Why kill him?'

Margaret hesitated. 'I don't think I'm going to say any more.'

'You might as well; none of it's admissible in court.'

She thought about it. 'I suppose you're right. Okay. Torrent was smart, you see. He twigged at once, after he heard of Anna's death, that something was up. He asked Natalie what she knew, and the stupid woman caved in and told him. So he had to go too; simple as that. I had already stolen the knife from the Goodchild woman's office. I had intended to use it to kill the girl, only it wasn't necessary. So when we were all at Miles's dinner party, I slipped a ground-up Mogadon into my husband's last brandy, then, once he was sound asleep, crept out and took care of the problem.'

'And that left only Natalie knowing what had happened?'

'Exactly.'

'And she, overcome with grief at her beloved uncle's death, horses a bottle of Stolychnaya in the bath, flakes out and drowns.'

'Exactly.'

'Which is where we came in.' I smiled at her. 'Would you like something for that headache, Margaret?' I asked.

'I'll get over it; I've had worse.'

'No you haven't, lady. It's going to get really bad when the police get here.'

'Why? What's my problem? I was visiting my friend Natalie when you people broke in and assaulted me.'

'What? You were visiting her dressed like the Milk Tray Woman?'

'I have an exotic taste in nightwear. The police will assume we're lezzies, and we won't deny it.' She had a point there. 'Natalie's too drunk to be interviewed just now, but when she sobers up she'll confirm it all. She doesn't have any choice; she's in it up to her neck.'

'Indeed!' I exclaimed. 'I'm impressed. You really do think on your feet . . . or on your arse in this case . . . don't you, Mrs Capperauld? There's only one small problem about that; no, sorry, one big one.'

For the first time, she looked slightly uncertain. 'What's that?' she challenged, brassing it out.

'My pal Mr Ross here; nothing is safe from him. He's the worst eavesdropper in Edinburgh. Do you know, he even has his own house bugged! He's so bad that he carries a bloody pocket recorder with him everywhere he goes. Isn't that right, Ricky?'

He stepped round from behind her and waved a small device in the air. 'Mini-disc,' he said. 'Broadcast quality; it's the same kind radio reporters often use. Would you like to hear?' He reviewed the recording, listening through an earpiece, made an adjustment, then paused and pressed a button.

I had already stolen the knife from the Goodchild woman's office. I had intended to use it to kill the girl, only it wasn't necessary. So when we were all at Miles's dinner party, I slipped a ground-up Mogadon into my husband's last brandy, then, once he was sound asleep, crept out and took care of the problem.

Margaret Capperauld went dead white as she listened to the sound of her own confession through the tiny, but effective speaker. 'But that won't be allowed in court,' she snarled, when Ricky switched off the recorder.

'Don't wager your life on it,' I told her, 'for you'd lose. But of course, you've placed your bet already, haven't you?'

55

As soon as Greg Oliver saw Ronnie Morrow's car arrive, as per orders from Ricky he got Ewan to hell out of there. No way did we want him to be around when his wife and his mistress were huckled into a police car.

We went with them, of course; not as suspects, but as witnesses.

It was almost eight by the time we finished making our formal statements. Ricky did a deal with Morrow for Alison to come in later that day, so that the charges against her could be formally binned. The young sergeant gave us a lift back to the Mound after that, and after I had called Miles and advised him to stand down the extras for another day at least, suggesting that he shoot Liam's bedroom scene instead.

Ricky came up to the apartment with me, but only to collect Alison, break the good news to her and take her home for what he hoped would be a bit of a celebration.

Tough luck, Richard. 'But I can go back to my own place now, can't I?' she said. 'I don't need minding any more, do I?' The way she chopped him off was pretty brutal; I could see why she had such a bright future in the PR business.

Just before nine, they left me on my own . . . almost. I was just beginning to think about a long sleep, when Liam appeared; from my bedroom. He looked at me, in a way I could only describe as shifty.

'All right then?' he asked.

'It is now. What about you? You don't look so good. Rough night?'

'Mmm. The thing is . . . I don't know if I should tell you this. Fuck, I don't know if I believe it. I was lying there trying to sleep, and then I hear you lot leave. *Thank Christ*, I thinks to myself, then five minutes later this Alison woman comes into my room and gets into bed beside me.

'I thinks about it . . . give her that . . . but then I says, "No thank you very much," gets up and goes across to your room.

'The light bulb's jiggered, but I thinks *So what?* and goes into the toilet to bleed the lizard. Then, when I came out . . . Whizz! Bang! I'm up in the air and on my arse and there's a bloody great naked woman lying on top of me!'

I kept my face straight. 'So what did you do about that?'

'What the hell could I do? I tell you, Oz, there's no bloody security in this building, none at all.'

56

The Capperauld scandal hit the fan twenty-four hours later, when Margaret was charged with the murders of David, Anna and Uncle James. Natalie was released; the crown office was going to need her as a prosecution witness.

Ewan was devastated; he really had known nothing about it, and, like the rest of us, suspected nothing.

With Miles's agreement he withdrew from the project, and the boss himself took over the part of Skinner. Okay, he's a bit short for it, but he has the charisma to carry anything off.

We finished the production on time; an achievement considering everything that had happened. Liam and I were even able to sleep easy in our beds, once Ricky had obliged us by sending Mandy O'Farrell on a temporary assignment as security chief on an oil terminal in the Orkney Islands.

We had a big close-down party of course. Everyone was there, even Nula, Liam's air stewardess, who fixed her schedule to accommodate it. Prim was not. She paid me one brief visit in Edinburgh to tell me, to my great relief and to confound Susie's suspicions, that she'd put her signature alongside mine on the divorce petition, and had it lodged with the court.

She surprised me then by telling me that she'd taken my advice, and decided to go back to basics. She had signed a six-month contract as a senior staff nurse in Ninewells Hospital, in Dundee, and she was planning to move back into Semple House, in Auchterarder, beside her parents, to draw breath, and do some serious thinking about what she wanted to do with the rest of her life.

She told me that although we'd been rotten at marriage, we'd been good at being friends, and hoped that would still be the case. I told her that as far as I was concerned, it would. Her new spirit of openness didn't extend to owning up to having it off with Mike Dylan, but I let that go. That, and he, were both history.

I was happy at closing off that chapter, but it didn't mean that there was nothing but roses in my garden. I had some serious thinking of my own to do. I was due in Vancouver in less than a month, and the central question of my life was still unresolved.

I was pondering hard, in my last few days in the apartment, about what it really meant to be my own man. When it came to it, there was only one place I could find an answer to that. So I went back to Fife, back to Enster, to see my Dad.

I told him what was at the core of it all. I reckoned that I loved Susie as much as I could ever love another woman, and that wee Janet was all my Christmases come at once. But I was scared, I said, plain scared about taking a chance on marriage again; even if my heart told me to do it, my head asked whether I could ever give up even a part of my independence.

Mac the Dentist thought about this for a while, and then he pronounced.

'Son,' he said, 'I'm a fucking backwoodsman, as you well know. I have a backwoodsman's simple attitudes to life, and his simple beliefs. And the way I see it is this. When you and the right woman have kids, you're not your own man any more; you're theirs and you're each other's, and that's how it should be.

'You don't actually have this independence that you talk about, not any more. Janet will be dependent on you, for the next twenty years and more. And Susie is now too, as you are on her. Whether you live together as a couple or not, you have a duty to bring that baby up together, unless death takes one of you out of the equation. So no, you are not independent, either of you; you ceased to be so the moment you made that child.

'What you are talking about is freedom. It's being the centre of your own universe, giving yourself the licence to do what you like, say what you like, go where you like, fuck who you like, without a thought to the consequences for anyone but yourself.

'Maybe you've done that for long enough, Oz. If you want to continue down that road, now that you're rich and famous, the opportunities to indulge yourself in such pleasures will be endless. But compared to the love that flows into you from your children, when you come home at night and sit them in your lap, the rewards of such a life are ashes, just ashes.

'What you're afraid of, son, is of finding out about yourself. You're asking yourself, and now me, whether if you choose family life, you'll be able to stay the course. I'm not a fucking fortune teller; some do, some don't. In my judgement, I'd say that you and Susie will make a go of it. Still, as you and I both know, nothing in life is certain but death and taxes, and a skilled accountant can avoid a good chunk of the latter.

'The last couple of years have made you a fatalist, Oz. They've developed a side in you that was latent, but lurking, before things went sour on you. And along the way, you've lost your belief in your own inherent goodness.

'Well, I haven't. Trust me if you don't trust yourself, and do what I would do if I was standing in your shoes right now.'

I looked into my Dad's coal fire, and for some reason I thought of wee Anna Chin, and her bowl of cherries. *Maybe it is*, I thought. *Maybe life is just that.*

I leaned over my father as he sat in his big comfy chair, and for the first time in around twenty-five years, I kissed him on the cheek. Then I climbed into my nice, shiny Mercedes and headed off to Glasgow to find out for myself whether, indeed, it is.

Now you can buy any of these other bestselling books by **Quintin Jardine** from your bookshop or *direct from his publisher*.

FREE P&P AND UK DELIVERY
(Overseas and Ireland £3.50 per book)

Autographs in the Rain	£5.99
Thursday Legends	£6.99
Gallery Whispers	£6.99
Murmuring the Judges	£6.99
Skinner's Ghosts	£6.99
Skinner's Mission	£6.99
Skinner's Ordeal	£6.99
Skinner's Round	£6.99
Skinner's Trail	£6.99
Skinner's Festival	£6.99
Skinner's Rules	£6.99
On Honeymoon with Death	£5.99
Screen Savers	£5.99
Wearing Purple	£5.99
A Coffin for Two	£6.99
Blackstone's Pursuits	£6.99

TO ORDER SIMPLY CALL THIS NUMBER

01235 400 414

or visit our website: <u>www.madaboutbooks.com</u>

Prices and availability subject to change without notice.